Worth The Fall

"So, let's do this. Let's talk about the elephant in the room," Petey said.

Well, crap. But she wasn't a shrink for nothing. She could shut this down easily enough. "Which elephant is that? The two-month-old elephant?" She paused, waiting for him to see where she was leading him. The moment he did, she lowered the hammer. "Or the eighteen-year old elephant."

Direct hit. He wouldn't be trying to push her anywhere she didn't want to go. She tossed the throw off of herself, got up and made to leave the room.

As she passed by the bed, he moved for her arm. She tugged, but he held tight. "If that's where you want to go, that's where we'll go," he said, and pulled her closer to him. "You can't just drop a bomb like that and walk out."

"Watch me," she said. He not only held fast, but also tugged on her hard, causing her to tumble into the side of the bed. He took advantage of her loss of balance and pulled her across his big body so that her butt was on the bed near his hip and her legs were draped over his lap. He anchored her with a quick arm around her waist, his other hand still gripping her arm.

He was so close. His eyes were so blue as they bore into hers. She'd always loved a black-haired, blue-eyed combination on a man. He smelled clean, if just a little antiseptic, probably from hospital shower soap. She thought she'd find it unpleasant, but she didn't.

"Not this time," he whispered. "You're not going to walk away from me this time." His eyes dropped to her lips and she knew he was going to kiss her.

And God help her, she was going to kiss him back.

OTHER TITLES BY
MARA JACOBS

The Worth Series
(Contemporary Romance)
Worth The Weight
Worth The Drive
Worth The Fall
Worth The Effort

Anna Dawson's Vegas Series
(Romantic Mystery)
Against The Odds
Against The Spread

Blackbird & Confessor Series
(Romantic Mystery)
Broken Wings

Countdown To A Kiss
(A New Year's Eve Anthology)

WORTH THE FALL

The Worth Series, Book Three

MARA JACOBS

Published by Mara Jacobs
©Copyright 2012 Mara Jacobs
Cover design by Kim Killion

ISBN: 978-0-9852586-3-4

For more information on the author and her works, please see www.marajacobs.com

For Holli

Prologue

The meeting of two personalities is like the contact
of two chemical substances;
if there is any reaction, both are transformed.

~ Carl Gustav Jung

ALISON JUKURI PULLED THE PILLOW over her face, trying to block out the rising sun. Wait a minute. Her bedroom window didn't face the east.

She slowly drew the pillow back and opened her eyes to a blinding light. Oh yeah, the hotel room. She'd booked a room at the hotel where Katie and Darío were having their wedding reception. She hadn't wanted to drive home after what would definitely be a fun night of partying. Even if she was the only one in the bridal party not knocked up and therefore able to drink. She smiled thinking about co-maid of honor Lizzie's water breaking just as the dancing got started.

Good God, how could smiling hurt so much? Why did her head feel as if it had been chopped off and sewn back on to her neck with a rusty needle and barbed wire for thread?

Hangover. Right, of course. She wasn't twenty-one anymore. She was a respected professor and therapist who had the occasional Scorpion at the Commodore. Not the crazy wild woman she'd become last night.

What exactly happened? She remembered Lizzie and Finn leaving to rush to the hospital. The rest of the wedding guests had been kind of on standby until Finn had texted that it was going to be a long night and all was well, so everybody should just stay and enjoy themselves.

She headed straight to the bar after getting Finn's text. Holding that cold glass in her hand was basically the last coherent memory Alison had.

Rough, stubbled cheeks scratching her face as hot lips sought hers.

Huh? She gingerly moved an arm—God, even her fingers hurt—and felt her cheek. There was a small tingle of pain and definite abrasion. But there was also a little frisson of pleasure with the pain.

Deep, wet kisses that stole her breath away. Her tongue being sucked on.

Her fingers slid down her cheek to her lips. Her puffy, well-used lips. What the hell happened last night? She tried to get her muddled brain to concentrate, but all she saw were flashes of memory. And flashes of lovely male flesh.

Her nails scratching down a broad, muscular back as she peaked. Grabbing hold of a sculpted-from-granite ass as she peaked. Again.

She must have had one doozy of a sex dream. The aftershocks were still vibrating through her body. But that didn't explain the puffy lips and stubble-burned cheeks. She shifted her legs slightly. Or her stubble-burned thighs. And other nicely aching things down there.

So, not a dream. She'd had a drunken hook-up. Alison started to berate herself, but a total of two in her thirty-six years didn't make her a slut. And given the last one had been eighteen years ago, it—

No. No way. It couldn't have been. There was no way she would have been so stupid. She slowly moved her arm behind her, more afraid of what she might touch than of the pain that moving brought. She came into contact with hard washboard abs. She slid her hand up to feel a wonderfully muscled and hairy chest.

A warm hand clamped down on her wrist and brought her hand and arm forward, a strong arm covering her, holding on to her wrist and pulling her back into said washboard abs. Alison looked down at the arm. If she'd had any doubt—not that she did—it was put to rest when she recognized the watch on his wrist.

She remembered years ago when he'd shown them all that watch, bragging about buying the crazy expensive thing with part of his signing bonus from the Red Wings. Alison had cracked something about it being too bad it wasn't digital so he'd be able tell the time instead of it just being a pretty bracelet. They'd all laughed.

Except him. He'd called her a name. She'd called him one back. Just their typical night out with the gang when he came home.

She started to move from his grasp but he only pulled her tighter against him. She held very still, trying to figure out how this conversation was going to go. Just as she was about to turn in his arms and face the proverbial music, he let out a snore.

Asleep. He was still asleep. Of course it would be second nature to him to pull the naked body he was with against him, even when unconscious. *Muscle memory* they called it when an action was repeated so often that the body took over for the mind.

Alison waited a moment, then tried again. This time his grip loosened and she slowly—oh, so slowly—eased out of the bed. She quickly grabbed her discarded bridesmaid's dress from the floor to hold in front of her in case he woke. She was relieved to see the condom wrappers (plural?!) on the nightstand.

And on he slept. Dreamt? Of last night? Of her? Or all the others?

She looked down at that glorious body and shook her head.

Alison Jukuri. Valedictorian. Summa cum laude. Genius IQ. Freaking Mensa member.

Or, as she was known all through school, the Smart One.

The label was doing her about as much good in adulthood as it did then, which was none at all. Because the actions Alison displayed last night were not smart. They were downright idiotic.

She'd slept with the man she least respected in the world.

Again.

One

A Freudian slip is when you say one thing
but mean your mother.

- Author Unknown

Two months later

"JUST LEAVE IT, HONEY, I'll get it." Petey Ryan's mom waved
him back in his seat as he stood to help her clear the table.

Petey reluctantly sat back down at the dining room table
with his father, not relishing the conversation to come. "Thanks
for dinner, Mom. It was great."

"Anytime, honey, you know that. We love having you, even
if it's only for a day or two," she replied as she made her way
into the kitchen. His parents were young compared to his friends'
parents—Petey'd been a shotgun baby. His mother was still trim,
with just a touch of gray in her hair, and she moved quickly,
efficiently, and with more ease than he did these days.

"Next time it'll be longer. I'll be here once a week for your
cooking if you'll have me." As soon as he said it, he regretted it.
For a couple of reasons.

"Oh, that would be wonderful. I'll plan on every Sunday,"
she said, popping her head around the corner from the kitchen, a
look of delight on her familiar face. That was one of the reasons he

regretted saying it. He didn't want to disappoint his mother, even though he loved her cooking and would like nothing better to be fed by her on a regular basis.

"You'll have nothing better to do. Probably need a free meal, too," his father said.

And that was the other reason.

He loved both his parents. He really did. And he had no doubt they loved him. And were proud of him. Even if his father didn't always know how to show it.

"I think I'll be able to handle my grocery bill, Dad."

His father gave a small snort, a signal to Petey to gird his loins—tape his ankles and strap on his pads, in his vernacular—for what was about to come.

"It just doesn't make sense. You've got three, maybe four good years left in you. Why would you hang up your skates now?"

Petey was already shaking his head. "I've got—*maybe*—two or three of those years in me, but they wouldn't be good ones." He sighed, smoothing the linen tablecloth. On the rare occasions that he made it home during the season, his mother always served dinner in the dining room with tablecloths and the fancy dishes. When he was in his own house over the summer, if he came for dinner, they would eat in the kitchen, or on the back deck. "I'm old, Dad. In the NHL, I'm ancient."

It was a full-fledged snort this time. "You're thirty-seven. Gordie Howe played until he was fifty-two."

He gave his father a leveling glance. "Come on, Dad. I'm no Gordie Howe."

Dan Ryan seemed to accept that—sadly, a little too easily. But Petey's father always was a realist, and most times he appreciated that. So why couldn't he be that realist now?

"Messier. Lemieux. They were well into their forties."

"Wings and centers. You won't find any defensemen playing that long." And before his father could pull out a name —and Petey just bet he had one waiting—he continued, "Dad. I'm done after this season. If I want to have any kind of life after hockey,

I have to stop doing this to my body." There was a little bit of pleading in his voice. Was he pleading for his father to understand? Or to give his permission?

The thought that maybe he still needed his father's permission to make a life decision pissed Petey off. But he couldn't put that on his father—that was on him.

And time for him to blow the whistle and call the play dead. "Dad," he said, raising his hand in a "stop" motion as he saw his father about to argue with him. "Stop. Really. I'm slower on the ice now. The younger guys are getting bigger and are faster. I do not want to go out on a low note. The decision's been made. I've told my coaches and the front office. Come May, or hopefully June, I'll have played my last game." He waited for a moment. When his father didn't make a comeback, Petey looked him in the eye and gave his shit-eating grin. "And I'll have my retirement drink out of the Stanley Cup."

After a moment, his father returned his grin. "Damn straight you'll be drinking out of the Cup!"

And that would help ease the sting for his father—Petey finally winning the trophy that had eluded him his whole career. Hell, it'd take the sting out of his body crying uncle for Petey, too.

"Now," he said, rising from the table, "I've got to go see that screaming, snotty brat of a baby or Lizzie will hand me my ass."

His mother, with her innate sense of knowing when any storm between Petey and his father was over, came back into the dining room. "You don't fool me. You're going to be a big pile of mush holding that baby. It's going to make you want one of your own. I guess I'm ready to be a grandmother."

"Bite your tongue," Petey and his father said simultaneously. They grinned at each other, the tension from their "talk" gone. They ran hot and cold, he and his father, but they always quickly found their way back to common ground.

He kissed his mother. "Thanks again, Mom." Making his way out of the dining room, across the living room and to the foyer to get his heavy winter coat, he added, "I shouldn't be too late. I doubt Lizzie's going to want to stay up late, drink some beers and shoot the shit."

"She will. You know she will Petey, just because she'll think you want to," his mother accurately stated. "Make sure you don't keep her up too late. I can't imagine she's getting much sleep."

She was right. His best friend Lizzie would sense he wanted to talk. She'd hide any yawn and have her husband Finn put the baby to bed—and anything else that needed to be done—and be totally there for Petey. Just like she'd been for years.

And he'd feel like a douche, but he'd totally take advantage of her friendship.

Just like he'd done for years.

She had to know something was up anyway. Petey rarely came home during the season, as there just wasn't enough time for the ten-hour drive from Detroit to their Upper Peninsula hometown when you were playing a game nearly every night. And these few days he had now—during the All-Star Game break— were days he usually stayed in Detroit, giving his body a much-needed rest.

But even though he'd just defended his decision to retire at the end of the season to his father, Petey was freaking out over the idea of giving up the only thing he did well.

Hell, the only thing he did period.

He needed Lizzie's calm perspective on it all to keep him from running to the front office and ripping up the paperwork. Not that he knew if there was actually any paperwork or not. See? He didn't even know how businesses worked.

All he knew was the ice. The glide, the cool, the feel of nothingness under his skates. And now he was going to give that all up because he wanted to be able to walk in an upright position when he was fifty.

He shut the front door behind him and stepped out onto the front porch. The temperature had dropped at least twenty degrees from when he'd gone inside hours ago to watch the All-Star Game with his dad. He'd been shoveling the front steps and walk, trying to prolong the task because he did not want to endure the torture of watching two of his teammates play in the elite game that Petey'd only played in once in his fifteen years in the league.

But his father had insisted Petey come in and watch the game with him and so he did, feeling a sense of doom, melancholy and pride for the game he loved all at the same time.

He shook off the game, the dinner and the conversation with his father. He'd always been remarkably good at not thinking too much. It'd served him well on the ice. Burrowing deeper into his parka, he made his way down the steps only to feel his feet go out from beneath him.

The ice. The substance on which he made his living. The hard surface he knew as home.

The cool glide betrayed him, and as he heard something in his knee pop he instinctively knew he wouldn't have several months to come to terms with retirement. No farewell games. No last wave to the cheering crowd at the Joe.

Petey Ryan lay at the bottom of the steps in a crumpled heap.

Retired.

—∾—

"And this is all of us last Fourth of July. See? That's you, there. And that's Mom." Alison pointed to the various faces in the family portrait she'd blown up, framed and placed in her father's room in the long-term care section of the hospital. "Do you remember that day, Dad?"

"Yes, of course, Alison. It was only months ago," her father answered with a touch of exasperation in his voice.

Good. That was good. He remembered, and he was pissed that she questioned his memory. A good day, then.

"It was the day before we shipped out to Korea. God, that was a fun day. Do you remember how Jimmy chased after you that day? But you weren't having any of it, were you? Playing hard to get, even then."

Not a good day. But not one of his worst, either.

"Not playing hard to get. Just not interested in Jimmy." She'd tried different tactics when her father was like this—lucid, but in a distant place. She'd corrected him, changed the topic, and pleaded with him to remember. She'd read up on the proper course of action, and there didn't seem to be a clear consensus on the topic. In the end, the kindest thing seemed to be to just go along with him.

"Why not? Jimmy was a *great* guy. A great guy," her father said. His attention drifted from the photo to a blank spot on the wall where he seemed to see the old gang because a smile lit up his wrinkled face.

Her father was eighty-five, and, up until a few years ago, had always looked a decade younger than his age. But the ravages of severe Alzheimer's had taken a toll on more than just his mind. He'd never been a big man, but now he was a shadow of his former self. Small and weak, a recurring lung infection had left him barely able to do the small tasks that would allow him to leave the hospital and enter an assisted-living facility.

That's what they'd been hoping for. An assisted-living place that could keep him safe, sheltered, and in comfort. They'd all discussed it—Alison, her mother Nora, and Charles, her father—years ago, back when he'd first been diagnosed. He didn't want the burden of his care to fall to Nora and they'd gone along with him.

But behind his back, Alison and her mother had formed an alliance of their own. They would do all they could to keep Charles in the family home as his disease progressed. And they were succeeding, until Nora became ill herself.

At first the doctors thought Alzheimer's for Nora too. Alison had just about lost it that day. She'd called her friend Katie, who was in Spain with her guy, Darío, and unloaded. She just didn't see how she was going to be able to handle it all. But it turned out not to be Alzheimer's but a slow-growth dementia of another kind.

Nora had the same sad bouts of not remembering things from the early past, but less frequently than her father did. Her mother's condition was not quite as debilitating as her father's.

But there was no way now that they'd be able to keep her father in the family home. Her mother was barely able to look after herself, even with a daily visit from Alison. There was no way she could care for her husband too.

"The trouble with you is you don't want the nice guys. Oh, you take 'em, but you don't really want them," her father said now, pulling Alison out of what was heading toward a self-pity reverie.

"What?" she asked, trying to remember what tangent her father was on. Oh, right. She was playing hard to get to Jimmy, who was bound for Korea. It did sound kind of bitchy. Poor guy heading to war and all. Least she could do was throw the kid a bone and let him steal a kiss behind the old oak tree.

"You think nice guys are weak and you know you can control weak." He looked at her with knowing eyes and she wondered if he was back.

"Dad?" she said softly.

"You've been doing it for years. Let the weak ones in, push them around, then dump them because you know deep down inside that's not what you want. Not what you need."

"Daddy?" she said a bit more strongly, trying to pull him out of the past. At least, she was hoping it was the past. Because if not, she was becoming uncomfortable thinking about her father's estimation of her love life.

"You need a strong man who won't let you push him around. But you won't—" And just like that he was gone. It was like a curtain had closed over his mind. When it happened it didn't seem to hurt him. He would just get a blank look on his face, which would turn to confusion and then acceptance. It was like he knew his brain just couldn't put any pieces together right now and it would be best to just power down.

It broke Alison's heart.

She patted his hand, said some soothing words to him, then got up to place the photo back on the shelf. She heard the rumbling of her phone vibrating in her purse and dug it out. Lizzie was calling. Odd. She knew Alison always spent the hours after having dinner with her mom at the hospital with her dad. Then she went back to her parents' house, where she'd recently begun spending the nights.

"Lizard, what's up?" she said when she connected to the call.

"Are you still at the hospital with your dad?" Lizzie asked. Alison felt a stab of fear at the tone of concern in Lizzie's voice.

"Yes. Why?"

"Petey's on the way there. He's in an ambulance. His mom just called me. He slipped on the ice and fell down the front stairs."

"In Detroit?" But no, that didn't make any sense. Still, Alison wasn't getting it. Her genius IQ seemed to shut down whenever Petey's name was mentioned. It was like her intelligence level dropped down to his or something. He didn't even need to be near, just brought to mind.

"No, here. He was home during the All-Star break. Just for the night."

"He drove all that way for one night?"

"He flew. He didn't—listen, Al, he's being brought in to the hospital right now. I need you to go find out what's going on. How he is. His parents are on their way. I'll get there as soon as I can."

"No, I—" But Lizzie'd already disconnected.

Alarm shot through her, but logic quickly prevailed. His parents' front steps were only about four or five high. He couldn't have sustained too serious of an injury—at least not life-threatening—from tumbling down them. Could he? Perhaps he was lucky and had fallen on his head—that way there'd be no damage.

She snorted internally at her own bitchery. Too bad she only used that one on herself and not on Petey. She sighed and started collecting her things. Due to Lizzie's command, maybe she'd get to bestow the zinger on the big man himself.

She kissed and hugged her father goodbye, promising to see

him the next day. He absently patted her on the back and called her Sally.

She left his room and started making her way to the other wing of the small hospital toward the little-used emergency room entrance.

Two

—w—

All hockey players are bilingual.
They know English and profanity.

~ Gordie Howe

HE WASN'T HARD TO FIND. For one thing, it was a pretty small hospital and thankfully there weren't a lot of emergencies in the neighboring towns of Houghton and Hancock, which shared the hospital. Or at least not a lot of emergencies from seven to ten most nights, because Alison could hear the ambulances arriving when she was in her father's room and she didn't hear them all that ofteThe other reason she found Petey fairly easily was that a crowd was already beginning to form around him. Local boy makes good. The town hero. And even more beloved because he never forgot where he came from, spending his summers in the U.P., giving to local charities, and helping out with summer youth hockey.

Yeah, a real freaking role model.

He was being wheeled down the hallway on a stretcher, coming right toward her. The EMTs were guiding him, one in front, one pushing from behind, with a nurse on either side of the gurney. Two more nurses were following.

Of course, the nurses were young and female. So was one of the EMTs. And they were all looking at him as more than a patient.

She supposed she couldn't blame them. If she was going to be completely objective—and she had to be for her patients, so she *should* be able to when it came to Petey—he was definitely worthy of gurney chasing.

At least physically.

It finally hit her that he was obviously really hurt or there was no way in hell Petey Ryan would be on that stretcher. He loved attention—the big ham—but not the hovering, concerned type. That would drive him crazy.

He was sitting up, even though the EMTs were trying to get him to lie back. They didn't seem to have a sense of urgency about them, though, wheeling him fairly slowly, which Alison figured was good news. He was wearing jeans, a flannel shirt, boots and an unzipped parka. He looked just like every other guy Alison knew.

And yet completely different.

Even on a gurney he had a presence about him. His size, of course, but even more than that.

His black hair was a touch on the long side. She knew that he always got it cut really short right before training camp then let it go for the season, only cutting it again once he got to the U.P. for the summer. Their little group had even had parties around it back when they were in their twenties. It was almost like summer only really began when Petey cut his hair.

She usually didn't see him mid-season unless she was watching a Red Wings game—which she only did if she was with her father or, in years past, at Katie and Ron's house where Ron would always be watching the game with a wistful "I coulda been a contender" look on his face.

Another reason she was glad Katie was now with Darío.

So, she usually only saw Petey with really short hair or really long hair. She had to admit the length he wore now—not quite to collar length, but just long enough to have a tiny bit of curl at the ends—made him even sexier. And it would be silky smooth, she knew that from exper—

"Alison? What are you doing here?"

There probably wasn't a huge emphasis on *you* like she imagined. Like why would the last person in the world he would want to see be here. But too many years had honed the defense mechanism in her where he was concerned, so she quickly said, "I was here visiting my father. Lizzie called me. I guess your mom called her."

The small parade had reached her at the end of the hallway and stopped, even though she'd stepped out of the way to let them pass.

"Is Lizzie on her way?" he asked with hope in his voice. Then he added, "No, she's got the baby now." There was defeat in his tone, almost petulance.

She knew how he felt. Alison's two closest friends had, in the span of a year, gotten married, pregnant, and were—or were about to be—new mothers. Lizzie's son, Samuel, was a few months old, and Katie was due any day now.

Of course Alison was delighted for her best friends, but there was no denying she barely saw them any more.

She stepped toward the gurney to reassure him. "She's coming. She's on her way. So are your parents."

The look of relief that had started to form on his face quickly departed. "Shit," he said, then looked around at the nurses seemingly trying to discern which nurse was in charge. They all looked to Alison like they were young enough to be candy stripers. "Don't let my parents back here. And they'll try, especially my dad."

"Well, you'll be in a private area until the doctor can get here, and then he'll either want to do X-rays or maybe an MRI, so they would be able to wait with you, no problem," one nurse informed him. Alison could tell the nurse was trying to reassure Petey, but she didn't know the relationship Petey had with his father.

"It'll need to be an MRI," Petey said with certainty. Must be all those years of injuries—he could probably diagnose himself. "It's shot. My knee," he said. Then he added so quietly that the whole group leaned toward him to hear, "I'm done."

Whatever their history—long ago, and the recent past of Katie's wedding—Petey was her friend, part of the same group she'd hung with since high school, and he needed somebody right now. She took a deep breath and summoned her inner Lizzie.

"You." She pointed to the two nurses who had been following the group. "You two go back to the receiving area. When Petey's parents come in, you tell them that they're not allowed to come back here right now. Tell them that Petey is fine and in good spirits, but the doctor just wants to run some tests."

They opened their mouths to say something, but Alison held up a finger stopping them. "And when Lizzie comes in— you'll know her, trust me—pull her aside and tell her Al said to run interference with Lieutenant Dan. But not so his parents can hear."

Petey chuckled, probably at the nickname the gang had given his father so many years ago because of his drill-sergeant ways about Petey practicing hockey. Everybody else looked confused, most likely wondering who Al was. "Do you have that?" she barked at the nurses. Okay, so, not *totally* Lizzie—she would never have barked—but Lizzie would have had this whole thing in hand a long time ago.

The young women looked just startled enough that they only nodded their heads, and when Alison twirled her finger for them to turn around and get moving they actually did.

"Channeling Lizzie, much?" Petey commented. Just when she was about to say that's exactly what she'd been doing, he added, "Plus a dash of bitch."

"Or, you could just say thank you."

He shrugged her off, grunted something unintelligible (big surprise!) and motioned for the EMTs to get moving. "Let's get the show on the road. If I'm about to move up my retirement date, I might as well find out now."

Retirement? Petey? Of course he'd have to retire from hockey someday and probably sooner rather than later, but it wasn't something he talked about. To be honest, Alison never gave it much thought. He always *did* play hockey, therefore he always *would* play hockey. Of course she knew that was ridiculous, but….

She was forced back and out of the way as they started to move the gurney and its merry band of travellers followed. As they went past her and through the doors leading to a different area, Petey turned around and nearly bellowed to her, "Well? Come on." Like it was her fault it was her and not Lizzie there.

A quick retort died on her lips when she saw the flash of pain that went across his face as he moved. "Coming," she said as she fell into line.

They wheeled him into an area with four curtained-off stalls with beds. She stood back as the EMTs transferred Petey over to one of the hospital beds and then started to move their own gurney back out the way they'd come. "Just ask him," the female one said to the other.

"I can't," he whispered back to his co-worker. "He'll think I'm an asshole."

"You *are* an asshole. But don't let that stop you."

Alison smiled, liking the feisty EMT. She was a tiny thing, too. It's a wonder she could even have helped Petey onto the stretcher as big as he was. "Petey," Alison said, catching his attention. "Give the EMTs your autograph. They did save your life, after all."

"Hardly saved his life," the young woman said as her partner stepped forward, taking his clipboard that had been on the gurney with him. He quickly found an empty sheet of paper, placed it on the top and pulled a pen out of his shirt pocket. He gave Alison a grateful look as he passed her.

Alison hated giving Petey his due, but he hid whatever kind of pain he was in—and she knew it had to be crazy pain if he would allow people to put him on a stretcher—and sat up a little taller, holding his hand out for the clipboard that the EMT was handing him.

"I'm a huge fan," the EMT said as Petey looked at the young man's nametag and then signed the autograph.

"I'm a big fan of yours now, Jeremy. I should probably be asking for *your* autograph."

This flustered the young man and he stammered just a little as he replied, "Oh, no sir, you're the star."

Alison caught the tiny flinch in Petey's face at being called sir, but he never lost his grin. "Maybe. But you're the hero, Jer. You and...." He looked pointedly at Jeremy's EMT partner.

"Sarah," she said.

"You and Sarah." He pointed at the nurses. "And you ladies, too. You guys are the real heroes. And you do it every day. No off-season for you guys."

Jesus. Lay it on a little thicker. But they ate it up, with ducked heads, shy smiles and "Aw, go on" waves of hands.

As the EMTs made their way from the area, the nurses made Petey comfortable and assured him the doctor on call would be with him soon. They then stood back and motioned to Alison, like it was now time for her to take over.

Take over what, exactly? Comforting him? Yeah, right, like he'd ever take comfort from her.

His hand pushing her knee up as he drove deeper into her, moaning her name in her ear then nipping her earlobe.

Holy crap, where had that thought come from?

She shook the disturbing—and oh, all right, arousing—thought from her mind as she stepped closer to Petey's bed. She could do this. She was a trained professional. She treated people in emotional crisis all the time.

But she hadn't had crazy monkey sex with any of them.

And Petey didn't really look like he was in emotional crisis. He did, however, look like he was in a lot of pain. "Do you want me to see if they can give you something for the pain? They'll need to wait for the doctor, but at least they can be prepared. They don't know how much pain you're in."

"How do *you* know how much pain I'm in?"

She gave him a stern stare. "Because you didn't just deny you were in pain. If it were manageable, you'd have given me a line about being a man, or some such shit."

He tried not to smile, and looked away from her, but she could see she'd made him chuckle, if only internally. She stepped a little closer to the bed. She could at least give him this. Comfort by insult was not a technique she'd ever use on her patients, but then again… "So, all those years on the ice, and you fall down icy stairs? Was it because you weren't on skates, or was it because it wasn't flat? Was it the, what, four, five-step incline that really threw ya?"

"Ha. Ha. You know, you—" He was cut off by the appearance of the doctor.

"Mr. Ryan. I'm a big fan. I'm sorry to meet under these circumstances. A fall, was it?" He said all this while writing things on a clipboard. When he finally lifted his head up he noticed Alison. "Alison? Hello. What are…you're a…friend of Mr. Ryan's?"

"Hi, Scott. I see it's your night on call." He nodded and Alison continued. "Yes, Petey and I've known each other since high school."

The doctor stepped forward and held his hand out, which Petey shook. "Dr. Thompson."

"You're not from around here," Petey said to the doctor. It wasn't a question. Scott Thompson was around their age, and they knew everyone in the small area who was around their age.

"No. Chicago originally. I moved here a couple of years ago."

"And you two know each other?" Petey stated the obvious, moving his hand between Scott and Alison.

"Yes," they both said. Scott smiled at her. "It's good to see you."

"You too."

"Are you her dad's doctor?" Petey asked with just enough curiosity to give Alison a tiny—*tiny*—shiver of triumph.

"No. Is your father ill?" he asked her.

"Late-stage Alzheimer's. He's been in and out of here with a lung infection they need to get under control before we can get him into a permanent assisted-living facility."

"Oh, I'm sorry to hear that." He looked between her and Petey again. "So, you were with Mr. Ryan when he fell? You—"

"No," she said quickly. "No. I was here visiting my dad when they brought Petey in. I just came to be with him until his parents get here. And his friend."

"What? You're not my friend?" Petey asked with a pissy voice.

"You know what I mean." She was about to go on, but Scott was done with whatever he'd written in Petey's chart and motioned for the nurses to come forward.

"The nurses mentioned you felt an MRI was in order. Have you had knee injuries before?"

"Several, but not like this. I heard the pop. I'm thinking the ACL is toast, and maybe even the meniscus, too."

"You seem to know your way around the knee."

"Doc, in my line of work...."

"Of course. And of course you've been at it for a good many years."

It wasn't an age slam at all, but Alison saw Petey's mouth form a thin line. "He's in a tremendous amount of pain, Scott, maybe you could—"

"Zip it, Al, I'm fine," Petey barked at her.

"You're not fine. You're—"

"Fine. I'm fine. Can we just get the show on the road?"

"We're going to take you down for an X-ray first, then the MRI most likely."

Alison stepped out of the way to let the nurses in. "I'll go find Lizzie and your parents and let them know what's going on," she told him.

"No," he said quickly, firmly. "I don't want them to know you're back here—they'll demand to be back here. At least my dad will. He'll...." He looked at Alison, knowing she'd understand.

And she did. She knew Dan Ryan would be in a very agitated state, and that was not a good look on him. "Okay. It's fine. I won't go out there."

"In fact, you can go home. Maybe you could just go out a back way or something, so my parents don't see you. Then text Lizzie that I'm fine and that she should keep my parents out there for now." He put on his trademark grin and said to the nurses, "I love my parents, but if they're back here fawning all over me, I *am* going to need those painkillers."

Right. Somehow Alison couldn't envision Lieutenant Dan fawning over his son, injured or not. It would be more like Dan badgering Scott to fix Petey up quick so he could get back on the ice.

But she was absolved from the duty that should have been Lizzie's anyway. She started to gather her bag and then saw... something...flit across his face. Relief? Fear? Pain? "I'll stay until you get back from your X-rays," she said, moving her bag from the chair she'd placed it on and sitting down.

"You don't have to."

"I know." A small look passed between them, but she couldn't have identified it if she'd wanted to. And she didn't. Textbook repression, but she didn't feel like analyzing herself right now.

He said nothing as they wheeled him away. "I'll text Lizzie. See if she can't get your parents to go home until we know what's going on," she called after him.

She heard a snort of laughter—or disgust—even though he was already down the hall. "Yeah. Good luck with that," she heard as Petey was wheeled through swinging doors off into the unknown.

Three

―∿―

The physical, whatever its nature may be, is itself unconscious.
— *Sigmund Freud*

OF ALL THE EMERGENCY ROOMS in all the world, Alison Jukuri had to walk into his.

Technically, Petey supposed, he'd walked—wheeled—into hers, since she was already here visiting her dad.

Still, hers was probably the last face he needed to see right now when all he wanted to do was howl at the injustice of surviving fifteen years in the NHL only to be brought low by his childhood home's front steps.

They'd taken his clothes off and put on one of those stupid gowns—though he'd insisted on keeping his boxers and tee-shirt on—and had done an X-ray and were now moving on to the MRI.

But he knew. He totally knew what the doc—*Scott*, for Christ's sake—was going to say. The tests weren't even necessary—his knee was shot.

He'd have surgery. He'd be fine. He'd be walking well in a few weeks. He could even lace up skates in probably six or seven.

And he'd never put on a uniform again.

If he were a younger man, it wouldn't be a problem. There would be rehab for the knee through the rest of the season and the off-season, and be ready to go by next fall. But he wasn't a young man—at least not by NHL standards. And to have that knee at full strength—full out, bruising defenseman, enforcer, goon-squad strength—wouldn't happen in Petey's remaining window of playing time. If he'd had any doubts about his body being on its last season, they were gone now.

There was a sense of irony to it all that he was sure he'd appreciate more if he weren't in excruciating pain. Something only Alison picked up on. Though if you tell nurses and doctors you're not in pain, that you're fine, they were probably supposed to believe you.

Not Alison. Damn, he hated that she knew him so well. Especially since he felt like he never knew her at all, even after years of traveling in the same set of friends. Even after what they had gone through—No. He was not going down that road again. He'd worn the hairshirt long enough at the time.

The irony of it all. Yeah, that's what he'd been thinking about as the technician situated his leg onto the MRI bed—*Fuck, that hurt*—while he smiled and said he was okay. The irony of just having told the front office, and then his parents, that this would be his last season. And then to have his season ended with one small fall.

No farewell visits to opposing rinks. No good-natured dirty hits from other teams because they'd never get another chance to plant Pete Ryan on his ass. No wave of his stick to the crowd at the Joe when he finished playing his last game in his home arena.

Christ, he'd never step on the ice at Joe Louis Arena again. At least not with a jersey on.

"Okay, Mr. Ryan, we're just about ready to begin," the tech said to him.

Petey gave him a grin and replied, "Take your time, 'cause I think I'm heading into surgery after you're done with me, and I'm in no rush for that."

The tech seemed startled at that and Petey saw him look to the little windowed booth where his doctor sat. He couldn't see what looks passed between them, but the tech was silent and a little more careful as he readied Petey.

"Okay, we're ready to begin. First, you'll—"

Petey held up a hand, interrupting the young man. "It's okay. This ain't my first rodeo."

Again, the tech looked beyond Petey and must have gotten the permission he needed to skip the preamble. He patted Petey's shoulder—which Petey should have found comforting but didn't—and left the room.

The machine started up and his bed moved down into position. They were giving him instructions through the intercom, but he didn't really hear them. He didn't need to, as he'd been through this a few times. And he didn't want to think about where he was and what was bound to come next.

Think of something else. Think of—

Her shapely legs wrapped around his waist as he drove into her, her ankles locked together like she couldn't get enough of him. Later, her sweet little ass curled into him, letting him hold her while she slept.

Aw, shit. *So* not where he wanted to go, even if it distracted him from the whirring of the machine that would be the messenger of bad news.

He'd relived the night of Katie's and Darío's wedding a thousand times in the months since he'd awakened alone in Alison's hotel room. Sometimes in frustration, sometimes in regret. Many times as a prelude to…well, the road could be a lonely place and there were nights where he just didn't want to go through the work it'd take to leave the room and find a willing bedmate in a bar somewhere.

And the memory of his night with Alison would be the final thought that got him off by his own hand in the shower.

To see her walking toward him down the hospital corridor— after fantasizing about her for months—had made him wonder for a moment if the pain in his knee had driven him to hallucinations.

She looked the same as she always did, petite but curvy body, smooth, flawless skin a few shades darker than most of the heavily Finnish population of the Copper Country. Alison was Finnish—and not just on the Jukuri side—but she was what was known as a dark Finn, her ancestors hailing from Lapland.

So she didn't have the white-blond, baby-fine hair that Katie—and many others in the area—did. Hers was a deep, rich brown that took on gold highlights in the summers when they'd all be outside all the time. She always wore it in a shorter style. Lately, it was cut with longer bangs in the front that kind of did this swoopy thing, but still short in the back, showing off her nape. Nothing sexier than a woman's exposed nape.

Nor did Alison have the blue eyes that so often accompanied the light Finns. No, Alison had the most amazing, huge, expressive brown eyes that could relay compassion (for others), and irritation (for him) with a single look.

And those eyes had looked at him once—well, technically twice, but he'd been too young and stupid to recognize it at the time—with such passion, intensity and all-around lust that sometimes just remembering that look in her whiskey-brown eyes was all it took in the shower.

But she wasn't there for him. Lizzie'd made her keep him company until the cavalry arrived.

He'd let her off the hook and told her to go, but she said she'd stay. He didn't really know what to expect as they finished up with the tests and wheeled him back to the holding area or whatever it was called.

Alison was there with one of those electronic book readers in her hands. She looked up as they drew near and then stood. "How'd it go?" she asked.

"They don't tell you anything there. The doc will be around in a few minutes to tell me I need surgery."

"How do you know that?"

He shrugged—*Shit, even that seemed to hurt his knee*—and said, "I know the drill."

She accepted that without question. They all knew when

he'd had surgery for lesser injuries before. Hell, Lizzie'd been at the hospital in Detroit through all of them. Katie and Ron had sent flowers. Zeke, Lizzie's twin and Petey's other best friend besides Lizzie, had flown into town for one of them.

Had Alison ever acknowledged any of his surgeries? A card? Anything?

No, he would have definitely remembered it if she had. Sudden pissiness overcame him. "I thought I said you could go home."

She gave him a look of stone. "I'm sorry. I must have missed the memo that said I listened to you."

"Did you at least text Lizzie and give her the scoop?"

"Yep. She and your parents are still out in the general waiting area. Your parents still have no idea I'm back here. Or that anyone's allowed back here with you."

"Let's keep it that way."

"What? I'm going to go out there and tell them I've been back here the whole time and they could have been, too? And deal with the wrath of Lieutenant Dan? Uh, that would be no."

And that's exactly how it would happen, too. "Jesus, he needs to get a life."

"He has a life," she said with the compassion he knew was there but seldom got to witness. "You. You're his life."

He let out a long sigh that felt good. "I know," he said softly. They both knew it to be true. "This is going to kill him. I mean, hours after I told him I was going to retire, you'd think it wouldn't be a big deal."

"That was for real? You *are* retiring?"

"Retired," he said, motioning toward his offending knee, which looked perfectly fine. From the outside.

"And you already told your parents?"

He nodded. "That's why I came home even though it's just a couple of days' break for the All-Star Game. I put in my paperwork this week. I'm done at the end of the season. I wanted to tell my parents face to face. Then I figured I'd need to see Lizzie after that."

She looked away for a moment, thinking. Always thinking, Alison. With that genius brain of hers that he never had a hope of matching.

"What exactly would have happened in the next three months or so if you hadn't fallen? Between now and your last game?" Her voice was low, soft and just a touch melodic, and he suddenly felt like her patients probably did—valued...important...safe.

But he didn't want her to see him as a patient. Had never wanted that.

"I don't know. Nothing much. Maybe a speech or something at the last home game. Hell, maybe even a bobblehead," he said

"You already have a bobblehead."

She knew that? Did she have one? And why did the thought that she did mean so much to him?

"Stevie has all your crap like that."

Oh. But still, how would she know what Lizzie's stepson collected unless—

"He insisted on showing off all his Pete Ryan paraphernalia when I was over for dinner one night."

The woman was never going to give an inch where he was concerned. A lesson he'd learned long, long ago. But had recently forgotten.

"I think there would probably be more than just a bobblehead. How many years have you been playing?" she asked.

They graduated from high school the same year, though she from Hancock and he from Houghton. They graduated from college the same year, though she with honors and he just squeaking through. They'd both begun their careers right after, though she went on for more degrees and he played a game for a living.

She knew damn well how many years he'd been in the NHL. Didn't she?

"Fifteen."

"Right. That's a long time for hockey, isn't it?"

"For a defenseman, yeah."

"And all those years with just one team. That—"

"I wasn't with the Red Wings the whole time. I got traded and then traded back." Christ, she really had no idea, did she? She'd been hanging with Katie and Ron up here all those years, and Petey knew they kept a close eye on his career. They wouldn't have mentioned that one of their closest friends now lived in a different city, played for a different team? Had missed the Stanley Cup years with the Red Wings?

Or was she playing him? Is this what she did with her patients? To do what—throw them off? Get them to open up more?

He needed to get her off this patient tactic she was taking with him before she started spouting words like "closure" and "acceptance."

He was not one of her patients. Had she moaned and arched while underneath one of her patients? Not damn likely.

"So. You and Doc Thompson? What's going on there? Fuck him yet?"

Her head came back and she pulled out of shrink mode. She blinked those huge brown peepers a couple of times. *Yeah, that's right. I'm not some poor sap who needs the couch.* He sat up a bit straighter, though it sent a flash of pain through him, and waited for her to hiss and spit like the wildcat he knew she could be.

"As if I'd tell you."

"Hmm, normally I'd say that meant yes. But with you...."

"Shut up. You don't know what you're talking about."

"Then set me straight. You and the good doctor...."

She looked like she wanted to spar with him, then he saw her glance at his knee and he knew the instant she decided to go easy on him. *Oh, hell no.*

"He's totally your type, you know. Safe. Boring."

"Educated. Civilized."

There she was.

"If you like that sort of thing."

She snorted a small laugh, and that familiar feeling he got whenever they verbally went at it came over him. Like her jabs were small tokens of affection.

"I do. I do like that sort of thing," she said quietly.

Or like small daggers to the soul.

"Listen, Al—" he began, not really sure where he was going, but also not sure how much of their seesaw he could take right now. He didn't get the chance to finish as the doctor chose that moment to make his way back into the area, chart and printouts in hand.

"Mr. Ryan, you were right. It is the ACL *and* the meniscus. You really did a number on this knee." He turned to the nurse who'd come from the desk area to join them. "Let's get some Percocet for Mr. Ryan right away."

"That's not necessary," he said.

The doc shook the papers in his hand, as if trying to remind Petey how messed up his knee was. Oh, he knew, all right. "Mr. Ryan, you must be in tremendous pain. I really think—"

Petey held up a hand, stopping him. "No meds. At least not until you have to put me under for surgery."

"Don't be an ass. Take the painkillers," Alison said.

He ignored her and asked the doctor, "How soon can you do the surgery?"

The doctor nodded as he said, "I'm glad you're okay with doing the surgery here. I assumed you'd want to have it done in Detroit. Maybe by team physicians?"

He waved that away. "This needs to be done ASAP. And I can't keep it immobilized for that drive or flight."

The doctor was nodding along with him, but also seemed surprised. Like he didn't think Petey had it in him to be so astute. Christ, did *everyone* in the room think he was just a dumb jock?

"Since it's so late, I'd like to keep you overnight and do the surgery first thing in the morning. I've already called Dr. Wright in Marquette and he's on standby to drive over tomorrow morning. I'll assist."

"You're not going to do it yourself?"

"No. He's an orthopedic surgeon. You'll be in better hands with him. For minimal invasion and a much smoother recovery, he'll go in arthroscopically. Which, given your scars, you've obviously had done before."

"But you'll be there?"

"Yes."

He didn't know why that would make him feel better, but it did. "Okay, Doc, let's get this show on the road. Find me a bed."

"Fine. Good. About the painkillers...."

"Nope. Nothing until the drip tomorrow morning. I'm good."

The doctor looked at him skeptically, but just nodded and walked away, giving instructions to the nurse who followed. He looked away from their retreating backs. He'd known what the doctor was going to say, had been dead on about the shape of his knee. So why did it feel so shitty to be right?

"Fuck."

He felt a small, warm hand gently touch his arm. "Want me to go get Lizzie?"

"No." He paused and shook his head slowly. "She'll care too much. So will my parents. They'll all be really upset."

"As opposed to me, who could give a shit?" she said with just a touch of sarcastic bitch in her voice. What had he called it? A dash. Yes, just a dash of bitch on that one. The hand stayed on his arm, though. And damn but he liked it.

"Exactly," he answered, not heeding her sarcasm. "That's exactly what I need right now. Somebody objective. Removed. Pretend I'm one of your patients or something."

"And when did you first know you wanted to sleep with your mother?" she said in a mock, low, smooth, therapist-y voice.

"Fuck," he growled. "Fine. Go get Lizzie. And my parents. Your shift is over. You've done your duty."

As always when they scrapped—which was pretty much whenever they were together—one of them went just a step too far and the other one quit. It was pretty much a running tie on who quit first.

Not that he kept score or anything.

She looked like she wanted to defuse the situation, to put the pin back in the grenade. He silently willed her to—to distract him, to stay with him. And it looked like she was going to. Her hand slid down his arm and, took his huge hand in her tiny one. He turned his over so her palm fit in his, gave hers a small squeeze and looked into her eyes.

And for a moment—just one, tiny moment—all their bullshit fell away and she smiled at him. Really smiled at him. And for just that moment, there was no pain.

And then she looked at their surroundings. A hospital bed. Holding hands. Fear. Pain. He saw the moment her mind went back there. Then something old, and familiar, flashed in her eyes and she stepped away from him. Slipped her hand from his. Removed the soft look from her eyes.

"Good luck tomorrow," she said. Then she gathered her things and walked away from him.

Four
—⚓—

Dreams are often most profound when they seem the most crazy.

~ Sigmund Freud

"AND YOU KNOW HOW MUCH I hate it when my mother calls."

Alison nodded agreement with her patient, prompting her to go on.

Denise Casparich looked at Alison for only a moment then dove in to her weekly tirade about her mother. "Well, it's just that she never listens…."

She went on, but Alison's mind wandered. That never happened with a patient—something in which she took great pride. Because lord knew, sometimes it wasn't easy.

But today, her mind was elsewhere. About two miles elsewhere. Across the bridge and at the hospital where Petey was probably just coming out of surgery.

Alison could easily be there soon—be there when he woke up. She'd be leaving for the hospital as soon as her session with Denise was over. She'd taken this semester off from teaching Intro to Psych at Tech to be able to deal more with her parents' situations. She only saw patients in the morning three days a week. It was the lightest schedule she'd ever had, but she was grateful to have the time now that she was shuttling from the hospital, to her mother's home, to her own, back to the hospital, and now to her mother's for the night.

Although she wouldn't need to be doing that much longer. Her sister Sherry had called just this morning and said she was able to come and stay with their mother for a few weeks. The absolute relief Alison felt also made her feel like crap.

And even though she may shortly be in the same building as a recovering Petey, she knew she wouldn't go to his room. Wouldn't be amongst the ones wishing him well, arranging his pillows, or making sure he had some ice chips nearby.

No. That was for his parents and Lizzie to do. Friends and family.

To the outside world, she and Petey were great friends. They'd been part of the same circle for years, always part of the crowd every summer.

Only they knew about the strain—or should that be *stain?*—on their relationship, which would never allow her the closeness he had with Lizzie, Zeke and Katie. Geez, Petey was even on speaking terms with Katie's ex, Ron, again.

"And I just can't help but think I should be a better friend, you know?"

Alison nodded agreement with her patient, then pulled herself out of her own thoughts. Oops. Denise was off the mother phone call. "Wait. What did you mean by that?"

Denise looked at her like it was a trick question. "That I should be a better friend?"

"Go on with that," she said, motioning with her hand for Denise to go a little deeper.

"Well, I mean, you know, being single and all."

"Mmm-hmm…." Alison mentally kicked herself for letting her mind wander. This may be something much more pertinent to Denise than her love-hate relationship with her mother. Not that the mother issue wasn't fodder for many of their sessions—warranted or not.

"When you're single, your friends become your family."

"In many cases, yes. Go on."

"But it seems like all my friends have either just gotten married or are about to. I'm feeling…very…."

"Left out," Alison finished for Denise. Which she absolutely never did. And honestly, was she finishing Denise's thought or her own? The situation might be babies instead of husbands, but there was no denying her tight circle of friends—yes, her family in many ways—was moving in a different direction. And Alison was feeling…what exactly was she feeling? Is that why she'd slept with Petey the night of Katie's wedding?

In the months since that night, she hadn't allowed herself to even try to put the drunken pieces of the puzzle together let alone *analyze* why she'd done it in the first place.

Enough. It wasn't the time or place to be thinking about… *Petey barely letting the heavy hotel door close behind them as he pushed her up against the wall of her room and started kissing her.*

"But why do you feel *you* need to be a better friend?" she asked Denise, trying to shake the flash of memory.

"Because…maybe then…." She couldn't finish, and this time Alison kept quiet. Denise was in her late twenties, and not originally from the U.P. She'd gone to Tech, fallen in love with the Copper Country, and decided to stay. Not entirely uncommon. Though most Tech grads with degrees in engineering found their way to larger cities.

Not being a native, and with most of her classmates gone, Denise had a smaller group of friends in the area, who were now apparently marrying off.

"How's your sleep lately?" Alison asked, glancing at the small wooden clock on the end table. Time to wrap it up.

Denise had a guilty look on her face as she said, "Fine." Alison gave her a questioning glance, which made Denise turn her attention to the window.

Alison paid more than she probably should for her office space, but it was high on a hill on the Houghton side of the bridge and had the most spectacular view of the Portage canal and lift bridge. In the fall, the colors of the Hancock trees were incredible. Even now, with the immense white blanket of snow and ice covering everything, it was breathtaking.

Unless you were suffering from seasonal affective disorder, as Denise was. Then the frozen tableau could be seen as one incredibly long emotional jail cell.

"Well, maybe not fine. But not as bad as last year."

"Did you try the special lamp I told you about? For light therapy?"

"Not yet."

Alison nodded. She could lead the horse to water.... She continued to go through the things that she and Denise had identified in earlier sessions as behavioral goals. Each week she gave Denise a new strategy or tool for dealing with the issues they'd targeted.

Denise had indeed used some of the tips Alison had given her during the previous week and seemed to feel they'd been beneficial.

They talked for a few minutes more about what things Denise could try in the upcoming week. Alison rounded out the session by asking, "And have you seen your doctor lately? Talked with him about medication?"

"Dr. Thompson? Yeah, he's great, but, you know...."

"There's no shame in antidepressants, Denise. I know you know that."

"I do. I know. But, you know, my mother says I just need more exercise."

"Of course regular activity can *help* with SAD, but—"

"Oh, wow, look at the time. I've got to get going. Thanks very much. I'll see you next week?"

"Of course," Alison replied, rising to walk Denise to the "out" door. She waited quietly while Denise donned her boots, parka, hat and mittens. It would have been easier for her patients to leave their outerwear in the reception area, but then they'd have to go out that way. Alison had made sure when she'd rented the office space that there were separate doors so patients didn't run into each other.

A good practice for any therapist, but particularly so in a small town where you were liable to see someone you knew. Whenever Alison took on a new patient, she always let them know that if she saw them out of the office it was up to the patient if they wished to acknowledge Alison or not. Almost always within the first few weeks she saw them in the aisle at Pat's IGA or at a hockey game.

Finally dressed for the freezing temperatures, Denise turned to Alison, seeming to want to say something, but eventually just pulled her knit cap further down on her head. Alison reached out and settled her hand on Denise's arm. "Hang in there. Spring *will* come."

Denise only nodded her head, turned, and opened the outside door. The blast of arctic wind nearly felled the slight girl and Alison heard her whisper, "When?" to herself as she braved the cold and left the office.

Alison shut the door on the wind and tidied up her office from the morning of patients. She washed out the used coffee mugs in the little kitchen off the reception area and dumped out what remained of the large pot of coffee she'd made this morning. She checked in the fridge to make sure she had plenty of cream, and looked in the cupboard for sugar. She eyed the different cookies and crackers she kept on hand, but the idea of food didn't appeal to her.

She returned to the office and fluffed up the pillows on the couch, then took her tablet, digital recorder, and files from the table next to her chair to her desk. It was on the opposite side of the large room from the sitting area of couch, two large comfy chairs, and end tables. No coffee table between her and her patients. No impediment to communicating, subliminal though it may be.

She took her time entering her notes into each patient's file. Often replaying parts of their conversations to make sure her interpretations at the time still held true.

Stalling. That's what she was doing. Plain and simple. Not wanting to leave her office for the hospital. Because even though she had absolutely zero intention of stopping by Petey's room, she'd know he was there. And she just didn't want to be tempted to swing by his room to see how he was doing.

Finally, she had every note transferred to their electronic file. Then she pulled out the folders of each patient that was scheduled for her next morning. After that, she made her way to the door, put on her heavy coat, boots and gloves, and wrapped her long scarf around her neck several times.

She told herself she was bracing for the cold like Denise had done. But as she walked out into the blustery afternoon, she knew she was bracing herself for much more.

—❦—

The blue of her bridesmaid's dress shouldn't have done for her skin what it did. Her dark Finn skin always looked hottest in yellows and reds. But Christ, the deep blue silk against her olive skin, made even deeper from her tan. He had to touch her. Had to touch that soft skin. Had to slide that blue strap off her shoulder...taste her...all of her....

"Mr. Ryan? Can you hear me?"

Of course I can hear you, baby. Say my name. Don't call me Mr. Ryan. Why so polite now? Call me Petey when my hands are on you like this. Scream my name.

"Mr. Ryan? It's Dr. Thompson. Can you open your eyes?"

Awww, fuck.

Petey slowly opened his eyes, coming out of his drug-induced fog. He hoped like hell he wasn't sporting wood and if so that his mom wasn't in the room with him and the doc.

He did a quick look around, and was grateful that it was just him, Doc, and Barb, the nurse who'd been with him in pre-op. He did a quick look down at Mr. Happy and was relieved to find that his dream, or haze, or whatever the hell it was, hadn't yet made its way south.

"How'd it go?" he asked.

"Very well. Dr. Wright had to do more repairs than originally thought, so it took longer than expected, but I think you'll be happy with the results."

Petey shot the doc a "yeah, right" look.

"Eventually."

Petey raised a brow.

"When you're eighty and able to walk without a cane."

He chuckled at that, but it came out rough and raspy and hurt his throat. Which made him cough, which made him hurt.

"Let's get you some water. How's the pain. Do you—"

"Fine. The pain's fine."

"Well, what we gave you will probably be wearing off shortly, maybe pretty soon with your size. We could—"

Petey grabbed the doctor's arm as he began to write something in his chart. "Doc. No pain meds. Do you understand? I am refusing all pain meds and I'd like you to put that in my chart."

The doctor stopped writing and looked at Petey. Really looked at him. It was all Petey could do to meet his gaze, but he did, not even mentally flinching. The doc was no dummy and he got it soon enough. Nodding, he wrote in the chart. "How about some Tylenol, if needed?"

"Without codeine?"

"If that's what you'd prefer."

"It is."

"Good. I'll make a notation." He finished writing and handed the chart to Barb, who did something with it near the end of the bed. He then looked at Petey again. "Dr. Wright will be in shortly to talk with you. He's in another surgery, and then needs to head back to Marquette. He'll want to give you some specific information about the surgery. The dos and don'ts, that sort of thing."

Petey nodded along. A knee brace for at least a week, maybe two. Shit, maybe a lot longer if it was as bad as the doc let on.

Keeping it elevated whenever he sat. He knew the drill. Knew it a little too well, which is why he didn't want to go anywhere near painkillers. After his last surgery a few years ago, he'd returned to the ice sooner than he probably should have and had gobbled the little bastards like candy just to get through the season.

It hadn't really gotten to problem proportions—thanks to Lizzie ransacking his house and flushing them all down the toilet then not leaving him alone for pretty much the next two weeks—but it'd had the potential to get out of hand. He wasn't about to take any chances now, when he had the rest of his life gaping before him. He'd need all his faculties to make some decisions that he thought he'd had months for which to prepare.

"Your parents and your friend are out in the family waiting area. It's okay with me if you'd like to see them."

He sighed, looked around the room, and sighed again. "Yeah, it's probably best to get it over with."

In seconds, his mom and Lizzie were flitting around him, fluffing pillows, checking on his ice-chip level. His father was at the foot of the bed, grilling Dr. Thompson and Dr. Wright, who'd arrived at the same time.

"There's over three months left in the season. He'll be ready to go before then, right?"

"Dad…."

"I don't think so, no," Doctor Wright said.

"But he's had knee surgery before. Sure, the first one he had the entire off-season to rehab, but the second one, he was back on the ice in two months."

"Dad, will ya—" Petey halted as his father raised his hand in a "stop" motion. Ignoring Petey, he continued to stare down the doctor who had just ensured that his son would walk normally for the rest of his life.

But that wasn't quite as important to Dan Ryan as his son ending his NHL career in a blaze of glory—not finishing it in a heap at the bottom of the front steps.

"It's because of those earlier surgeries and all the damage

done to his knee that he won't be playing hockey again," the doctor said to Petey's dad. He then moved to the head of the bed and addressed Petey. "I'm sorry to be the bearer of bad news, Mr. Ryan, but your professional hockey days are over."

"That's okay, Doc," he said with way more nonchalance than he felt. "I was going to hang 'em up at the end of this season, anyway."

"What?" Lizzie said. That's right. He hadn't made it to her house last night to let her in on the news.

"I told them this week. I'm done at the end of the season." The room, which had already been quiet, fell absolutely silent. "Well. Yeah. I guess I'm done *now*." He tried to conjure up a grin, but it wouldn't come.

Lizzie reached out and took his hand, stroking it. His mother smoothed back his hair. The doctors nodded and conferred with each other.

His father looked like his head would explode.

"That wasn't a final decision. We hadn't finished discussing it. When you came back from Lizzie's, we were going to talk about it some more."

"No, we weren't."

"Yes, son, we most certainly were."

For the early part of his hockey life, Petey would have capitulated at this point. He might not have eventually gone along with his father, but he would have placated him for a while. Then there were the rebel years, his early and mid-twenties, when he would have just told his father to fuck off. But they'd turned a corner somewhere in there, and even though his father was still an emotional guy where his son's hockey career was concerned, Petey was better able to understand and deal with him.

"Dad," he said softly, but firmly, and waited until his father was really looking at him. Really listening. "It was going to happen. But it doesn't really matter now, anyway." He waited, but his father just stared at him. Petey felt his father fighting it— hell, he had too when he realized he'd had enough of the bruising punishment. "Dad. I'm done."

His father looked at him for another few seconds and then nodded his head, but it was like he didn't really see Petey. Nobody else said anything. Petey was about to try to break the mood when his father turned back to him, laid a hand softly on Petey's foot, and said in a small voice, "How are you feeling, son? Are you in much pain?"

That. Right there. That's why even through their stage-father history, their screaming matches about Petey's play in a particular game and their months of pouting after a fight like little kids... *that* was why Petey loved his father.

Because his father loved *him*.

"It's not bad," he lied to his father. His body felt like a log, except for his knee, which burned like a mother.

Dr. Wright, who hadn't been there when Petey'd briefed Dr. Thompson, said, "You're bound to be in pain for quite some time. We'll make sure you have—"

"No," Petey and Lizzie said at the same time. They didn't yell it or anything, but there was firmness in both their voices, which caused his parents to look at them and then at each other. "The pain is manageable," he added. He looked at his parents. "Seriously. It's no big deal."

They looked from him to Lizzie, wanting confirmation that all was well. Lizzie, of course, came through for him like she always did. "It's fine. Not even worth mentioning. He just liked the pain pills a little too much after his last surgery, so it's probably better if he could just suck it up and live with the pain this go round."

"What? Why didn't—"

"Seriously," Lizzie said to his mother, placing a hand on her arm. She then looked at his father before she went on. "If it had been a problem—a *real* problem—you know I would have called you."

They all looked at her, then each other and then at him. "No big deal. Just don't want to rely on them. Especially now that I don't have...won't have...anything." Christ, was that his voice catching?

Thank God his surgeon spoke up. "I'd like to keep you in here for at least a couple of days. I'm back on Wednesday, and if it looks good, you can go home then."

"My other surgeries were all outpatient," Petey said.

"They weren't this severe," the doctor continued. "We really need to keep it immobilized for forty-eight hours. After that, you should be able to move about fairly well. I wouldn't suggest trying to travel back to Detroit any time soon, though. A flight would be detrimental given the lack of legroom, and driving would be way too long of a trip, even with frequent stops."

Petey sighed and ran his hand through his hair. It felt stiff and matted. When was the last time he'd showered? Yesterday morning in Detroit before his flight? God, it felt like a thousand years ago. "I guess there's no rush to get back to the D now."

"I'll call your cleaning lady and let her know you'll be up here for a while. She can take care of things down there." She looked away, and Petey knew she was already four steps ahead of the rest of them. "I'll have someone at the firm write up a press release. No. I'll write it myself, it's too important." She stepped away from his bed to where she'd set her purse. She rummaged through the huge bag and pulled out—he knew without even seeing it—a note pad, onto which she immediately began jotting down notes.

Lizzie owned Hampton and Associates, a pubic relations firm, and Petey'd been her first client years ago when she'd branched out on her own. Now she had many clients with bigger names than him, but he always got her special attention.

"You won't need a cast, but we will definitely want a brace on it for at least a week. Limited movement...." The doctor was rattling off instructions and he was trying to grasp them, but his brain was still a bit fuzzy from the anesthesia. He glanced at Lizzie, who caught his meaning, flipped to a new page in her tablet and looked to the doctor, pen poised like she was a member of the steno pool. He went on about when to have it propped up, how to shower, all that kind of crap. "And try to stay away from icy steps," the doctor concluded with a smile on his face, a feeble attempt at humor. When it fell flat, he cleared his throat and added, "Actually, stay away from steps of any kind for at least a week."

"Oh no," his mother said, her mind obviously going where his went—to their Victorian home with its *many* stairs.

The home he'd built for himself that he lived in during the summers had a main-floor master bedroom, but a family was living there during the winter, keeping an eye on it for him. The husband was doing a year as a prof at Tech. They only needed a place for nine months, and didn't want to move their furniture and everything. He wasn't sure about the details because Lizzie had set it up, saying it would be nice for him to have someone in the house to take care of it. Of all the years that he'd been away during the hockey season, he'd done it maybe four or five times—have somebody in house during the season.

Just his luck that it'd be this year.

Of course, if he was able to stay at his house, his mom would most likely move in to take care of him, and his father would surely follow. He didn't think he could take the constant hovering from them. That would have him reaching for painkillers for sure.

"Okay. Right," Lizzie said, quickly coming up with a new plan. "Well, you'll just come and stay with us. Annie's able to do stairs now, so she can have Stevie's room upstairs and you can have the one she used downstairs. Stevie will take the couch—he'll love that, actually—and…." Lizzie was already planning everything. That was okay with him. Given the choice of kicking out a family from his house, grappling with the steps at his parents (both of those choices coming with his parents' constant company), and crashing at Lizard's….

"But, Lizzie, honey," his mother piped in. "What about the baby? Is he even sleeping through the night?"

"Um, no, not entirely," she answered, and Petey noticed for the first time just how exhausted his close friend looked. It could have been from the late night holding vigil in the waiting room, but it looked deeper than that. And he wasn't about to add to her burden.

"Lizard, I can't stay with you. Not with a baby in the house."

She waved a hand in dismissal. "It'll be fine. We'll just... um...."

"Lizzie," he said in his best cut-the-crap tone, "it's not an option. That damn thing squalling all night will seriously mess with my recuperative sleeping patterns."

Both Lizzie and his mother playfully swatted at him, but he noticed Lizzie didn't push the idea of having him stay in her already crowded household.

"I'll just...." Shit, what would he do? And how much would it mess up his knee to fly back to Detroit and just hang out in his one-story condo for the weeks of recuperation? But now that he was done—really done—he didn't want to be back there during the hockey season. Like he could go in to the rink each day. He hadn't thought that far ahead, but he knew the day after the season was over, he'd be heading out of the D, most likely for good.

"Oh, well, here's the perfect solution now," Lizzie said as she stepped aside. Petey was shocked to see Alison standing in the doorway. "Alison, Petey will be staying with you for a little while."

Five

I watch a lot of hockey. There are some good hockey players and there are some awfully stupid hockey players.

- Ted Lindsay

SHE KNEW SHE SHOULDN'T have come to the hospital today.

Standing in the doorway, she tried to play dumb. "How are you feeling?" she directed at Petey, like she didn't hear Lizzie. "Looks like things went well."

"That's what they tell me," Petey answered her while motioning to Scott and a physician she didn't know. She nodded to them both.

The two men made their way toward the door, and Alison reluctantly moved forward into the room to make a path for them to leave. "Dr. Thompson will check in with you later today. I'll be back on Wednesday morning and we'll see about getting you out of here."

"You have to be here until Wednesday?" she asked.

Petey shrugged, like it was no big deal. Alison didn't have a ton of experience with surgery, but she was pretty sure one like Petey's was done outpatient most of the time.

"Once they got in there, it was more of a mess than they thought," Lizzie explained. "Recovery time may be a lot longer than normal, too."

Petey visibly bristled at that. God, he must hate this. Having people hover around him like this. He loved attention, that's for sure, but not like this.

She desperately tried to think of something to say to Lizzie to distract her from the train of thought she'd obviously been on when Alison had come in. "Umm…you…." Shit. She had nothing.

It didn't matter, because Petey's mom chimed in with, "Alison, we were thinking that maybe Petey could stay at your place for a few days once he gets out of here. Just until he's able to negotiate steps a little better."

She glanced at Petey. His glower was just daring her to…. "Doesn't look like he's real able to negotiate steps on his best days," she hurled out while motioning to his wrapped and elevated knee.

Petey's eyes flashed with what looked like grudging respect at her zinger. His father snorted. His mother and Lizzie looked at her like she'd just kicked a puppy. Yeah. Right. A six-three, two forty-five puppy.

"I can stay with Ron," Petey said. "He's in a first-floor apartment."

"Ewww," was out of her mouth before she could think about it. Gut reaction whenever she thought about Ron since he'd destroyed Katie. Not that she wasn't loads better off now.

"The guy fucked up. It cost him. Big time. Cut him some slack," Petey argued. Of course he argued the point with her.

"It doesn't matter," Lizzie said. "He's got Amber and the baby with him."

Petey shook his head. "Why do I keep forgetting about that?"

Because you're an idiot was just about out of her mouth before she caught herself. No need to kick the puppy even further. Her mind started racing through all the people she knew who would take Petey in. A bunch came to mind. Then she started weeding out the ones with lots of steps in their home. Crap. That was most of them. The area was loaded with older two-story homes. Tall and narrow, with smaller roof areas to have to shovel in the winter.

"Alison's will be fine. Perfect in fact, because you wouldn't even have to do the front steps if we pulled right into the garage."

Damn. Why'd she have to have that attached garage added a few years ago? Because she was sick to death of shoveling her car out every morning. But she'd take that right now over where this conversation was heading.

"I can stop over in the mornings to see how you're doing while Al's with patients," Lizzie started in with whatever master plan she was brewing. "Of course I'll have to bring Sam with me. Or maybe Finn can adjust his time with the horses to be in the house with Sam for a while." She waved a hand, dismissing that possible impediment. "Mrs. Ryan, do you still leave work after school gets out?" At the woman's nod, Lizzie barreled on. "So you can stop over while Alison's here with her dad and then at her mom's."

She saw Petey give her a questioning look at that. He must not be aware that her mom needed looking in on. She kept quiet.

"Oh, but you're spending the nights at your mom's now, aren't you?" Lizzie asked her with compassion in her voice.

Say yes. That would end the whole thing right there. No way should Petey be left alone overnight when he'd barely be able to walk. *Just keep your trap shut and this farce will be over with.*

"Actually, Sherry's coming in tomorrow. She's going to be staying with Mom for a few weeks." Wow. Okay. She typically tried never to play shrink with herself, but that just begged to be analyzed.

Later.

"See? That couldn't have worked out any better," Lizzie said, like everything was concluded.

"Alison still hasn't said if she wants me to stay with her," Petey said, looking right at her.

His parents and Lizzie looked at her, puzzlement on their faces. Or course they'd be puzzled. To them, it'd be like Lizzie taking Petey in—automatic. To them, she and Petey had been best buds for years. They had no idea. None of them knew about....

She looked back at Petey. Was that a challenge in his expression? His strong chin tilted up ever so slightly, a gleam came into his eyes. Yep. The son of a bitch was challenging her.

She just wasn't sure to what.

"Of course I want you to stay with me," she answered with absolutely no hint of sarcasm in her voice. His parents and Lizzie all looked as if her answer were no big deal, like it was a foregone conclusion that she'd want to help out her dear, dear friend.

But the look in Petey's eyes. It seemed like part shock that she'd called his bluff. Part irritation that he'd now be under her roof, at her mercy as it were. But the other part of that look....

She trembled just a tiny bit, feeling a shock of awareness go through her. The other three people around the bed didn't notice, as they were gathering things or settling into chairs.

But Petey noticed. And his look of triumph had her scurrying for the door.

—⚉—

"So let's see your ring," Mr. Jukuri said to Petey late on Tuesday afternoon.

"I don't have a ring, Mr. J. I wasn't with the Red Wings when they won the Cup, remember?" Wrong thing to say apparently, as Alison's father got a confused look on his face and then turned to look out the window of his hospital room.

Petey and Lizzie had spent all morning crafting a press release about his injury, talking on the phone with the Red Wings front office—who'd been incredibly understanding, even though they'd need to call up an inexperienced defenseman to finish out the season—and working out logistical details of him not returning to Detroit for the foreseeable future. She'd brought the baby with her, in one of those carrier things. Petey had to admit it was a cute little thing. He. Sam. Sam was a cute little thing. Being an only child himself, and Lizzie being the first in their close group to have kids, Petey didn't have a lot of experience with babies. Yeah, sure, his teammates had a bunch of kids, but Petey'd never been one to hang out at a teammate's home and intrude on family time during the season. They got it so infrequently with the crazy road schedule.

And Sam seemed to have inherited his mother's love of plans. Lizzie announced when she'd entered his room that Sam would be awake just long enough for he and Petey to become acquainted and then sleep while they conducted business, and damn if that wasn't exactly what happened.

But after she left, and before his mother was due to arrive after her day of work as Houghton's elementary school's chief administrative assistant, Petey felt a little stir crazy. Dr. Thompson had said he'd need to get out of bed and move around a bit with the brace and crutches before they'd let him leave tomorrow. So he'd asked a nurse to set up a wheelchair for him a little bit outside his room and then hobbled to it before collapsing into it.

It'd been a lot harder on him than he'd thought it'd be. He was so drained he didn't put up any argument when the nurse started wheeling him around. To give him a change of scenery, she'd said. It all looked the same to Petey—depressing as hell—until he thought to ask to be brought to Mr. Jukuri's room for a visit.

Mr. J had always liked Petey. Had always loved talking hockey with him. And Petey liked talking with Mr. J. because he wasn't nearly so obsessive about hockey as his own father was.

But now, looking at the frail man, confused by his own failing memory, Petey wondered if he should have come at all.

"Lots of people do that," he tried to reassure him. "Assume I won the Cup. But no, I was with the Stars during those years."

He'd hated Dallas. The guys had been all right, and the front office had been good to him. But the lack of seasons bugged him. It just didn't feel right to leave the ice rink and walk out into ninety-degree heat. He'd missed Michigan and was grateful when he'd been traded back to the Wings.

He'd never even bought a place in Texas, just rented. It'd never felt like home.

"Yes, that's right. You were with Dallas during those years. I forgot about that."

"Yeah, I'm still trying to," Petey said with a wink that caused Mr. J to laugh. Ah, good, he was back. Or maybe he'd never left.

"And will you be able to finish out the season, Pete?" he asked, nodding toward Petey's knee.

"Doesn't look that way."

"There's always next year."

"Actually, that does it for me. I'm officially retired. They'll make the announcement tomorrow."

"Oh, that's a shame. They'll miss you on the blue line."

Petey felt a lump form in his throat, and his good-natured aww-shucks comeback died on his lips. Holy shit, this was for real. Lizzie's group would take care of the details, but he was going to be bombarded with looks like Mr. Jukuri was giving him right now.

It wasn't quite pity—who would pity a hockey star making two mil a year? It wasn't just compassion. He didn't know what the hell it was, but suddenly he was grateful he'd be hiding out at Alison's for the next week and be able to dodge all of it.

Speak of the devil—in she walked. And dressed in red, too. The smile she directed at her father faltered when she saw Petey sitting in the wheelchair next to the older man's bed.

"What are you doing here?" she asked him as she took off her red coat, draped it over a chair, then moved to the other side of her father's bed and kissed his wrinkled cheek.

"Stretching my legs," he answered. Mr. J laughed, but he got a "humph" from Alison. "Doc said I needed to move a little, so I walked with crutches and the brace to the chair."

"How's the pain?"

Like you wouldn't believe. "Manageable."

She looked closer at him. She started to say something then stopped. Turning to her father, she asked in a much nicer voice than she'd used with Petey, "And how are you today, Daddy?"

"Fine, dear, fine." He gave his daughter a warm smile and Petey noticed the brief look of melancholy that flitted across her face.

That sweet, round, almost angelic face that contorted with near pain as she climaxed beneath him.

"I was just talking hockey with Petey. Sounds like he's hanging up his skates. But you probably already knew that."

"I did, yes."

"I guess we all grow old," he said, then let out a weary sigh. "I'm feeling pretty good today, Alison, are there things we should go over?"

"Should I leave?" Petey asked and made to move the wheelchair.

"No, no, you're fine," Mr. Jukuri said. It looked like Alison was about to trump her father's choice when he added, "I've enjoyed our chat and would like to talk some more if you have the time."

Petey could see Alison warring with wanting him out of there—wanting him gone, in general—and her father's enjoyment. She finally shrugged, turned around and pulled the guest chair up to the side of the bed and sat down.

"I've got nowhere better to go," Petey said and made a show of reclining a little and putting his hands behind his head. Shit... even that hurt.

"Sherry's coming in tomorrow. I'm going to pick her up at the airport and bring her to the house to see Mom. Then she'll have your car to come see you tomorrow evening."

"Oh, that's wonderful. Is she bringing the babies?"

Petey watched Alison open then shut her mouth, a sadness coming to her face, which she quickly tried to hide. Al's sisters were much older and had grown kids of their own. "No, Dad, the babies are grown up. Jake got married two years ago. And Taylor just graduated from college last spring. They're both out east, like Sherry."

Charles Jukuri looked at his daughter with concentration, then looked over to the wall where someone—it had to have been Al, right?—had blown up a family photo of the Jukuri clan from whenever they'd last been together.

The photo looked to be a few years old, with Mr. Jukuri looking much healthier than he did now. It'd been taking in the summertime on the front lawn of what had been the old Jukuri cabin. Alison had taken it over about ten years ago and slowly refurbished the whole thing. It was on the small side, but it was cozy and on the lake.

And had no stairs.

"Yes, that's right. Sherry sent us video of Taylor's graduation from Rutgers."

"Yes, yes she did," Alison answered her father with near glee in her voice at her father's memory of something that happened less than a year ago.

And suddenly, sitting in a wheelchair with only a few months before he was whole again—even though he would be out of work—Petey felt like a total shit for the feelings of self-pity he'd been having since waking up after surgery.

"Anyway," she went on kind of quickly, as if trying to cram things in during this lucid moment. "Sherry's able to stay for a whole month with Mom."

"That will be a nice break for you, Alison. You've done so much."

Had she? He'd had a sense of things going downhill with her parents when he was home last summer, but hadn't really digested how much. Or how bad.

She waved her father's statement away with a flick of her little hand. "It looks like we'll be able to get Mom moved into the Ridges during the time that Sherry's here. In the type of apartment we all talked about. Do you remember that?"

He nodded. "And when will I be able to join her there?" There was a fear in his voice, like maybe she'd tell him he wouldn't be able to join his wife in the assisted-living facility.

"Soon, we hope. In fact, Dr. Simms mentioned that your infection seemed to be responding to the meds better than he hoped. You might even beat Mom to your new place."

"And the house? You'll sell the house?"

She looked down at her lap, seeming to gather her thoughts. Petey was both riveted to the family scene and embarrassed that he hadn't left. He hadn't realized these were the types of things Mr. Jukuri would want to discuss because he was having a good moment.

God, this could so easily be him in only twenty or thirty years, with as many concussions as he'd had on the ice and the links they were making between NFL players with several concussions and early-onset dementia. He'd thought about it. It was one of the reasons he'd decided to retire after this season. But holy shit, the thought of his children having to remind him of important things like Alison was doing now?

Assuming he ever had children.

He started to have a mini flash of panic, so he tried to zero in on what Alison was saying so he wouldn't think about himself.

"That's what you both wanted when it got to this point. But we don't have to, I can—"

"Yes. Sell the house. I remember the plans your mother and I made. We don't want to be a burden on you, Alison. And we want to be together if possible. They were sound plans then, no reason to change them now." He gave Alison a questioning look. "Is there?"

The man was looking for hope. Looking for Alison to tell him the situation was so much better than they'd planned for.

She ducked her head, her short hair falling like a curtain over her eyes, only her chin visible. Then she looked at her father straight on and said, "No. There's no reason to change the plans you and Mom made."

She had balls and didn't hide. Never had. It was a quality that he both admired and was irritated by, depending on the day.

They talked some more about lesser things, then she gathered up her things, kissed her father goodbye, and said she'd be back that evening to see him again.

Jesus, she was making two trips a day to see him, plus her

mother, plus her patient load? He couldn't remember if Lizzie'd mentioned if Alison was still teaching at Tech or not. Probably not with all she had going on.

Again, sitting in a wheelchair for a couple of days and lying around in bed for a few weeks was starting to seem pretty good.

After Alison left, he chatted hockey with her dad for a little while longer and, when it was getting close to the time his mother was expected to show, he started to say his goodbyes. As he maneuvered the wheelchair past the bed, Mr. Jukuri reached out to stop him. He leaned over and said in a low, conspiratorial voice, "I've seen how you look at her, you know."

Fuck. For years he'd masked how he looked at Alison, had practically made a science of it, only to have her father call him on it now?

"Don't worry, she can't tell." *Thank God.* "But I can." *Oh, shit.*

Was it polite to burn rubber out of an old man's hospital room? "Listen, Mr. J, I think you've got it—"

"I'm telling you, Jimmy, Sally's the type of girl you just have to take charge with."

Oh. Okay. So, was this better or worse? And how was he supposed to respond? And did Mr. J. really know "*Sally*"? She would eat alive any man who tried to control her.

"Um, yeah, I know, but...."

Mr. Jukuri took his hand from Petey's arm and waved it with more strength than he'd have guessed the old man had.

"See what I mean? 'Um, yeah.' That's not the type of thing that's going to get her. She needs somebody just as strong as she is, someone who will peel off that armor she's built around herself." He pointed a bony finger at Petey. "I'm telling you, Jimmy, Sally is not the type of girl you steal kisses from."

Petey knew that.

"She's the type of girl you *take* kisses from."

Petey didn't know *that.*

But he wouldn't mind finding out.

Six

—ᴍ—

Who looks outside, dreams; who looks inside, awakes.

- Carl Gustav Jung

LIZZIE STOOD IN THE DOORWAY to Alison's bedroom and laughed at Petey, who had just been tucked into bed by his mother like he was a toddler. "Oh, God, I didn't think Alison even owned pink sheets. I'm pretty sure she bought them just to mess with you."

He had no doubt of that.

His mother and Lizzie had picked him up from the hospital and brought him to Alison's cottage, where they found the door unlocked, flowers on the kitchen table and a note stating she wanted Petey to take her room because of the television in there.

She'd put a PS on the note that had cracked his mom and Lizzie up—"Stay out of my panty drawer, perv."

It made sense for him to stay in her room. It was closer to the kitchen and the bathroom, and there was the television bonus. But a flicker of…something…went through him at the thought of spending time in her bed. Until he quickly realized she'd moved her personal things down the hall to the other bedroom.

And that she'd frillied up the room she'd stuck him in. It had to be on purpose. He could so not see her with pink sheets and pink comforter and pink…well shit, just about everything.

Lizzie's dropped-jaw look at the bed and her subsequent chuckles had confirmed it. "My God, when did she even have the time to do this? It's good, though, she needed a good laugh."

"Yeah, except you're the one laughing, as will be anybody who comes to visit and sees me in this Barbie Dream House."

Lizzie hooted with laughter. "Oh, she laughed, all right. You just know she was busting a gut standing in line at Shopko with these in her cart."

He couldn't help smiling at the thought of that. Yeah. Okay. She got him on that one.

His mother came back into the room, stifling a grin as she looked at her bruising hockey-player son surrounded by pink shams.

It was a sham, all right.

"I put the casserole in the oven on timer, so it'll go off by itself when it's done, in case you're sleeping. It'll be fine until you're ready or Alison gets home."

"Thanks, Mom. You know you didn't have to do that."

She came over and sat on the edge of the bed. Petey was propped up against the headboard on top of the comforter—no way was he going to crawl into the pile of Pepto Bismol until he had to. His mother pulled a throw (pink) from the foot of the bed and draped it across his legs to his waist. He saw her eyes fill with sadness as the throw covered the brace on his leg. At least he was able to wear track pants and have the brace fit over them.

"It's the least I can do, bring some meals over for you. And Alison. It kills me that you can't be at the house."

"Dad and I would be at each other's throats within twenty-four hours."

She looked like she was going to argue with him but then just shrugged and gave a small smile. "You're probably right."

"Plus, all those damn stairs. Not to mention the ones that did me in in the first place."

She put a hand on his ankle. "Oh Petey, you have no idea how sick your father is about that. He was beside himself. He still is."

"Why? It's the end of January in the Copper Country. What outside steps aren't icy? I just wasn't paying attention. Too much of a Southern boy now."

"They don't have icy stairs in Detroit?"

"Not for hockey stars—we're exempt! We do our share of ice time in other ways."

She swatted his good leg and chuckled. His mother's laughter was better than any Vicodin. "Seriously, Mom, you've got to get Dad to ease up on himself. It never occurred to me that it was in any way anyone's fault."

"That's right," Lizzie said, entering the room. "If you think about it, he was on his way to see me. One could say it was my fault."

"Yeah, let's go with that," he said, winking at his best friend, who flipped him the bird behind his mother's back.

"I need to get back home. I have a conference call."

"It's after five. Didn't you promise Finn you'd keep normal work hours now?"

"West coast."

That sparked his interest. "Who ya going after?"

A coy smile played across her face. "Can't say, it's too early. Let's just say Darío made the connection and it would be a *Major* coup for Hampton and Associates."

What Major-winning golfer lived on the west coast? "Phil?" She only smiled wider. "No shit? Lizard, that's great."

"Petey," his mother said, swatting him again as she rose from the bed. "Watch the mouth."

"Sorry," he said, though they both knew he wasn't. "Good luck with the call."

"Thanks. Like I said, way too early. We're just going to talk about some of his charitable foundations and if we could help him out."

"Which of course you can."

"Of course," she said with no hesitation. She came over,

bent down and kissed him on the forehead, and ruffled his hair. Yep, definitely a toddler. "Al thought she'd be home around eight after having dinner with her mom and sister and stopping by the hospital for a quick visit with her dad."

"How long has she been keeping this up?"

Lizzie sighed, placed her hands on her hips, and looked out the window like she was counting the passage of time via the seasons. Maybe she was. "Jeez, I think her dad's been in and out of the hospital for nearly a year now? Maybe a little less. Her mom didn't start going downhill until this past summer, and it's been a lot slower."

"Jesus," he said under his breath.

"Yeah," Lizzie agreed.

He looked around at the stupid pink sheets. Where *had* she found time to do this? "This seems like a lot to ask. Maybe we should figure something else out. A motel or something? Call Jules and see if she has any rooms available for long-term. I know it's snowmobile season, but she loves me. She'll find me a room."

"You are not staying in a motel, nice as Jules's place is. You'll go stir crazy. At least here you can hobble to the kitchen and living room for a change of scenery. Plus, you can't beat the view," his mother said, motioning out the large window to the ice-covered lake. If he weren't pissed at ice in general right now he'd agree.

"Honestly," Lizzie said, "I think this might be good for Al, too. She's been in such a rut lately with the hospital, her mom's situation and her private practice."

"So, what? Another patient for her to look after?"

"You mean like her parents' kind of patient, or her patients' kind of patient?" Lizzie joked. "'Cause I'm thinking you could probably use both kinds of attention."

"Ha fucking ha," he said, and shrugged as his mother arched a brow at his language, then left the room.

It was Lizzie's turn to sit on the bed and pat his foot. "Seriously, though, you know she'd be a great listener if you want to talk about this all."

"Talk about falling down the stairs and having my knee twisted all to hell? Doesn't seem like a lot to talk about."

Lizzie pinned him with a look. Her no-nonsense stare that she'd pulled on him numerous times. And which he'd ignored numerous times.

"You know what I mean. Obviously you wanted to talk about your impending retirement with your folks and me, or you wouldn't have gone through the huge hassle of flying up here for a day when you could have just called or emailed with the news. And that's when you had several months to come to terms with it. Well, guess what, those terms are now upon you. It'd be no wonder if you went through some sort of...."

"Of what?"

She waved a hand around, as if trying to capture the right words. "I don't know. A phase or something."

"A phase? Like puberty?"

"See? This is why you should talk to Al about it. I'm not the best at figuring out emotions. Hell, I ate mine for fifteen years." She looked away from him, out the window, and he knew she was a step away from beating herself up inside.

He nudged her hip with his good knee. "Hey," he said quietly. He nudged her again until she took her gaze off the wintery landscape and looked at him. "All in the past, Lizard. You're in a good place,now. You. Finn. The kids. Baby Sam. It's all good."

She blinked at him, and then, as if coming out of a trance, a huge smile lit her pretty face. "You're totally right. Nothing but rainbows and lollipops."

"And Major-winning clients, unless you blow it by being late for your call."

She glanced at her watch and nodded. "Yep, gotta go." She moved from the bed just as his mother came back into the room with a pitcher of water and a glass, which she put on the bedside table.

"I can stay if you want me to," she said. "Until Alison comes home."

Part of him wanted her to. Not because he feared being alone, but because he'd like some buffer when Alison first arrived. They'd have to be alone together, of course, but if his mom were here then she'd have to be semi-cordial to him. Jesus. He needed his mommy to make sure the big bad girl was nice to him?

"Nah, but thanks. I'm pretty wiped and I'll probably just zonk out for a while, anyway."

"That's good. The doctor said you should get as much rest as possible for the next few days."

They said their goodbyes and the ladies left him in the pink cauldron to stare out the window at the frozen landscape and think about what he was going to do with the rest of his life.

—⚒—

Alison quietly let herself into her home, hoping not to wake Petey. Hoping Petey would be asleep. The kitchen smelled amazing and she glanced around the room from where she stood in the foyer divesting herself of her winter outerwear. No sign of whatever smelled so good. Boots off, she padded across the hardwood floor and peeked in the oven. Nothing. She looked in the fridge. A casserole dish, with a large portion of the cheesy concoction removed, sat covered with a glass lid. She peered at the sink, but there were no dirty dishes. Opening the dishwasher she saw a rinsed plate, glass and some silverware.

Lizzie or Petey's mom must have stayed a while and gotten him fed and cleaned up. This was just as well, since she was exhausted after her dinner with her mother and Sherry. She put the bag of warm soup she'd gotten to go from the restaurant into the refrigerator. He could have it tomorrow.

"Al?" she heard him call from her bedroom. "That you?"

Who else would it be, she wondered, but then mentally cut him some slack upon realizing that her home would probably have a revolving door for the next few days. His parents and Lizzie and others would want to come and see how he was faring. And leave yummy-looking casseroles.

"Yep," she answered as she made her way down the hallway to the bedrooms. "Sorry if I woke you, I was trying to be—" The words died in her mouth as she rounded the corner and saw him propped up in her bed naked from the waist up, a vision of pure male amidst the pink bedding.

She'd bought it as a joke. She'd been at Shopko picking up her mom's meds yesterday when she'd taken a U-turn with her cart and ended up buying anything pink and lacy that would fit on a queen bed.

But now she played shrink for just a second and wondered if she hadn't done it to protect herself. To temper the vision of him in her bed.

And she hadn't even factored in the naked part.

God, he was so big, so strong, with a chest full of dark hair that trailed down and down into…a mass of…frilly pink cotton. Yep, that helped. A little.

"You didn't wake me. I slept most of the afternoon and evening after my mom and Lizzie left. I just woke up about an hour ago."

She nodded, trying not to stare at his chest. "Wait. So you got that dinner by yourself?"

"Well, my mom put it in the oven on timer. I didn't make it or anything."

"But you got out of bed, got the thing out of the oven, ate, and did the dishes?"

He shrugged, like it was no big deal, and Alison took a step closer, really looking at him now, not just at his amazing physique. "That seems like a lot on your first day out. Are you feeling okay?" She went to place a hand on his forehead like a mother checking a child for fever, but stopped herself.

He tracked her movement with his eyes, staying on her dropped hand as he said, "Doc said I should move around a little more each day."

"Yes, but he probably meant, like, working up to getting to the john or something, not standing in the kitchen doing dishes."

"I just put 'em in the dishwasher. It's no big deal. I'm fine." There was an edge to his voice and she knew to drop it. She moved around the side of the bed, to a small alcove that looked out onto the lake. She'd placed an upholstered chair and ottoman in the little nook, thinking she'd read case files on that chair while watching boaters on the lake. She'd even spent extra money on beautiful windows. But instead, the spot had become her sanctuary from the outside world and she never brought work into the space. She used it for pleasure reading and to just sit and be calmed by the sight of the lake.

Getting comfy in the chair, she studied Petey while he watched her. "Do you want to talk about—" She saw the panicked look in his eyes and realized he thought she was going to bring up the night of Katie and Darío's wedding reception. She quickly finished her thought. "—Setting up some ground rules while you're staying here?"

"Like what? You'll put a necktie on your bedroom door if you've got someone in there?" There was some humor in his voice, but also just enough petulance to make her burrow into the chair, pull the cashmere throw from the ottoman up and around her, and give him a small, coy smile and shrug.

"Well, yes, I guess that's what I mean."

It wasn't at all what she'd meant. But the way his shoulders tensed and his eyes narrowed...well, she really couldn't be blamed for a little exaggeration, could she?

"Are you seeing someone right now?"

"I...."

He held a hand up. "Wait. Were you seeing someone that night? The night of Katie's wedding? Is that why you bailed in the morning without a word?"

Where had that idea come from? Had he been thinking about why she hadn't stuck around for the post-mortem? Wasn't it obvious? That there was no way in hell she could face him after....

The best night of sex in her life.

Wow. How could she even know that if most of the night

was still hazy at best? But she knew it was true.

And suddenly she didn't want to play this game with him. "No. I wasn't seeing anyone then. I'm not seeing anyone now."

He relaxed. Just a small movement, a tiny shifting of the shoulders, but she saw it. He ran a hand through his hair, took a deep breath, then let it out. "So, let's do this. Let's talk about the elephant in the room."

Well, crap. But she wasn't a shrink for nothing. She could shut this down easily enough. "Which elephant is that? The two-month-old elephant?" She paused, waiting for him to see where she was leading him. The moment he did, she lowered the hammer. "Or the eighteen-year old elephant."

Direct hit. He wouldn't be trying to push her anywhere she didn't want to go. She tossed the throw off of herself, got up and made to leave the room. If the man could fix himself dinner and put his dishes in the dishwasher, he didn't need her waiting on him. She could make an early night of it in the guest room where she'd moved some of her things.

As she passed by the bed, he moved for her arm. She tugged, but he held tight. "If that's where you want to go, that's where we'll go," he said, and pulled her closer to him. "You can't just drop a bomb like that and walk out."

"Watch me," she said. He not only held fast, but also tugged on her hard, causing her to tumble into the side of the bed. He took advantage of her loss of balance and pulled her across his big body so that her butt was on the bed near his hip and her legs were draped over his lap. He anchored her with a quick arm around her waist, his other hand still gripping her arm.

He was so close. His eyes were so blue as they bore into hers. She'd always loved a black-haired, blue-eyed combination on a man. He smelled clean, if just a little antiseptic, probably from hospital shower soap. She thought she'd find it unpleasant, but she didn't.

"Not this time," he whispered. "You're not going to walk away from me this time." His eyes dropped to her lips and she knew he was going to kiss her.

And God help her, she was going to kiss him back.

Seven

—⚏—

Figure skaters have awful perceptions of hockey players.
- *Kristi Yamaguchi*

SHE SMELLED SO GOOD. Not at all like the hospital soap and shampoo that he'd used this morning before he'd been discharged.

God, was that just this morning? Sitting here now, with Alison in his arms, it seemed like everything else was light years away. That everything came down to this one moment in time. When he could kiss Alison Jukuri again.

It'd been eighteen years between the first and second time they'd kissed, so two months between the second and third time should feel like nothing. But it didn't. It felt like a very long time indeed.

"Petey," she said with warning in her voice.

Typically he'd heed that warning tone, knowing that the barbs would soon come out. But the moment he saw her walk through the bedroom door, he knew he was going to try out Mr. Jukuri's advice. Even if that advice had been for Jimmy and Sally.

Hard-headed woman and a befuddled man? Same diff.

"Alison," he said softly. He ran his hand up and down her back trying to gentle her, like a mare that could bolt at any minute. "Easy. It's so easy." And it was. That was the shitty part about the whole thing—the physical had been easy, and so, so good, between them. It was the other stuff—the real-life stuff—that caused them to steer clear of anything more than friendship.

His hand released her arm and slid down, over her little wrist, to her hand. He twisted his palm up so hers rested in his. He didn't assert any pressure, didn't circle his fingers around hers, he just waited while he watched her.

Her big brown eyes left his and travelled to their hands. God, he loved to watch her think, to see that million-dollar mind grapple with something so basic, so simple. Like holding hands with a man she was hot for. She may have a genius IQ, but when it was her own life, she was as clueless as everybody else.

Something clicked inside her. He wasn't sure what, but he knew the moment she decided. She bit her lip—Jesus, that sent a shock straight to his dick—and slowly moved her hand so that their fingers aligned on top of each other, though hers were much smaller and shorter than his. Then she put just the slightest pressure on hers so that her fingers split his and their hands were intertwined.

She looked from their hands back to him and he thought he'd lose it. She was so breathtaking to him right then, her eyes shimmering with passion, her little chin raised just a tiny bit in challenge. Her lips parted slightly in anticipation. God, those lips. *Must taste* was all his non-million-dollar brain was capable of computing.

He started to dip his head slowly, to be gentle so she wouldn't turn away, and then Mr. Jukuri's words ran through his head. *Take it. Take.* His body paraphrased. His hand quickly slid from her back to her nape, holding her in place as his mouth descended on hers. She let out a tiny gasp of surprise just as his lips took hers and he knew he'd made the right move.

Holy shit, she tasted good. A little coffee, something sweet, but mostly she tasted of desire. He'd slept with more women than he could remember, but this little firecracker had always been the kiss he thought of the most. For her being so tiny, and he so huge, their mouths fit together perfectly. His lips moved over hers, quickly finding a rhythm. He slid his tongue inside her mouth to find hers waiting to play, to tangle, to taste him back.

He tightened his grip on the back of her neck and she moaned. A fleeting memory of her moaning with pleasure as he held her down that night two months ago passed by him. Did his girl like to be taken?

Increasing the pressure of his mouth on hers, he moved their intertwined hands behind her back, arching her against him, taking away some of her control. And damned if she didn't like it, breathing more heavily, devouring his lips in return.

Christ, could it have been that easy all these years? Just take the control from a woman who was always in control of her own emotions? A woman who wore biting comments and her high intellect like armor against all those who got close?

Instead of trying to slowly pierce it, should he have just ripped the damn armor off?

The hand on her neck loosened and she whimpered her disapproval. "Wait," he whispered to her. "I've got it now. I know. I've got ya." She didn't acknowledge his words other than claiming his mouth and sucking on his tongue, but that was enough. He moved his hand from her neck to her shoulder, then pushed her down—not very gently—to her back, following her down, hovering over her, blocking out any sight but him. Her legs slid up over his turned hip, dangling along his ass.

He pulled his lips from her. She had her eyes shut tight. "Look at me," he whispered, but she only licked her lips, inviting him back. Not good enough. "Look at me," he growled, and nipped her bottom lip. Her eyes sprung open, glazed with desire and something else. Embarrassment? Shame?

No. He wouldn't allow that. If she needed it this way, he could do that for her and not let her feel badly about it. He pulled their still joined hands from behind her—sadly, because the arch of her back pushed those sweet tits nearly in his face—and pinned their hands above her head. He quickly grabbed her other hand and brought it up to join her other, holding them both down with his. He skimmed his free hand down the underside of her arm, against her soft, baby-blue sweater. Down along her ribcage, to the petite, but curvy waist. He held her firmly there, letting her know he was in charge. She briefly tried to free herself, but she didn't put much effort into it and she licked her lips and watched his face as he pushed her hands deeper into the pink sheets.

"Don't," he said firmly. Her chest started rising more heavily, almost begging for his touch, but he wouldn't give it to her. Not yet. He swooped down to taste those lips again, but she moved her head slightly to the side at the last moment. Oh, she wanted to play. He tightened his grip on her hands. "Kiss me," he demanded, and she turned her head and looked at him, confliction in her gaze. "Now," he said more strongly, and dipped his head so his lips hovered over hers. "Do it."

And damn, she did, raising her head off the bed to devour his mouth with hers. She moaned again as his hand left her waist to cover a soft breast. He squeezed, then rubbed his thumb over the already hard nipple. He broke away from her kiss so he could watch as his continued stroking caused her nipple to tighten up and peak behind her sweater. He tried to pinch, but his fingers slid on the soft material. He didn't want to let go of her hands to get the sweater off, but he had to get his mouth on her. Pushing the sweater up to her chin, he didn't even take the time to reach behind her and undo her bra, instead pulling down the cup so that her luscious globe became visible to him.

And available to his mouth.

He kept his eyes on hers as he took that sweet nipple into his mouth, pushing her joined hands further down on the bed.

"Oh, God," she moaned, her neck arching, head driving into the mattress. Her hands wrapped around his and he wasn't sure if he was holding her down, or she was holding him to her, but it didn't matter. All that mattered was that hard nipple in his mouth pebbling up under his tongue. The soft flesh surrounding it tightening and growing as he sucked.

He switched sides, going through the same jerky movements

to bare her other breast and feast upon it. God, she had amazing tits. Full-sized for such a petite woman, soft yet firm and so, so responsive. He could have stayed like that for hours, just moving his head from time to time to lick and play and suck on the other one. But she wanted more, his Al. She started moving her hips, which, given how awkwardly situated they both were, basically jammed her ass into his crotch—not that he was complaining.

He needed to be on top of her, and he sensed she needed it too. Forgetting everything except the need to dominate her little body, he slid her legs from his hip down....

"Fuck," he yelled as excruciating pain shot through his leg. His hands left her to reach down and move her legs from on top of his bad knee just as she realized what had happened.

"Oh, holy crap, I'm so sorry," she exclaimed. She tried to scoot away from him, but it only caused her foot to come in direct contact with his knee, even more unprotected since he'd taken the brace off for the night shortly before she'd come home.

He hissed through his teeth, wanting to throw her legs and body well away from him, and yet not wanting her gone from beneath him. He just needed to move his damn leg away....

But it was too late. She did some kind of gymnastic half-twist, half-roll away from him and she was off the bed on the other side. He pawed at the sheets, like he could pull her back to him, but she was shaking her head. She pulled down her sweater and stepped further away.

"It doesn't hurt. I mean, it did at first, but it's fine now." He held his hand out to her, still off balance from her sudden departure. "No damage done."

Wrong thing to say. Her head was shaking and it sounded like a small snort of half disgust and half laughter escaped from her. Her hand flew to her mouth as if to take the strangled sound back. Her fingers moved over her lips, puffy from their rough kisses.

She walked quickly around the bed and to the door.

"Al, wait," he pleaded, but she was nearly out the door. But then she stopped. Thank God she stopped, though she kept her back to him. Her movements in front of her body indicated that she tucked her breasts back into her bra. What a waste.

She slowly shook her head. "I'm so sorry, I never meant for that to happen."

"My knee's fine. I don't even feel it anymore," he replied, though he knew that's not what she'd meant.

"That's not what I meant and you know it," said the frickin' Mensa member.

"Come back, Al," he said quietly, but she was already shaking her head, still not even looking back at him. "Look at me, for Christ's sake."

She slowly turned around. Yep, her breasts were safely back in her bra cups. But it was the resolved look on her face that bothered him the most.

"I have no problem with you being here, Petey." At his raised brow, she went on, "Really. Whatever else, you are my friend, and it really does seem to be the best solution. But—"

Did any good sentence ever start out with "but"? He motioned for her to continue, wanting the set-down over with.

"But what just happened cannot happen again." Her voice grew firmer as she spoke, like she was gaining momentum. "I'm happy to have you stay here while you recover. But it's obvious you can get your own food and get yourself in and out of bed by yourself."

"I never said I couldn't. Nobody expected you to play nursemaid."

"Right. Exactly. And I'm gone so much of the time anyway, and you'll need to be resting. Well, it shouldn't be a problem." She waved her hands between them. "This much proximity. But, Petey, seriously, it's not going to happen again." She gave him her schoolmarm look and left.

Eighteen years of trying—granted, not very hard and not very often, but still sometimes trying—to get close to her on more than a friendly level. Whenever he did, she'd pull that look on him and walk away.

And he always let her, figuring after what had happened all those years ago that he didn't really have the right to ask for more.

But as she walked out that door, and as he sat with the rest of his life ahead of him, he knew that he wasn't going to let a pouty look stop him this time.

"Walk away then, Alison," he said loudly though he knew she'd hear him in the hallway of the small cottage. "I can't chase you *now*." He emphasized the last word and waited to hear her bedroom door shut—or more likely slam. When he heard nothing, he loudly added, "But my knee is going to heal. And you won't be able to walk away then. And if you do…I can chase you."

Now he heard the door slam.

—ᵡ—

That…that…super-ego, super-sized neanderthal.

Alison took off her slacks and threw them in the general vicinity of the guest room hamper. Her fury grew as she pulled her sweater over her head and remembered the rough way Petey had shoved it out of his way. She cursed herself as she pulled her bra off and reached for her thermal top, wanting to cover up her aching breasts. Breasts *he* made ache.

How *dare* he insinuate he'd come after her, whether in the literal or metaphorical sense. Where was he all these years? Oh, sure, there were a couple of times each summer when he'd sniff around a little bit after a night of too much beer and friendliness. But only because he was bored out of season and probably horny without all the groupies around.

She'd pretend not to notice, or quietly shut him down, not wanting to be just a warm body at the end of the evening. She'd been that once and look where it'd gotten her.

But he always went back to Detroit for training camp. And she wouldn't hear from him again except through Lizzie, Katie, or a group email to the whole gang.

She slid off her panties, trying not to notice her other achy parts. Peeled off her socks and pulled on her flannel pajama bottoms. She went to the drawer in the dresser where she'd hurriedly thrown a bunch of things this morning. Damn. She'd forgotten to throw in a pair of her fuzzy sleeping socks.

No way in hell was she going back in there—she'd just suffer through cold feet tonight.

Chase her? Right. He'd never chased a woman in his life— had never needed to. He just sat back and waited as they flocked to him, his good looks and sports-star profession doing all the heavy lifting.

She pulled down the comforter and top sheet and slid into bed. She knew she'd need to use the restroom and brush her teeth at the very least, but right now she didn't want to go anywhere near the hallway bathroom. Not that she didn't trust herself. No. There was no way in hell she'd make her way back to her room. Still, it might be best to wait for a while. Until she absolutely *had* to use the bathroom.

She rolled onto her side, trying to ignore her body's cravings. Trying not to think how close she'd been to…all of it. Holding on tight to this new side of him and doing exactly what he told her.

She couldn't even blame his aggressive behavior on pain meds. He'd never been like this with her before when he'd been home for a stay.

Oh, but wait. He wasn't going back to Detroit this time. This wasn't a summer break, but the end of his life as he knew it.

Ah…seemed like some ego functioning at play. Because he's lost control of his life he needs to be in control elsewhere.

With perhaps a dollop of transference thrown in. He wouldn't be tussling with defensemen on the ice anymore, so why not….

And oh, the tussling had been very, very nice.

But tussling with Petey *had* been nice…both times. Or at least what she allowed herself to remember from the night of Katie's wedding. The actual tussling wasn't the problem.

But you couldn't spend your whole life…tussling.

Eight

—∿—

If one does not understand a person,
one tends to regard him as a fool.

- Carl Gustav Jung

Eighteen Years Ago

ALISON LOOKED AROUND at the stragglers still at the party.
Lizzie had left hours ago, wanting to be with the boy she was
currently dating. Some guy named Finn that Alison and Katie
hadn't even bothered to meet. Didn't seem worth it—he was
older, from Houghton, and Lizzie would have some fun with him
for a couple of months, tops, then they'd all head off to State.

Katie had left, too, with her boyfriend of the moment. Alison
had ridden out to the Lily Pond with them for their graduation
party but had assured them she'd get a ride home with someone
else when they'd wanted to leave a couple of hours ago.

Not having a boyfriend to go make out with, Alison wanted
to spend the evening chatting with friends around the bonfire and
having some laughs while remembering the past thirteen years.

The Lily Pond was a public-access area about ten miles out
of Hancock off the road that ran alongside the Portage canal. By
day, it was used for people to launch boats onto the canal, since
it was only a mile or two downstream from the entry to Lake

Superior. By night, it was where high school kids came to party. Not to make out, as it wasn't private enough for that. It was really nothing more than a large circular parking lot, a long dock and boat launch and—and this was a godsend to said partiers—public johns.

They'd all had their various graduation parties and open houses earlier in the day. Those were the events for relatives and your parents' friends. Alison's older sisters had come home for their baby sister's big event. They were several years older than she was—she'd been a change of life surprise to her parents—and both had husbands and children. Her grandparents were long gone, with Alison's parents being so much older than her classmates'. She hadn't wanted an open house, had wanted the freedom to visit all of her friend's events. After Alison returned from hitting those up, the Jukuri family had gone out to Gino's for a celebratory dinner.

Which quickly turned into a lovefest for Sherry and Janis, who were very close but hadn't seen each other in a year. Alison loved her sisters, but she hadn't known them very well, being only three when Sherry left for Central Michigan and five when Janis had gone off to Ferris State. Both had met their future husbands at school and had never returned to Hancock for anything longer than a week here and there in the summer. They came back a bit more frequently once they'd had children, so her parents would get to see their grandchildren. Alison's oldest nephew was only seven years younger than she.

So, even though the family dinner was in her honor, she'd felt like an invited guest to the Sherry/Janis reunion. Still, the ravioli was good, as always.

Once the mandatory events were over, the majority of the small class met out at the Lily Pond for their own party. Somebody's older brother had bought the keg, and Alison had nursed a red plastic cupful for most of the evening. She'd had a great time chatting up her longtime classmates, most of whom she'd known since kindergarten. Small town, small graduating classes, meant you grew very close. That's why so many of them dated kids from different grades, or neighboring towns.

Which is what Lizzie had done last year with Petey Ryan. They'd dated a few months, gone to the junior prom, and then at some point decided they'd be much better friends than lovers (not that they ever were actual *lovers*—that wasn't in Lizzie's "plan" until college). By that time, Petey had become tight with Lizzie's twin Zeke, so he kind of became another brother to them all.

So when Petey loped up to her at the Lily Pond, announced he was leaving and asked if she wanted a ride, it was no big deal. He'd driven them home from places lots of times. She couldn't remember ever being alone with him, though.

Oh, who was she kidding? She'd have definitely remembered some quality alone time with Petey Ryan in a truck. She'd developed a super-huge—and super-secret—crush on the hulking boy when Lizzie'd dated him. One she would have never acted on while her friend dated him, and one she didn't know how to initiate once they'd become just friends.

Besides, boys like Pete Ryan didn't date brainiacs like Alison. They really didn't even date nice, cute, but no-great-beauties like Lizzie. She had to admit, Petey's stock soared in Alison's estimation when he had dated Lizzie, she so seemingly not his type. Though now she suspected that Petey was originally drawn to Lizzie by her niceness. He didn't know that a boy and girl could be only friends so tried to pursue her in a romantic sense before realizing he really just wanted the deep friendship that Lizzie offered just about everybody.

No, boys like Petey tended to date stunning girls like Katie, but to Alison's knowledge, Katie and Petey had never felt drawn to each other. Which raised his stock a little bit more in her eyes.

But if drop-dead gorgeous Katie wasn't who he wanted, and neither was everyone's best friend Lizzie, there was no way in hell that smart—and smart-ass—Alison stood a chance.

"Yeah, sure, a ride would be great, thanks," she told him when he asked. She emptied her cup into the bushes then threw the cup in the garbage bin as she followed him across the lot and to his truck. She half expected to see the other Houghton boys who had good-naturedly crashed their party an hour or so ago follow along with them, but they stayed behind. Must have driven in separate cars.

Petey held the passenger-side door open for her. She'd noticed that about him, that he had good manners. It was a big red Ford truck and usually when he gave them a ride home, Lizzie or Katie, or even Zeke, would give her a boost up. But they weren't here and she hesitated for a moment and then felt his hands on her hips helping her up. As she moved into the seat, one of his hands slid from her hip to her ass, but that was surely only to help guide her. Wasn't it? It really wasn't different from when Lizzie would do it.

But it felt very different.

In fact, the whole truck felt different. Smaller somehow, when it should have felt bigger with just the two of them instead of their entire posse. He got in and started the truck then looked over at her. "Are you cold?"

She shivered as she shook her head. He chuckled and turned on the heater. It was early June, but summer was slow to come to the Copper Country this year. She'd worn jeans and a tee-shirt but had brought a fleece pullover with her, which she'd put on a while ago. He wore jeans and a long-sleeve gray tee with some hockey equipment company's logo across the front. "I'm sorry I don't have a jacket to offer you. Wait," he said and turned to rummage in the space behind the seat, allowing her a look at his long back and tight butt. Levi's were made for a body like his.

He turned back around and handed her a plaid flannel blanket. "Here you go," he said turning the heat up even more.

"Really, I'm not that cold," she said but took the blanket and placed it on her lap. It had been a cool evening, but that wasn't why she'd shivered.

They pulled out of the circular area and drove down the quarter-mile dirt road back to the main road, which would lead them back to Hancock.

When they got to the road, Petey stopped, looked both ways, then put both hands on the steering wheel and looked over at her. "Right or left?"

What was he talking about? He had to know this road as well as she did. Right was the direction back to Hancock. Left took them further out on the canal road, eventually to Lake Superior and then Calumet.

"Right or left?" he asked again. "You decide."

Decide. Choose. So he wasn't asking her for directions, but rather asking her where she wanted to go. With him. Alone.

"Left," she said firmly, and he quickly pulled the truck out onto the road and away from their hometowns.

They rode in silence for a few miles, past the entrance to the state park. About a half-mile farther, he pulled the truck to a stop. Which was fine to do on this low-traffic road, in the wee hours of the evening. "Left or straight," he asked.

Straight would take them in a more direct route to Calumet. Left would take them eventually to Calumet, but via a road where at points you could pull over and view Lake Superior. Not that there'd be any viewing this late at night.

"Left."

He turned.

They both stayed silent, which was unusual. She usually always had something to say about everything, and Petey was typically the life of the party. But on he drove, not saying a word.

She still didn't have a good bead on what was going on. Was he just bored and not ready to go home, looking to extend the evening with a game of "you decide where we'll end up"? Or was it something more?

And was he leaving that up to her to decide? That thought scared the bejeezus out of her. When they got to the Calumet Water Works public area, she was about ready to jump out of her skin wondering if he'd...yep. He stopped the truck, again in the middle of the road, and said, "Left or straight."

"Left," she barely whispered. He pulled the truck into the deserted area, coming to park facing the lake. He put the truck in park, then placed his hand on the key.

He looked over at her, made sure she was watching him, watching his hand, and softly said, "On or off."

She swallowed. Crap, why was he making her make all the choices? What if she was building something up in her mind that wasn't going to happen? What exactly would happen? And why now? Why after a whole year of hanging around together?

Damn him, she didn't want to have put herself out there like this.

"Alison?" Her name had never sounded so soft and tempting as when he said it. "On or off?"

"Off." He turned the ignition off and the truck went silent. Except she was sure he'd be able to hear her heartbeat, crazy fast as it was. He turned, leaning his back against the driver's door, his arms open wide, one along the door, resting on the dash, the other along the top of bench seat.

He took a deep breath and his exhale sounded a little shaky, which made her feel both better and worse. "Here," he said, tucking his chin down to where he sat. "Or there?" He bobbed his chin in her direction.

Holy crap, this was going to happen. Whatever "this" was. She quickly thought out all the ramifications, did some calculations and realized she just needed to turn her mind off for the duration. Yeah, it wasn't a smart move. She'd just been named the class valedictorian earlier in the day, in theory proving her smarts, but...she wanted this.

"Here," she said with more confidence than she felt. She moved back on the seat to give him room.

The truck cab was huge—which had been so convenient when he'd played taxi to the whole group—with a bench seat that now seemed very small when his large body moved across it.

He shifted his legs so that they were splayed into her side of the foot area. He slid a foot under hers and lifted so that she moved her legs, one sliding up on the bench, one dangling below. He wedged in, allowing her leg to move behind him, along the back of the seat.

He was so close now she could smell his scent. A little bit of smoke from the bonfire, the outdoors, even the detergent his mother used on his clothes. A heady combination that had her breathing even more heavily.

He reached out slowly, tentatively and put his hands on her waist, catching fleece and denim. The blanket slid from her lap to the seat beside her. As he lifted her slowly, she realized where he wanted her, and put her knee down to leverage herself up enough to straddle him, which she did while he slid under her, essentially taking her spot in the passenger seat.

His right hand left her waist and dropped down, fumbling for...oh, the seat went back. She'd never known that. But why would she.

It didn't lie down flat, but it did give his long legs more room and tilted her into him in the most delicious way.

She'd had a few boyfriends through high school, and many make-out sessions, but was still a virgin. Somehow she sensed with Petey that this was going to go beyond a make-out session.

It wasn't like she had a master plan of when she was going to "lose it" like Lizzie did. She probably would have by now, but she hadn't felt any particular drive to go further when making out with her boyfriends at the time.

Now, she *definitely* felt the drive to go further. And they'd barely touched. She couldn't imagine even being coherent enough to say stop when Petey put his hands on her body.

If he ever did.

His head came up from the back of the seat. Even straddling him and sitting up a bit on her knees, she only came up to eye level with him. But it was enough, because it was lip level, too. And oh, what soft lips he had, she realized as he brushed them against hers. It was quick and tentative. And then again, with just a bit more pressure. And then a third time that had her wishing he'd just do it, already.

But no, he pulled back, took her face in his hands and held her until she looked at him.

"Yes or no?" he asked. It would seem to be his final question of the night. And the most important.

She licked her lips, happy to be in this position—literally—but not thrilled about having to call all the shots. She guessed it was kind of chivalrous of him, but really, couldn't he just start ripping her clothes off?

"Yes," she said and leaned forward. His hands slid from her face to the back of her neck as they kissed. One hand squeezed, surprising her…in a good way. She squirmed a little and his touch eased.

"Sorry," he whispered, but before she could tell him it was okay—preferred, in fact—he was kissing her again. Their mouths fit perfectly. And she loved that his body was so big and strong. Very Darwinian, she thought randomly, but she wanted this big, strong boy to cover her up physically. To be on top of her. But she just didn't know how to convey that message.

So she kept kissing him, which he seemed to like just fine, if his growing erection underneath her was any indication. Which of course it was.

She settled down onto him, and rubbed her jeans on his, trying find that…yes, there it was. Good lord, he was large. She'd given Roger Camden a handjob on New Year's Eve when they'd been dating and there was no way that he'd ever been as big as Petey was even at half-staff.

"Al…yeah…God, that feels good," he groaned as she shifted again, aligning the seams in the most delightful spot. His hands pulled her tee-shirt from her jeans and then skimmed against her bare waist. Up over her ribcage to her boobs, which he massaged and kneaded all while tangling his tongue with hers.

She let out a soft sigh and played with his hair. So soft, with a nice bit of wave. Moving her hand underneath to his nape, she pulled on him, wanting him to take the lead and lay her down on the bench seat. What would it feel like to have all that male hovering over her?

Or deep inside her?

But he didn't take the hint, and she wasn't experienced—or assertive—enough to tell him what she wanted. She wasn't even sure herself what that was. Instead he lifted her pullover off of her, taking her tee halfway up with it. It felt automatic to try to pull it down, but his hands were already there and stilled hers.

He broke away from the kiss. "Okay?" he asked as they both held her shirt. She nodded and held her arms over her head, like a child. But she was no child and neither was he. And God, how could they have been going at it and she not have her hands on that amazing chest?

It was too early in the year for beach weather, but she remembered that physique from last summer. Almost down to each hard plane and contour of his young body. She grabbed at the cotton of his long-sleeve tee, pulling it hard from his waistband, which caused him to hiss.

"Let me," he said, and eased the shirt out of his jeans and over his head, throwing it somewhere in the truck. She barely had her hands on his chest before he was crushing her to him and reaching behind her for her bra clasp, which he had undone in a flash. Then his mouth was on her breast and she arched back, the sensation was so intense.

He followed her with his mouth and she rewarded him by grinding down on him. "Fuck, yeah," he moaned, then sucked hard on her nipple.

She tried pulling him again and this time he followed, holding on to her back as he eased her down across the bench seat, scooting her up so that her head was even with the steering wheel. His mouth was back on her breast, one hand holding it, the other finding its way down her stomach to the opening of her jeans. She heard the snap and felt the zipper open and knew that if she was going to stop him, it should be now.

Instead, she lifted her hips as he reached with both hands

to shimmy the denim off of her, pushing the pants to the floor of the truck cab. He moved up her body and she wrapped her arms around his neck, reveling in the sheer volume of him hulking over her. His hands took her face again and he whispered, "Okay?"

"Yeah," she whispered back. "Good."

He nodded his agreement and kissed her again, deeply and yet softly, as his hands roamed all over her body then slid into her panties. He fumbled a bit, but then, oh then, he found a spot... the spot...and she moaned her approval. He continued to rub, but then moved from the magical spot to one that still felt good, but wasn't quite as...magical. She twitched her hips, wanting his hand to return, but instead he pulled his hand completely away and started unbuttoning his own fly.

She did want to feel him, take him in her hand, but she'd been so close.

"God, I can't believe this is happening," he said as he rose up and yanked his jeans and boxers down. "I've...it's like...you're...."

What? She wanted to scream, desperate to know what was going through his mind. She always wanted to know what he was thinking and feeling. And never as much as now—to know if this meant anything more to him than a little extended celebration on their big day.

Or if *she* meant more to him.

—⚬⚬—

Petey couldn't believe Alison Jukuri's naked body was laid out beneath him. As he fumbled in his wallet for a condom, he tried to think about anything else other than how badly he'd wanted her for the past year.

Hockey. Think about hockey or you'll come before you can even get the condom on.

So he thought about hockey...and ice...and how hot she'd look lying naked like this on the ice.

His fingers shook as he rolled the condom on while looking down at her. Jesus, she was a cute little thing. He hadn't thought so at first. In the beginning, she was just his girlfriend Lizzie's smart-ass, short-stuff best friend. But she'd grown on him in the past year. And in the past few months, he'd been dying to get her alone, separate from the pack of friends that he and Lizzie had somehow formed after their break-up.

And now they were alone, and he was pulling her panties off of her. It wasn't his first time, but he suspected it was Al's, and he'd like to make it a bit more special for her. But dear God, if he didn't get inside her soon....

She kept her hips tilted after lifting them for the panty removal and all thoughts of taking his time and making it special—yeah, right, in a truck?—flew from his brain, much like the blood flow had. All thoughts and blood flow found their way straight to his dick, which was now prodding along her opening.

He saw her flinch just a tiny bit. "Is this okay? Do you want to stop?" he asked. *Please say no, please say no.*

"No," she answered, to his overwhelming relief. "I'm okay. It's just...."

"What? What do you want? What can I do?"

He'd been having sex since he was fifteen. Not regularly (he *had* dated Lizzie for several months), but with enough girls that he thought he could provide what Alison was asking for...if she'd ask for it. He wasn't experienced enough to know what would do it for her on his own. Truth be told, all that stuff south of the border on a girl's body was still pretty much a mystery to him. But he wanted to make it good for her. It meant more to him than just getting his rocks off with a willing partner.

She meant more to him than that.

She shook her head. "Nothing. Just...um...can you come down here to me?"

He'd been kneeling on the seat while he'd struggled with the condom, so he lowered himself, careful to keep his weight on his forearms. Her breasts, which had tasted so fantastic, nestled against his chest, her belly along his.

And that mouth of hers. Usually used for witty and biting remarks, its purpose tonight was so much better. He lowered his mouth and kissed her again. She was right there with him, kissing back, tangling her tongue with his. She wrapped her arms around his neck, her hands running up and down his back, across his shoulders, driving him fucking insane with want.

He reached down and guided himself into her slowly. Or, he tried to go slowly anyway, seeing if it'd be too much for her. He looked down into her eyes, and she licked her lips, then bit the bottom one as he pushed in further.

"Okay?" he whispered and she nodded. He pushed again, lodging himself all the way in. Holy shit, she felt so good. Warm and wet and oh, so very, very tight around him. "I'm sorry," he groaned as he started rocking into her. "I'm not going to last very long. I just…you just…feel so good."

She wrapped her arms tighter around him, nuzzled his neck, then licked him—fuck, that was amazing—before whispering back, "It's okay. It feels good like this. Just let yourself…um…just do what feels good."

Shit, it all felt good. But it was even better when he picked up his pace and slid in and out of her little body with more force. She wiggled under him and tilted her hips a little. To his great embarrassment, that was all it took.

He poured himself into her. She clung on tight and he collapsed on top of her when it was over. He was barely able to comprehend that she hadn't come, but he was drained and it felt so good to just lie on top of her body that his mind wouldn't quite compute it all.

He knew he didn't fall asleep, but it was several minutes before he could move. "Sorry. Am I squashing you?"

"No. It feels nice," she answered, but shifted underneath him.

Damn, this could not be comfortable for her. He started to pull out of her, but she held him tight. "Just a little bit longer?"

Like she had to ask. "As long as you want," he said and held her close, not fully believing what had just happened. What it'd been like to be inside her body.

To still be inside her.

After a while, she wiggled again, and he knew he was getting too heavy for her. She made a sound of protest when he pulled away from her, but he was determined to get his weight off of her. As he pulled out, the condom started to slide off his now depleted dick, and he quickly reached down and retrieved it, feeling the warmth and wetness that their bodies had created.

He knew they'd be good together. Nobody would have guessed it, they were so different, but he knew. Giving her some space to get dressed, he left the truck and disposed of the condom in a trashcan. Lake Superior glowed in the moonlight in front of him. He breathed in the fresh air and listened to the waves lap onto the sand.

It was supposed to be a night to say goodbye, graduation and all. But all Petey could think was this was the night when his life began.

Nine

—ᗯ—

A puck is a hard rubber disc that hockey players strike when
they can't hit one another.

~ Jimmy Cannon

ALISON SHOOK EIGHTEEN YEARS of cobwebs from her mind
as she drove to Katie's house the next morning. Damn Petey for
making her remember something she'd done a pretty admirable
job of forgetting.

And it hadn't been easy.

She didn't have patients this morning. Normally she'd either
be doing much-needed chores around her house or be over at her
mother's. She chose not to go to her parents' house because she
wanted to give her mom and Sherry some time to catch up alone.

And there was no way she was going to stick around at home
this morning.

She could have gone to the hospital to visit her dad, but her
visiting times were pretty regular and she didn't want to mess with
his schedule too much. She'd go see him in the afternoon at her
normal time.

So she'd quickly dressed and tip-toed past Petey's room,
feeling a little better when she heard deep snores coming from
behind the door.

At least *he* hadn't been up all night thinking when he needed some rest.

She'd left the house and started driving, not really knowing where she was going. She could go to her office and catch up on paperwork, but there wasn't much with the lighter patient load right now.

She ended up calling Katie from the car to see if she wanted to go out for breakfast, and Katie' talked her into coming over to her house. It hadn't been a hard sell.

"So, Sherry's home? That's great, right?" Katie asked her after Alison was settled at the kitchen table. Katie poured her some coffee, bringing it to her and then settled her large, pregnant girth into a chair. She leaned over and breathed deep from Alison's cup. "God, I miss coffee."

"Not too much longer and you'll be able to have a cup."

Katie's already gorgeous face lit up even more as she rested her hands on her belly. "The doctor says two more weeks, but I think I could go any day. I mean, obviously we know exactly when she was conceived, but I think she's going to be an over-achiever like her father and show up early."

"How do you know exactly—" Alison began and then stopped. It seemed like Katie and Darío had been together a lot longer than nine months, but they'd had a one-night stand that had created the little bun in her oven.

A thousand smart-ass retorts ran through her mind about usually conservative Katie getting knocked up, but they died in her throat. Looking at her dear friend, so happy to be with child, Alison was overcome with feelings of...of....

"Is that nissu I smell?" she asked when she didn't want to think any more.

"Yep, made it this morning. It should be cool enough to put the icing on now." She made a move to get up, but Alison waved her down.

"I'll get it. You just relax, little mama." Katie beamed and Alison got up and set about putting the icing Katie had made onto the still slightly warm Finnish breakfast bread. She had her back to Katie but heard her deep sigh of contentment which filled Alison with happiness and something else. Envy? Maybe a touch, though oddly enough she'd never been envious of the breathtakingly beautiful Katie before.

She slathered on more icing than was probably needed, but it felt like a morning that called out for sugar.

Something in what Katie had just said came back to her. "She? Did you say 'she' when you were talking about the baby? I thought you guys decided not to find out the gender?"

"We did. We haven't." She got a cute smile on her face when Alison turned around to look at her. "We've just always called her a she. We really don't know. But I think we may have willed her into a girl."

"You know that's not possible, right?" she joked. At least she thought she was joking, but by the look on Katie's face she wasn't sure. Katie fairly glowed with emotion.

"Oh, Al, there's so much about my life that shouldn't be possible, and it suddenly is, so I'm not counting out something like willing a baby's sex."

"So, will you be disappointed if it's a boy?"

Katie waved her question away as nonsense as Alison set the plate with the nissu on the table, then returned to the cabinets for plates and forks.

"Of course not. I'm delirious at the thought of either. I think Darío put the idea of a girl in my head and it just stuck. We'll be very blessed no matter what." Alison set the gathered plates and forks on the table and took her seat as Katie continued, "My God, after all these years of wanting a baby, I couldn't care less about the gender."

"I know. I'm so happy for you, Katie," she said, patting her friend's arm. Katie looked at her like she was waiting for the shoe to drop, or the "but". There was no but. There was no other shoe.

Katie and Lizzie were both new wives and new mothers and were deliriously happy. And Alison was genuinely delighted for them.

And yet she felt just like her patient Denise—that everyone was getting on with their lives but her.

She dug in to the nissu.

A few bites later she thought to ask, "Should you wake up Darío while it's still warm? And awesome, by the way."

"Thanks. And Darío's been awake and gone for a couple of hours now. He went to the SDC to work out, then he's going to meet Mark for breakfast to talk golf."

Their friend Mark managed the university's golf course, which was currently buried under three feet of snow.

"If you can't play it, might as well talk about it?"

"Something like that. Poor Darío. He's never really seen much of a winter and certainly not a U.P. winter. But I really wanted to be near family—and you and Lizard—when the baby came. He's been a real trooper about it."

"He'd do anything for you and you know it."

She smiled dreamily. "I know. I'd feel badly about it, except I'd do anything for him, too."

Alison shoved another bite of the pastry into her mouth and just nodded.

"God, I feel so awful, I didn't even ask how Petey's doing. They got him to your house okay? He's settled in?"

The nissu got stuck in her throat. She took a large drink of coffee, then another before answering Katie. "Yes. His mom and Lizzie brought him home yesterday afternoon. By the time I got there he'd been up, fixed himself something to eat, done the dishes and got back in bed." Her voice caught a little at the end when mentioning—and thinking about—Petey in her bed. And the lovely things they did there.

"Wow. Not surprising, though. A little thing like surgery's not going to keep Petey down."

"It didn't seem to, no." Not if his flinging her body down on the bed was any indication. And oh, had she enjoyed being flung.

"And stuff like showers and that kind of thing? His dad coming over to help with that, or are you going to hop in the shower and soap up that amazing bod?"

She nearly choked on her coffee, but Katie was already laughing. Ah, yes, that would be quite a joke, wouldn't it? Brainy Alison and brawny Petey getting hot and sticky in a shower together.

"I guess his dad's probably going to come over. I didn't really get many of the details." Because she'd been too busy kissing the man. "We barely spoke when I got home last night before I went to bed." That was true, there hadn't been much talking. "Oh man, I thought having Petey around would be bad enough, but Lieutenant Dan, too?"

Katie reached for her phone and hit a button. "Let me call Darío and ask him to stop by and see if Petey needs any...man help."

"Thanks," she said, more for Petey than herself. She'd be out of the house most of the day (even if she had to sit in the parking lot of Pat's IGA and read a book!), so she wouldn't really have to deal with Petey's dad. But she knew Petey would much rather have Darío help him out than have to deal with his father one day out of the hospital.

With no pain meds.

Katie spoke to her husband for a few minutes, and Alison gathered that Darío was fine with swinging by her house to check on Petey.

"Let me ask Al," Katie said then turned to her. "Door locked or anything?"

She shook her head, and Katie relayed the info to Darío. They said a few more things, then Katie giggled, said something in Spanish that Alison didn't want translated, and disconnected.

"He's just finishing up breakfast with Mark, then he's going to head to your place."

"That's nice of him."

"He's a nice guy," Katie said as she smiled a cat-that-ate-the-canary smile and lifted a forkful of nissu to her still grinning mouth. She paused and winked at Alison. "A *very* nice guy."

Alison took another sip of her coffee, thinking it had gone a little bitter.

—〰—

Petey woke up not knowing which was more painful—his knee or his raging hard-on. They could probably both be eased by a good rubdown, but he was pretty sure the person he most wanted as his private nurse this morning wasn't going to be putting her hands on either of his aching body parts.

"Al?" he called out. He glanced at the clock—ten in the morning. Surprised that his knee had allowed him to sleep so late and so deeply, he eased his body slowly to a sitting position. He was pretty sure Lizzie said something about Alison not having patients on certain days, so she was probably just ignoring him.

Again.

"Come on, Al, I know you're probably still pissed about last night, but we've got to talk about it at some point," he boomed loudly enough for her to hear him down the hall even if she still had her door shut.

"Do we really have to talk about it? Because I'm prepared to pretend I didn't hear a word you just said," Darío Luna said from the doorway, scaring the crap out of Petey.

"Jesus Christ, you can't just sneak up on a guy like that."

"Hardly sneaking. I've been here for nearly an hour waiting for you to wake up."

"Still. A little warning would have been nice."

The Spaniard shrugged, walked into the bedroom and settled into the upholstered chair by the window.

The same chair Al had sat in last night when she'd snuggled up with that throw-blanket thing.

"What are you doing here, anyway? Shouldn't you be painting a nursery or something?"

"We did that weeks ago. I was out anyway, and Katie called and said to stop by to see if you needed anything."

"Did Alison let you in?" He was totally going to be in the dog house if Alison knew Darío had overheard him talking about what happened last night. Or what didn't happen.

"She's not here. She's at my house having breakfast with Katie."

Oh. That little sneak had dashed out before he had a chance to...what? Talk with her? Or pin her to the bed again and not let her up this time, even if she ground her foot into his knee? Actually that sounded pretty good—the pinning her down part, not the knee-grinding part.

In fact, now that his cock had gone down with Darío's arrival, the pain in his knee was ratcheting up. He tried to edge it off the bed a bit and hissed in pain.

Instantly, Darío was off his chair and around the bed to Petey's side. "What can I do to help?"

"I think there are some of those heating pad thingies that you put in the microwave out in the kitchen. Could you put one in for about three minutes?"

Darío was out the door before Petey had finished his sentence.

While he heard the rummaging in the kitchen, Petey gently massaged his thigh above the knee, then tried again to stretch it. Probably better to wait until the heating pad did its magic.

Darío soon returned with the piping hot pad and a cup of piping hot coffee, setting the cup on the night stand and handing the pad to Petey.

"Do you need any help getting to the bathroom?"

Petey gingerly layed the pad across his bandaged leg. "Eventually, maybe. Probably. Let me see if the heat can limber it up before I put the brace on."

Darío left the room and came back a moment later with his own cup of coffee, which he drank from, and then sat back in the chair.

Petey leaned back against the headboard doing the tiny leg lifts the doctor had advised him to do as he drank from his cup.

"Shit, that's strong," he said, to which Darío only shrugged again.

"I'm trying not to drink it in front of Katie, so when I get a chance...."

"So, you're coffee cheating on Katie with me?"

He chuckled. "In a way. She told me she didn't care if I drank it in front of her, but I try not to."

"No drinking in front of her either?"

"*Sí*. But that isn't quite as hard."

"Hmmm. I don't know. It'd be pretty hard to give up my beer." He took another long gulp of the black stuff. "Yeah. No. Giving up coffee would be harder during the season. I live on it. Beer would be harder to give up in the summers." He grinned. "I live on *it*, then."

And then he remembered that every day was summer from now on, even if the wind was blowing and snow was falling as it was outside the window behind Darío.

Darío shifted forward in his chair. "Do you want to talk about it? Being done with hockey?"

Did he? Should he? Would Darío even understand? As a professional athlete, maybe. As a professional golfer who could play well into his forties and then on the seniors' tour once fifty, maybe not.

"Do you ever think about life after golf? What you'd do?"

The golfer looked out the window, took a drink of coffee and slowly shook his head. "Not much, no. At least not until lately."

"Why lately? You still have a lot of years left to play." Golf. Not hockey.

He took a deep breath, let it out, then turned from the window to Petey. "It all changed when I met Katie."

"You mean when you found out she was preggers."

He was already shaking his head. "No. No. Before that. I know it now. My life—the rest of my life—changed the moment I first saw her in the gallery on that golf course."

"Jesus. Whipped much?"

Darío's brows knitted together. "I do not undertand what is this 'whipped'. As in a lashing?" His Spanish accent got a bit thicker, and his grin told Petey that he understood just fine.

"Don't play dumb Spaniard with me."

Darío laughed. "*Sí*, I am *muy* whipped. And happily so."

Petey laughed along with his new friend. He didn't know Darío very well. He'd golfed with him this summer and hung with him a bit before he'd had to go back to training camp. He liked the guy. Certainly wished he could golf like him.

Petey had been tight with Katie's ex, Ron, too, but liked the pairing of Darío and Katie better. Ron and Katie had been too much alike, total king and queen of the prom. Boring in their perfection.

People would look at Darío and wonder how he ever got a woman like Katie. Petey liked that. Liked the unexpected in a couple. Added a little bit of spice.

So just when the hell was his little unexpected piece of spice coming home?

Ten

—〰—

Being entirely honest with oneself is a good exercise.

- Sigmund Freud

AFTER TOURING KATIE'S NURSERY to see what had been done since she'd last visited and clearing away their dishes, Alison said her goodbyes and left.

As she pulled out of the driveway, seeing the beautiful new home that Katie and Darío had only been in for a few months, made Alison think about how quickly life could change.

This time last year, Lizzie and Finn had just gotten back together after thinking they'd never make it as a coupleRon had just left Katie to be with the girl he thought he'd knocked up.

Petey'd been in the middle of a good season, the thought of retirement still just a distant one.

And Alison? The only thing that had changed in her life in the past year was the measurement of her parents' downhill progression.

She'd dated a man named Brandt, a professor at Tech, for a while the summer before that when Lizzie'd been home with her half-assed plan to sleep with Finn for a few months. But things had begun to fizzle with Brandt just a month or so into the fall. Not too long after they'd started sleeping together.

Alison drove out of Katie's new neighborhood near the top

of Quincy Hill in Hancock, not sure where she was headed but still thinking about Brandt.

Well, not really Brandt, but about all the men she'd dated. She was driving past the Quincy Hill roadside scenic view, when she pulled in at the last second, put the car in park, and looked out over the valley of Hancock, the canal, and Houghton below her. Though the snow was falling thickly, it was still a lovely sight, so fresh and pristinely white.

Man, she hadn't parked in this place in a long time. She wasn't even sure when was the—Oh. Right. She remembered the last time she was here and decided that even picking apart the reasoning behind her failed relationships with men was better than remembering that long ago day.

So, then, things went south with Brandt after they'd begun sleeping together. And before Brandt? There'd been Philip, a doctor from Marquette who had a satellite practice in the Copper Country. And before him? Rob, a geology consultant to one of the mining companies.

This had been over the course of the past six or seven years. Alison took a deep breath, turned the car heater up a bit, and, trying to forget it was herself she was thinking about, put on her shrink cap.

It was something she normally didn't do, believing you couldn't truly see yourself objectively, as an uninvolved outsider like a therapist would. But she tried now.

Was there a commonality to these relationships? All three men were highly educated and with off-the-chart IQs. Just like herself.

All three men were not from the area originally. And what inference could she take from that? Perhaps she chose to be the person she wanted to be, and not the person the small community had pegged her as for all these years?

Or perhaps she wanted to be someone else completely? Somebody different?

Crap, she really didn't like this. No wonder she so seldom

did it.

Skipping the deeper self-introspection, she tried to analyze the more surface stuff.

How long did each relationship last? Aha! No pattern after all. They'd varied pretty widely from a few months with Brandt to almost three years with Rob. Of course, when you added up all the time she and Rob were actually together, due to him living in Minnesota and only being in town sporadically for his consulting job, it was probably more like…shit.

A few months.

Philip? Yep, a few months if you added up actual time spent together.

Okay, almighty shrink. Time to pull out the big guns. How did each of the relationships end? Okay, good. No pattern there. Brandt had dumped her, amicably. Philip had met someone in Marquette he wanted to see exclusively, which he and Alison discussed like the civilized adults they were. And she had ended things with Rob, mainly because of the limited time they saw each other. It hadn't felt as much like a relationship as just a prolonged series of booty calls.

Which brought her to the grand finale—sex. It would take months, perhaps years, of therapy before a patient trusted a therapist enough to be really honest about their sex lives. Not just the nuts and bolts, but about understanding their desires and making sure their needs were truly met.

Or not, as the case may be.

As *her* case may be.

She'd specifically chosen smart, educated men with whom she shared an interest in literature, the way they viewed the world—basically talked the same language.

It'd been satisfactory, sometimes fulfilling, but ultimately pretty boring in bed.

She knew. Of course she knew. But the denial had been buried so deep, for so long, that she could easily ignore it. And she had.

But now, a few years from forty, all her friends happily settled with their men and growing families, it was time for Alison to face the truth.

Brainy, introspective, oh-so-civilized Alison Jukuri really just wanted a caveman.

—∞—

Darío helped him hobble out to the kitchen for an actual breakfast then stood just inside the bathroom while Petey struggled to shower. After he'd dried himself off and put on some boxers, Darío assisted him in putting a new bandage on his knee, then the ace bandage, then his track pants and then the fucking brace. At least the damn thing allowed him to stand, albeit with crutches.

He hated that he needed help with the simple tasks but had been around injuries long enough to know that the more you follow the rules the doctor laid out, the sooner you were back on the ice.

Except he wouldn't be back on the ice.

By the time they got all this accomplished, he was hungry again, so they made their way back to the kitchen and Darío made him a sandwich.

"You don't want one?" Petey asked him when he placed Petey's in front of him but then sat down without anything for himself.

"No, thanks. I'm picking up something for myself and Katie on my way home. She has a craving."

"For what?"

Darío let out a sigh and said, "Pasties. Again."

"Not a pasty fan?"

"They are fine. But not every day. And I do mean every day."

Petey laughed. He loved the meat pies, but even he wouldn't want them more than once a week. "It'll be over soon," he said. Darío got a look of sheer happiness on his face, and Petey felt a pang of envy.

Trying to change the subject before the golfer launched into baby clothes and birthing methods, Petey asked, "What were you meeting with Mark about? Just wanted to shoot the shit about golf since you couldn't be out playing it with the snow up to your balls?"

Darío chuckled at what was a pretty accurate visualization. "That, but a little more. I wanted to get his take on an idea I had."

Petey motioned for him to continue as he took a large bite of his sandwich.

"I was thinking it might be nice for the area to have an indoor driving range since the winters are so long here."

Petey took a drink of milk and swallowed. "You mean it would be nice for *you* to have an indoor driving range."

Darío shrugged, but grinned. "*Sí.* But I truly believe it would be good for the community. For as short as the season is here, there are a fair amount of golfers."

"Right, but they're all playing league hockey during the winters. Or going to their kids' hockey games. And hockey practice."

Another shrug. "So I've been told. Mark is for the idea in theory, and the university has looked at it, but they don't think the numbers will work. Plus, it would take a large chunk of land to do it, and they don't want to take that away from the existing golf course, which I agree with."

"Can it be land anywhere?"

"The flatter the better, or at least the cheaper to develop. Which is not as easy as it sounds around here. You have a lot of hills."

"That we do. But, I also happen to have a huge plot of land up by the airport that I've been hanging on to for a while. Nothing ever presented itself as a good opportunity for it. I bought it as a write-off years ago."

"Flat?"

"Very."

"How large?"

"I can't remember for sure. My business manager would know and I can call him, but I want to say it was around two or three acres. Would that be large enough?"

"And then some. And you'd be willing to sell this land? To me?" Darío leaned forward, resting his forearms on the table. Surely no longer tan from daily golf, his arms were covered in a thick sweater. The man probably hadn't even owned a heavy sweater before this year.

Petey took another bite of the sandwich and took his time chewing, thinking furiously as he did. Gulped down some milk, then wiped his napkin across his face.

"Okay," he finally said. "What do you think about a partnership on this thing? My land. Your idea. Our venture?"

Darío blinked several times, taking it in. He sat back in his chair, his arms dropping to his sides. Then, just as quickly, he sat back up, placing his arms once again on the table. "You don't want to just sell me the land?"

Petey shook his head no.

"You want to be involved?" Petey nodded. "How involved?"

Now Petey pushed the plate and glass aside, put his own arms on the table and leaned forward. "Very involved."

"Why?"

"Because you're going to be spending the next three months changing diapers and being sleep-deprived. Then you're going to spend the spring and summer on the Tour, if Katie lets you go." He looked pointedly at Darío.

"Katie wants me to go. She said she and the baby will try to travel with me. I'm happy to take a season off, but…"

"She's not going to let you do that."

"No."

"So, you, and hopefully Katie and the baby, will be gone most of the spring and summer, right when they'll be able to break ground and start building. If we get a really aggressive contracting company—" He stopped at Darío's raised hand. "What?"

"You're really serious? You want to be that involved in something you didn't even know existed a minute ago?"

"Yes."

"Again, I must ask. Why?"

He shrugged, and massaged his upper thigh where the brace pinched him a tiny bit.

"I was never going to stay in Detroit after I retired. I'd always planned on living here full time, I just hadn't given much thought to what I'd do up here." He moved his suddenly throbbing leg to a slightly different angle trying to ease the pain. "Well, it's time to give it some thought. And I'm thinking 'local business owner' has a nice ring to it."

And more proximity to follow up on his threat to chase down Alison.

"Besides, who else is qualified to hand out those buckets of balls to kids if not a former jock?"

Eleven

Hockey players have fire in their hearts and ice in their veins.
- Author Unknown

Eighteen years ago

ALISON COULDN'T BELIEVE she'd finally see Petey again after their night together. The Monday after graduation, she, Lizzie and Katie had taken their gift money and gone to Green Bay for three days of shopping and lying by a hotel pool. When they'd gotten back, she'd found out through the grapevine that Petey was in Ann Arbor at a hockey camp for two weeks.

So here they were, three weeks after that night in his truck, finally facing each other.

She had no idea what to expect. When Petey had dropped her off at home, he'd kissed her sweetly and whispered, "See you soon." She'd been in her bedroom before she realized how cryptic that farewell had been.

Of course, she hadn't said anything to Lizzie and Katie about it. It would probably blow their minds, the thought of her and Petey together—as a couple or even for one night only. And of course those questions—what it was, what they would be—would definitely come up. So until she had the answers, she kept mum.

Hopefully she'd get some sense from Petey tonight. They

were all hanging out at Katie's house in the finished basement—
the scene of many of their youthful misdemeanors. Katie had
rented some movies, and they were all just going to chill. They
all held various summer jobs, some daytime, some night, so these
nights of just hanging out were becoming harder to schedule.

Alison was the first to arrive according to Mr. Maki, who
let her in and waved in the general vicinity of the basement door.

She was assaulted by loud music—more like screaming—as
she made her way down the stairs and into the large, open room.

"What is that?" she said loudly, getting Katie's attention.

Her friend, who'd been standing next to the stereo moving
with the music, startled and then turned the volume down. "It's
Nirvana."

"Hardly!"

Katie shook her head, her blond mane loose and flowing as
she laughed. "No. The band's name is Nirvana. Aren't they great?"

Alison listened for a minute. Obviously her friend had
different taste in music than she. "I can't understand a word
they're saying."

"I know. It took me, like, twenty times, and I'm still not sure
I've got them right."

"They are not coming to State with us."

Katie stuck out her tongue at Alison and said, "That's what
headphones were made for."

"Then may you and Nirvana end up in…nirvana together."
She made her way over to the corner of the sectional that she
always sat in and staked her claim. "But can you tear yourself
away from it for now?"

Katie turned the volume down even further until it was just
an irritating buzz, and then joined Alison.

"How was work today?"

"Good," Alison answered and started telling Katie about
her day in the biology lab at Tech where she'd snagged a summer
internship. Typically they went to college students after they'd
completed at least their freshman year, but usually their sophomore

year. It had only taken taken one look at Alison's SAT scores for them to give her the spot.

A few seconds in, Katie held up a hand for her to stop. "Let's just say it was a rhetorical question."

Right. Of course. Nobody really wanted to hear about the things that were fascinating to Alison. They wanted to talk about sports, movies, and Nirvana, apparently.

She rubbed her hands on her khaki shorts, suddenly more nervous than before about the thought of seeing Petey again.

Who was she kidding? He would never go for a girl like her for anything more than a one-night stand. Just a warm body to nicely pass the evening with.

Still hopeful, she decided to waive judgment until he showed up. Maybe, just maybe, he was more than the dumb jock everybody thought he was and could see her for more than just the class brain.

God, she hoped so.

Katie's boyfriend showed up next, and they cuddled together not far from where Alison sat. Curtis was his name, he was from Houghton and was on the hockey team with Petey.

He seemed to like Nirvana just fine. Or at least he told Katie he did.

Zeke, Lizzie's twin, came down the stairs next, leading a girl by the hand. Valerie, a sophomore from Calumet that Zeke had been dating for a year. Tiny little thing, even shorter than Alison. They said their hellos and plopped down in the La-Z-Boy that was adjacent to the sectional. Zeke sat down first, then he pulled Val onto his lap.

"Let's start the flick," he said, his hands already up the back of Val's shirt. They would soon be up the front of her shirt when the lights went out and the movie began.

Great. It was shaping up to be a couples' night and there she sat in the corner of the couch alone.

And apparently no Petey.

"Isn't Lizzie with you?" she asked Zeke.

"She's coming, she and Petey."

"They're together?" she asked a little too quickly.

Zeke pulled his face out of Val's neck long enough to answer, "Outside. She came with us, and Petey pulled up at the same time. There's something weird going on with them. They huddled together pretty quickly and just stayed out there talking." He then poked his head all the way around Val. "They're not back together are they? It was okay the first time, but now? I don't know. It would feel weird. Verging on creepy."

Creepy? Try shattering. She'd faked not liking Petey well enough when Lizzie had been dating him, but now? After she and Petey had...but wait. "Isn't Lizzie dating that guy Finn?" she asked anyone who had the right answer.

"Not any more. I'm not really sure what happened or when, but that's off," Zeke said.

Alison looked at Katie. "Did you know that?"

Katie shook her head. "No. It must have happened fairly recently. But you know, it's been a few days since I've actually talked to Lizzie. And she's back with Petey already? Fast worker."

"We don't know that she and Petey are back together," Alison said, hoping that the panic she was beginning to feel wasn't heard in her voice.

Just then, the door at the top of the stairwell opened and Lizzie and Petey descended. Petey's hand was on Lizzie's shoulder and, when his face became visible, the look on his face as he looked at the back of Lizzie's head sent a shiver of dread through Alison.

Affection. There was so much affection there. She craned her neck forward over the back of the couch to see more closely. To see if it was "best buddy" affection or "I finally got my girl back" affection. She couldn't tell for sure. As they both reached the bottom of the steps, Lizzie turned to Petey and put her arms around his waist, hugging him and saying something to him which Alison couldn't hear. He hugged her back, and a strange look came over his face.

Lizzie leaned up, kissed Petey on the cheek, patted his chest and then moved into the sitting area greeting everyone with her usual smile and cheer.

Still. It could be nothing. Alison wasn't going to jump to conclusions.

She'd wait and see where Petey sat. There was a seat next to her, and another on the other side of Katie and Curtis, next to Lizzie.

He rounded the corner slowly, looking in her direction. She sat and watched him, willing him to come her way, but not daring to say a word. Finally he said, "What's up, all? Let's get this flick rolling so Zeke can start feeling up Val," and plopped down on the sectional.

Next to Lizzie.

Alison stared at him, becoming more and more pissed off. Not sure if she was pissed at Petey or herself.

He stared back at her for a moment. She couldn't read his look, and then he looked away.

Definitely more pissed at *him*.

"What's on the bill tonight?" he asked. Before Katie could answer him, Alison said, "We wanted to get the foreign film everybody's talking about, but it was subtitled."

"So?"

"Well, that would involve reading, and we knew you were going to be here, so...."

Everyone laughed at her joke.

Everyone but Petey.

—∞—

Well. Petey guessed that jab from Alison settled that.

Fuck.

He'd been so excited to see her tonight, could hardly wait to get to Katie's for their first official night of being...*them*...in front of their friends.

But Lizzie had grabbed him as they were entering the house to be her sounding board about her being dumped by some loser named Finn who obviously didn't know a good thing when it stood right in front of him.

He'd given Lizzie a bit of a pep talk. He'd never really seen her down and it kind of threw him. She was the one who gave out the pep talks. Still, he tried his best, and soon she was nodding along with him and saying things like, "You're right. It's nothing. I'm going to State in two months. I'll never even think about him again."

Petey was nodding, but the thought of the girls—okay, Alison—heading off to State so soon had him regretting the two weeks he'd spent at hockey camp.

He should have called her before he left and locked things down, but she'd been in Green Bay with the girls and he didn't know how to get ahold of them.

"Okay," he'd said to Lizzie. "Let's go on in. It's just us guys, right? Not a big group?"

Lizzie nodded as she moved toward the house. "Yep, just us."

"But Alison?" he said wanting to make sure.

"Yep, Al's here," she said pointing to a little car across the street.

"That new?"

"Yep, she got it for graduation."

"Ended up being quite a night, graduation," Petey said with humor in his voice.

This was good. He and Lizzie could get any awkwardness about Alison and him—not that he thought there would be much, if any—out of the way before going in.

"I guess. But she got the car the next day, not graduation day."

"That's not what I meant," he said pointedly.

Lizzie looked at him with puzzlement. "What are you talking about?"

"You know. Graduation night…Alison…."

"What? What do you think you—oh my God! Did she leave the party with somebody?" She grabbed the front of his shirt. "Who? You have to tell me."

He shook his head, confused.

"Petey," she whined, still holding on to his shirt. "Tell me."

"She didn't tell you?"

"No, she never said a word. Who was it?"

He just stood there, slowly shaking his head, trying not to read too much into the fact that Alison hadn't told her two best friends—who told each other *everything*—that she'd lost her virginity. Even when they'd spent the following three days together in Green Bay, with presumably lots of girl talk.

Why?

"Let's see…" Lizzie was saying to herself. "Who was still there when I left? Who would she have made out with but been too embarrassed to tell us about?"

Bingo.

His worst fear—that Alison would be embarrassed she'd slept with a dumb jock like him—seemed to be coming true.

He'd had to repeat third grade, making him a year older than all his classmates. It had helped him with hockey, developing earlier than every other boy, but he'd never been able to shake that feeling of inferiority. At least when it came to books and grades.

The things Alison excelled at.

He'd barely made the grades to get into Tech. Coach had said they'd have tutors available to help him, and of course he wouldn't be taking the courses most of the engineering-geared students would be taking. But it still weighed on him—whether he'd make it through four more years of school.

They walked into the house and to the basement, Petey still in a daze. They started down the stairs and he saw Lizzie take a deep breath, as if bracing herself. Shit, she was hurting, too. And she was such a great person.

He put his hand on her shoulder and squeezed while they made their way down the stairs. At the bottom she turned to him and gave him a hug.

"Thanks for listening, Petey. Not bad for a hockey player."

She meant it as a tease and even kissed him on the cheek after she said it, but it rubbed him the wrong way.

Lizzie made her way to the large connected couches and sat at one end. Petey followed her, his gaze searching out Alison, who was seated at the opposite end.

A smile. One meaningful look or a pat on the empty seat next to her. God, give him something to go on so he didn't make a fool out of himself.

But she gave him nothing, and so he sat next to Lizzie.

Alison did look at him, with cool brown eyes. Not anything like the night they'd lit up with desire.

He looked away, not able to bear that she'd looked at him so unfeelingly, as if the best night of his life had been nothing more to her than ridding herself of her pesky virginity before heading off to college.

He then asked about the movie, afraid his voice would give him away.

And then, bam, she hit him with the illiterate zinger and everyone was laughing with her.

Except him.

Twelve

—ᴍ—

Love and work…work and love, that's all there is.
~ Sigmund Freud

ALISON SPENT THE REST OF THE DAY and evening in her usual routine, but it was far from ordinary.

The time she normally spent with her mother was today spent with Sherry, their mother, and Alison going to the Ridges senior assisted-living facility and finalizing paperwork. They were allowed to get the keys of the tiny apartment her parents would soon be moving to.

Alison had made the choice to get the unfurnished option and have as many of her parents' belongings moved in as would fit to try to add some familiarity.

That had been a hard day. Realizing there was no reason not to move her parents' furniture and personal belongings into this place. That they wouldn't be returning home once they moved here.

Just like today was a hard day, seeing what would be her mother's and father's new home.

Their last home.

Sherry seemed to be taking it much more in stride than Alison.

"I had no idea it was this bad, Al," she said while their

mother was checking out the bathroom. "They really should have been in here months ago. I wish you'd kept us better informed."

"I called you and Janis once a week and sent several emails between calls. I don't know how much better informed I could have kept you."

Sherry seemed not to hear her as she opened the bare cupboards of the kitchen.

"God, there's hardly any cabinet space in this place. Though I suppose she won't be cooking much."

"She has the option, if she'd like too, but they'll also have the full meal plan, so they can easily walk down the hall and eat, or even just pick up the phone and have something sent to their rooms." She'd gone over the different plans with the housing director for hours, making sure the best option was available. "And if they don't come to meals, somebody checks on them later to make sure they did eat and didn't...you know...."

Sherry looked at her with a blank stare. "Leave a burner on. Or a dishcloth near it. Or the sink running full blast. Anything like that."

"Don't you think you're being dramatic?" Sherry asked, then continued to poke around the room.

"No, Sherry, not at all. Those are very real possibilities when dealing with dementia."

She saw Sherry's back stiffen at the word. She'd never sugar-coated it with her sisters, had told them exactly what the doctors had said. She had, of course, added her own opinions, limited in this field as they were.

Sherry looked in the empty fridge and oven, and then turned around to face Alison. "Okay. So, we get them in here soon. This week if we can. Do you know some movers that we can use?"

Alison nodded. "I've already hired the moving company. They're ready when we are. I've measured and figured out what pieces should come here. I packed a bag with some of Dad's belongings and already took it to my place."

"Why did you do that?"

"I didn't want Mom to see it and be confused."

Sherry was shaking her head. "You should have done this a lot sooner, Alison."

"It wasn't necessary before. And we all agreed they'd stay in the house until it became non-viable."

Sherry turned away from her, toward the living area. "And then we'll put the house up for sale? We might still be able to do that while I'm here if we get them moved in this week."

Alison hadn't thought they'd sell it quite so soon after her parents had vacated, but there was no reason not to. With Sherry here to help clean it out and get it ready to show, she might as well.

"Yes, we can do that."

The back of Sherry's head nodded, and she took a step further from Alison.

All her years of studying patients' body language had Alison guessing what was coming next.

"And the cabin? We'll put that on the market after that? Or do them at the same time?"

Yep. She'd seen that one coming a mile away. Had actually been prepared for it since Sherry announced she'd be visiting and able to stay for so long.

Alison took her time walking to where Sherry stood looking out the window. The view overlooked the little park area that the residents used. It wasn't as spectacular as looking at the lake, but it was nice and scenic. There were benches and even a gazebo, though of course they were all covered with snow.

She stepped around Sherry and turned back to face her. She waited until Sherry met her eyes and then put on her best soothing, reasoning voice. "No, Sherry. You know that isn't what was decided. I'm going to keep the cottage. It's my home now. We all talked about this ten years ago. We all agreed."

Sherry had the decency to look guilty, but blustered on. "Things are different now."

The cottage was different, that's for sure. It had been a

ramshackle mess ten years ago when Alison had talked her parents into letting her fix it up.

They all decided then that Alison would get the cottage when her parents passed and Sherry and Janis would get the house.

Alison had spent the next ten years pouring hard work and her own money into the cottage, making it the cozy, stylish, shabby-chic place it now was.

So of course now Sherry and Janis wanted it back on the table.

Not going to happen.

"We have it all written down, Sherry. Mom and Dad's wishes on their care. Who gets what. Everything."

They'd done it just to avoid a situation like this.

And Sherry must have known it too, because she let it drop pretty quickly.

And even though she kept her calm, cool appearance up through the rest of the afternoon, and throughout her evening visit with her father, by the time Alison got home to her beloved cottage, she felt like she'd been pulled in eighty different directions.

—⚍—

Petey heard the garage door open, the car pull in and then the door go back down again. But no Alison appeared through the door. And he was sitting at the kitchen table facing it, waiting for her. After what seemed like an hour, he reached for his crutches to go check on her when the door finally opened and in she walked, bundled in that red coat. Jeans and Uggs sticking out beneath the hem.

Always tiny, she looked even smaller tonight as she unwrapped herself from her coat, scarf, gloves, and hat.

Her short hair followed the knit hat up with static, then finally fell into its slick, short 'do.

He'd been ready to spar, ready to pounce, but looking at her he felt that it'd be an unfair fight, like she had one hand tied behind her back.

The thought of binding her was a nice one, and something

he'd pull out later and fantasize about. For now though, he just softly said, "Did you eat any dinner?"

Her body relaxed a little and he realized she'd been on guard, expecting him to spar.

She shook her head. "No, not yet. I thought I might nuke some of your mom's casserole. Can I get you some?"

"No, thanks. My parents came over this afternoon bearing even more culinary delights."

"So you ate with them?"

"Yep."

She sat down at the table with him. Then she got back up and poured herself a glass of red wine. She motioned the glass to him, asking if he wanted any. He held up his beer bottle in answer. She sat back down and took a fairly large gulp from her glass.

"How'd that go? With your father, I mean."

He let out the breath he hadn't realized he was holding. Good, they were going to do normal. He could do normal with her. It didn't always have to be bob and weave.

"Actually, not too bad. Darío had helped me this morning, so my dad didn't have to, which probably helped. It was just a nice family dinner." He paused and took a swig from his beer. "In which no one mentioned the word hockey."

Alison laughed. She had the cutest little laugh, breathy and light, like it always surprised her when it came out and she had to suck it back in.

"How red did his face get, trying not to mention it?"

Ah, she knew his father well.

"On a scale from pink to crimson? I'd say fire-engine red."

Another small laugh. The color was coming back into her face now and she looked at him—really looked at him—for the first time since she'd walked in the door.

"And the knee?" she asked, pointing to his leg propped up on one of the kitchen chairs.

"Not too bad. If I keep it propped up, it just aches a little.

Kind of a dull ache, but really not bad. The brace pinches a little bit when I stand for too long, so I don't."

Wow, that had felt good, to give a truly honest answer instead of the "fine, fine, no problem" answer he'd given his parents, teammates, friends in Detroit, the media and the other gazillion callers he'd talked to throughout the day.

Even Al seemed surprised he'd been so forthright. She drank some more wine, then proceeded to fix a plate for herself from the pan of lasagna his mother had left heating in the oven.

"She made you a salad and put it in the fridge." Alison nodded and got it out as well as a bottle of dressing. She went back to the oven and pulled out the tin foil bundle next to the pan.

"Garlic bread?" she asked him even though she was already unwrapping it.

"Yep."

"Mmm. God bless your mother," she said, putting two slices on her plate, then wrapping up the bread and putting it on the counter. She put the metal lid on the baking pan and started to put the rest of the lasagna into the fridge, looking back at Petey before she did. "Sure you don't want some more before I put it away?"

He shook his head and she turned back to her task, made harder by his mother's five bags of groceries that she'd brought with her today. And the case of beer his father had.

Alison had to bend over and lean in. Gazing at her ass in those jeans had Petey hoping she'd never find room for the pan and have to stand like that all night.

Sadly, she finally found a spot, put the pan in, and brought her plate and salad bowl to the table, then topped off her wine glass.

"Ready for another?" she asked, indicating his beer.

He gulped down the last bit and nodded. "If you don't mind."

She brought him a new bottle and took his old one, careful

not to touch his hand.

She finally sat and started eating. Her moans at the good food had him fidgeting in his seat, which sent a shot of pain down his leg.

"So, how was your day?" he asked. "No patients today?"

She shook her head, her mouth full. She eyed him suspiciously as she chewed and swallowed, as if her schedule was a state secret that had fallen into enemy hands.

"Lizzie mentioned you were taking on a lighter load right now because of your parents."

She seemed to accept that. She wiped her mouth on her napkin, then placed it back in her lap. She took a sip of wine, her tongue reaching out to swipe a stray drop off her lip.

Jesus, she was killing him just by eating frickin' lasagna and drinking wine.

"My day. Let's see. My day sucked," she said.

"Sorry to hear that." She looked at him like there was some hidden jab coming. "Really," he said and held his hands up in a surrender motion. "I'm sorry you had a sucky day."

She leaned back in her chair, taking her glass of wine with her, arms crossed, measuring him with her eyes.

"Thank you," she finally said.

Two simple words, and yet it felt to Petey as if the earth had shifted, and they were entering into another plane or something.

Yeah, maybe they were on another plane…adulthood.

She told him about her day as she finished eating and nearly finished the bottle of wine.

"And here I thought having some Spaniard standing and watching while I showered in case I fell was about as bad as it could get."

She chuckled. "Nope. I trump ya there, pal."

She cleaned up after herself, putting her dishes in the dishwasher. She brought another beer and what remained of the wine to the table and sat back down.

He'd thought for sure she'd have retreated to her room by

now or at least moved away from him into the living room.

But no, she stayed at the table. With him.

He reached out slowly across the small table and peeled her hand from around the stem of the wine glass and held it. Squeezing her fingers, he looked up and waited until she looked up, too.

"Can we talk about last night?"

She didn't pull them away, but her fingers did clench a little in his.

"I'm not sure there's much to say," she quietly said.

"Oh, I think there's a world to say. I think there's eighteen years worth of things to say, but I'm willing to keep it to just last night."

He took a swig of beer, giving her a moment to digest that, but still clung to her hand.

"What would you like to say?" she asked and then quickly added, "About last night."

He entwined his fingers with hers, much like she'd done last night. "I want to say that I meant what I said."

"Which part?"

"All of it."

"That you'd chase me?" She pointed to his raised leg. "If your knee was better."

"I think we both know I was talking in the metaphorical sense, but yeah." She raised her brows at him. "What? You didn't think I'd know a big word like metaphorical."

"I meant it last night when I said it couldn't happen again," she said. But there was just...something in her voice.

"And now?" he said, trying not to let the smidgen of hope he was feeling come through.

"And now. Let's just say I've been doing a lot of thinking today."

"Oh, Al. Baby, you do a lot of thinking *every* day."

She ducked her head in a shy way, and he squeezed her hand. And holy shit, she squeezed back. "But what were you thinking about today?"

"Choices. Control. And how sick and tired I am of making choices lately."

"Your parents."

She nodded, then continued, "But more than that. I've been thinking about my relationships with men, too."

He held his breath, not wanting to go all caveman with the surge of jealousy that pulsed through him. "In what way?" he asked nonchalantly.

"How I was never satisfied with them in bed."

"Umm...umm...I got nothing."

She chuckled. "I didn't expect you to say anything to that. I'm just trying to tell you what state of mind I'm in right now."

"And what is that?"

She took a deep breath, then slowly let it out. Her chest rose and fell, but he tried not to notice as he held her eyes.

"Like I said, I'm tired of making choices, of controlling things. I'm tired of not getting what I want out of a sexual relationship simply because I'm afraid to tell my partner what I need."

"And what do you need, Al?" he asked softly, leaning as far toward her as he could with his leg still in its brace. "Do you want to lose control?"

She shook her head just a tiny bit and leaned forward. "No. I don't want to *lose* control." She waited and he held his breath not knowing, not daring to guess, where she was going.

"I want to have my control *taken*."

Thirteen

—⚭—

If you never change your mind, why have one?
> *~ Edward de Bono*

WERE THE GODS cutting him some slack? Was the universe making up for his career ending sooner than he'd planned?

Or did Alison Jukuri just tell him she wanted him to control her in bed?

Okay. Don't freak out. And more importantly, don't freak her *out.*

He held her gaze and squeezed her hand again. "So...you're thinking not so much this..." He gently rubbed his thumb over hers—a soft caress, a whisper of a touch. Then he turned their hands so hers was against the table. He disengaged their fingers and slid his hand up her palm and to her wrist, which he then tightly encircled, pushing her hand further into the hard table. "As this..." he said, tightening his hold even more.

It was tiny. But oh, he heard the little gasp that left her mouth.

"Say it."

She nodded.

"Say it," he said more firmly.

"Yes," she whispered.

Excitement like he couldn't believe rushed through him.

Fuck, it was better than stepping out onto the ice at the Joe to a packed house chanting his name.

She was breathing a little deeper now, her sweater rising and falling. Brown and fuzzy, the sweater looked like it would be incredible to touch.

He couldn't wait until it was wadded up on the floor.

"So...how do we...how does this work?" She looked away from him, embarrassed.

"Don't worry, Al, I've got it. I'll get us through it. You won't have to ask for a thing. But we should talk through a few ground rules, first."

"Ground rules? Like what?" Her eyes were huge and the exact shade of brown as her sweater. Puzzlement and a bit of anticipation came through in both her voice and body language as she leaned closer.

He also noticed that she hadn't made a move to loosen her hand from his grip.

"Like what...acts...are on the table. Like choosing a safe word. Stuff like that."

"So, you do this a lot?"

He thought that might kill the deal. That she would be turned off by the thought. But nope, she was genuinely curious.

"Not a lot, no. But, come on Al, you don't become a defenseman in the NHL without wanting to dominate."

She smiled at that and then looked as if she'd done something wrong. He jostled her leg under the table with his good leg. "Hey, this can be fun, too. We can enjoy it and laugh and it can still be intense." She nodded. "We can make this up as we go, Al, now that I know what you want."

He thought about that for a minute. Yeah, no. She wasn't going to want him to ask her every few minutes if she liked it or if she wanted something else. That was the whole point. She was sick of making choices, of telling people what to do, of giving life advice. She wanted to be told what to do. "So maybe even more reason to have a safe word. Just something you can say so I'll know if I've gone too far."

"Okay. What do you suggest? Is there a standard safe word used in these types of situations?" She was mocking it all, but that was out of insecurity. She wanted this.

"Let's just get this straight," he said, squeezing her wrist. "Nothing about us is standard, so don't bullshit yourself."

"I know," she softly admitted.

"Let's see…how about puck? Nice, short and near and dear to my heart."

She thought about it a second—leave it to Alison to overthink a safe word—then shook her head. "No. Something else."What's wrong with puck?"

"If I call it out, you might confuse it with 'fuck.'"

"You planning on calling out 'fuck' a lot?" And didn't the thought of that just make his already twitching dick sit up and pay attention.

"Maybe," she said in a little coquette voice that was so unlike her.

Actually, the whole night was unlike her and a complete one-eighty from her parting words last night.

She must have had one shitty day of introspection after visiting Katie and her mom and sister.

Or…and this was just starting to come to him…maybe this was the real Alison. Maybe all the bullshit she showed everyone was just that—bullshit.

A mini-eureka went through his head, but he didn't want to veer off track now. He'd definitely file that thought away, though.

"So, not puck. You choose," he said.

She looked around, seemingly looking at objects, sizing them up, as if they were playing a game of I spy or something.

"Coffee," she said.

"Shorter. One syllable."

She seemed exasperated. Her eyes roamed around again then came to rest on him. "Jock."

He raised a brow at her. "Fine. Jock it is. So now that—"

"Wait. That's the word we use if you're going too far, right?"

"Yes."

"Well, what word do I use if you're not going far enough?"

Jesus, he was going to come before they even kissed if she kept putting provocative images like that in his head.

"More?"

She shook her head. "Too commonplace. That could pop out without me even realizing it." She narrowed her eyes playfully at him. "Assuming you're doing it right."

"Alllll," he groaned and she giggled.

"Speed. That's the word for stepping it up. Good enough?" she asked.

"Perfect. Anything else? Anything…you know…verboten?"

"That's what I've got 'jock' for, right?"

"Well, yeah, but maybe I should know up front if—"

"Let's just leave it with jock."

He nodded, sensing he was going to lose the moment entirely if he didn't get this show on the road.

"Now," he said, "Put your wine glass and all this other shit that's on the table over on the counter."

"Why would I—"

"Do it. The time for talking, the time for asking and the time for you thinking is over. Just do what I tell you." He released her wrist, sat back in his chair and took a long drag from the beer bottle. He tried to slouch down, but it was a little hard to do with his bum leg out to one side and propped up on a chair. But he thought he pulled off the bossy lover okay. He took another drink of beer and watched her as she rose from the table and began clearing the table of the salt and pepper shakers, napkin holder, and all the other crap that was perpetually on kitchen tables.

Alison Jukuri did as he told her.

Well, holy shit, this might be the night of his life.

When she'd finished her task, she returned to the table but didn't sit back down. Instead, she stood tentatively by the side of her chair.

"Now, if I were able, I would throw you over my shoulder, carry you off to the bedroom and fuck you three ways to Sunday."

She bit her bottom lip, then swiped her tongue across it.

"But, I'm not really capable of doing that tonight. That will have to wait until I'm back on my feet completely."

Something passed across her eyes. Doubt. Damn, she was thinking this was just another one-night stand like the night of Katie's wedding. It wasn't, but he didn't correct her. They'd have time for that later.

Much later.

"So, we're going to have to improvise. And I'm thinking this table will do just fine," he said as he put his beer bottle down on the worn oak table.

"Besides," he added. "There's no way I'm going to fuck you hard on pink sheets."

She barked out a quick nervous laugh, and he relaxed a little.

"Come here," he said in the low voice he used on players from opposing teams when he wanted to intimidate them.

She walked toward him.

He lowered his bad leg from the chair, brushing her off as she tried to help him. "It's fine. Really. It aches a hell of a lot more about two feet higher."

"The brace?"

"Ah, no," he said as he brought his hand to his erection. "Here."

"I can help with that ache," she said and stepped closer to him. When she started to go down on her knees, he reached out and put a hand on her waist, stopping her.

"Not yet. Not until I tell you. This is my show."

Her eyes went wide. She shifted her stance, then nodded.

He could demand the whole "call me sir" spiel. He'd done it before with a couple of women who liked power games. But something kept him from taking that step.

He scooted his chair back from the table and opened his legs. "Closer," he said.

She moved between his legs, he put his hand on her stomach. He caressed the warm and fuzzy sweater and gently pushed her back a step, so her ass hit the edge of the table.

"Hop up on it," he told her. She did, nearly toppling his beer bottle, but he reached out and snatched it in time. He then scooted his chair closer to the table. Alison had to spread her legs to allow him in, like he was seating himself in front of a gourmet dinner.

He drank from the bottle, then offered it to her. As she took a drink he said, "Let some of it spill out of those lips. Just enough for me to lick up."

She did, and as he leaned forward and up, she leaned forward and down, and their mouths met. Two nights in a row he'd kissed that mouth—a record for them.

But thinking about their past, how she wanted it tonight and all that other bullshit flew from his mind when she opened her mouth and their tongues finally found each other. Twirling, pushing, frantically seeking the other, their tongues tangled while Petey deepened the kiss. It was a low table, she was a short woman, and he was a big man, so there wasn't much stretching as he reached out his hand and wrapped it around the back of her neck. She groaned into his mouth. He tasted the beer as he licked it from her lips, but he also tasted the wine and garlic. Yes, indeed, it was just like he had sat down to a feast.

He could have kissed her all night, but she started squirming, as did his hard-on. He sat back in the chair, grateful to hear her small whine as he pulled away.

"Take off your sweater," he said. He held his hand out for the beer bottle, which she handed him. He drank the last of it, set the bottle on the floor and gently rolled it out of potential harm's way.

She watched him get rid of the bottle, but she still hadn't moved. "Do it, Al. Lose the sweater."

She kept her eyes on him as she lifted the hem. "Slowly," he added. He saw the shift in her when she started to lift in a slow, teasing manner, dragging her hand up her bared skin. She wanted to tease.

When she got to her bra, she added her other hand to the other side and lifted. Then she stopped, just as the bottom of a black satin bra came into view.

"Why, you naughty girl," he whispered. "Do your panties match that bra?"

"You'll have to wait and see," she said, easing the sweater up a bit more so the entire cup showed now, but not the flesh above it.

"More," he commanded. "All of it."

She pulled the damn sweater off in one smooth motion. "Jesus, you're beautiful." He reached out and ran a finger across the bounty at the top of the black satin, dipping into her cleavage. She shivered but didn't move away from him. No, she moved deeper into his touch. His fingertip kept the glide going to the side of her breast, then he shifted his hand, cupping the side of her, and down underneath, lifting and shaping her. His thumb flicked her nipple, the small bud hardening at his touch. He flicked a couple more times then pushed his thumb in, right onto the nipple, circling, grinding.

"Ahhh," she sighed, her head falling back. She braced her hands on the outside edges of the narrow table, causing her to arch into him. Practically begging for his mouth.

He reached behind her, having to put his face right into her tits to do so. Which he was so okay with him. He undid her bra and yanked it down away from her. She raised one hand just long enough for him to slip the strap through. He left the other strap around her arm and the bra stayed there, still on the table. She didn't seem to care and it wasn't about to slow him down from getting his mouth on her.

He cupped both of her tits and pushed them together, lashing them both with his tongue as he handled them with a fair bit of force.

"Yes," she gasped, and he squeezed them harder and sucked

deeply on one of her nipples.

God, she was so responsive, so ready for this. He moved his thumb under and up through her cleavage made tighter and higher by his hands. He stroked his thumb up and down through the warm, fragrant passage.

"This is going to be my cock, baby. Right between your tits. And you're going to like it, aren't you."

"Yes," she sighed.

"Look at me," he said sternly. Her head snapped up. Her eyes were dazed, her mouth wet from his kisses. "Watch me taste these amazing tits."

He put his mouth on her again, but kept his eyes on hers. She took a hand off the table to run it through his hair. Then she stopped and began to take it away. "Don't stop," he said. "Put your hands in my hair. Hold me to you. Pull on my hair when you want it harder."

She did as he told her, her fingers digging into his scalp, holding his head to her. It spurred him on and he took a tight nipple back into his mouth and sucked. Her breasts were soft and firm as his hands molded them. Her fingers played in his hair, losing some of their bite.

So he bit her.

Not too hard, but just a tiny bite on her nipple had her hands clutching him once more.

"Yes," she moaned. He moved to her other breast and bit again, this time tugging on it as he pulled away. Her ass rocked on the table as she gasped.

His girl liked a little pain with her pleasure.

He knew how exhilarating pain could be. He fairly flew down the ice after being painfully checked in the boards.

He wouldn't go too far with her and would certainly never hurt her, but damn if all these revealing desires of hers didn't have him dying to be inside her.

"Enough," he said, abruptly pulling away, pleased when she clutched at him. But he ducked out of her hands and pushed the chair from the table, awkwardly standing up.

She just watched him. She didn't even offer to help, so dazed with lust. Her sweet tits heaved from her breathing, wet and glistening.

He pulled his tee-shirt over his head and sent it flying. God, he loved the way she looked at his body. It made all the hours of training worth it just for the gaze of hunger she was giving him.

He grabbed one of his crutches from the chair they'd been resting on and propped himself up, standing in front of her but just out of reach.

"Unsnap your jeans."

He noticed her hands trembled as she reached for her fly and undid the metal button. Good, 'cause he sure as hell was shaking on the inside.

"Unzip." She did.

"Now take them off, but don't leave the table. I want you to squirm 'em off."

Her big brain seemed stumped.

"Scooch and rock. I want to see those gorgeous tits jiggle while you do."

More heat infused her already flushed face, but she began to rock and lift and squirm her way out of her jeans while she remained seated.

And Jesus, it was a sight to behold. Her breasts swayed with the motion and jerked when she tugged. Petey put a hand on himself over his track pants and started to slowly stroke. The sight caused Alison to stop her progress.

"Keep going," he firmly said.

She did, her movements faster now, tits bobbing from side to side.

He squeezed his cock so he wouldn't end this too quickly.

When she had the jeans past her thighs he tipped the arm part of his crutch forward, catching the denim and pushing them down and off her. He brought the crutch back up and used the toe of it to push the jeans under the table so as not to fuck up his traction.

"Pretty as a picture," he said as he looked at her, meaning every word. She leaned back again, posing for him. Her bra still lay on the table, one strap loosely hanging from her arm. The black satin bra matched her panties, which was all she was wearing. Her legs were spread a little—not as wide as they soon would be—with just a tease of what awaited him showing. She reached to the waistband of her panties, but he growled, "Leave 'em on." She halted her progress.

"Slide one hand in," he told her. "Slide your fingers along those plump lips. But don't dip inside. Not yet." Her head tilted to one side and a little back, almost resting on her shoulder, as she did what he commanded. He watched the movements of her hand through the black satin, gliding, light, but not going deeper. Her wrist and the top of her hand moved in and out of the satin and he began to lightly stroke his cock.

She had the most beautiful skin; flawless and the color of a latte with too much milk. His eyes went back to her breasts, still red and heavy from his mouth.

"Put your other hand on your tits," he said, his voice rough with arousal. She moved quickly, the bra strap falling away as she moved her hand from the edge of the table and to her breast. She had one hand on each place he wanted to feel, to taste, to lick. He didn't need to direct her. She started pinching her nipple, tugging on it as he had. Shit, she was rougher with herself than he'd been.

"Okay," he said as he pushed the waistband of his track pants down, letting his cock spring free. "Slip a finger in." She must have been on the edge as much as he, because in a flash her hand disappeared into her panties.

"Wet?" he demanded.

"Yes," she gasped.

"Show me." She whimpered at the thought of leaving that warm heat—he didn't blame her—but removed her hand, holding up her fingers. He leaned the crutch against the chair where the other one rested, then stepped forward, grabbed her wrist and sucked on her fingers. She inched her ass closer to the edge of the table, closer to his erection.

"You want this?" he asked, stroking himself as he continued to hold her wrist.

She nodded and he squeezed her wrist. "Yes," she said.

He let go of her and grabbed the top of her panties with both hands. "Rock back," he told her. When she did he slid the panties off her and down her legs, which he pushed together. Once the black satin scrap lay on the floor, he linked a hand under each of the knees, stepped closer to her, slid his hands down her shapely calves, and then twisted his hands so he could push her legs up in the air.

The movement threw her off balance and she put her arms behind her, bracing herself. He put her feet over his shoulders, which pulled her even closer to him, then slid his hands down her legs to her hips. One hand grasped a hip and the other circled under her legs to grab ahold of his hard dick and guide it into her.

The heat of her. She was like a furnace and he wasn't even inside her yet. And then he realized why it felt so amazing even just being next to the wet heat. He was riding bareback.

"Christ. Shit."

"What? What is it?"

"No condom. I mean there might be one somewhere in my shaving kit, but…fuck." The thought of picking up his crutches, hobbling back to the bathroom, rummaging…shit. And if Alison hopped off that table to go get one, he had the sinking feeling she wouldn't come back.

But still, there was no way he—

"Are you okay? I mean, are you clean? Disease-free?" she asked.

"Yeah, I am. We have a physical at the start of every training camp, so I know I'm clean."

"And you've worn a condom every time since?"

No need to tell her she was the only one he'd had sex with since reporting for training camp. "I wear a condom every time…

period."

"Then we're okay. I'm on the pill."

He didn't want to think about that—why she'd need regular birth control. And then he thought about it and it made sense.

"You're okay with just that? The pill?"

She inched herself even closer to him, half her ass nearly off the table. "Yes," she said. "I'm okay with that. Just do it. Now.

"Speed," she said and smiled up at him. "Speed, speed, speed."

Fourteen

A good hockey player plays where the puck is.
A great hockey player plays where the puck is going to be.
~ Wayne Gretzky

ALISON COULDN'T BELIEVE IT. It was as if she'd finally figured out the missing piece to the puzzle that was sex. Or at least sex for *her*.

Petey took his erection, guided it just inside her, then pulled it back out. She groaned. He smiled that cocky, sexy smile and drove into her.

He inched closer to her and his hand came up and slid behind her neck pulling her to him for a kiss. She leaned forward, still needing to keep her balance, which sent her legs up higher along his chest.

Which drove him deeper inside her.

She could barely kiss him through her gasp of satisfaction.

She sucked on his tongue, her kisses a bit frantic as she tried to make him move. Her position was such that she was at his mercy, not able to control the pace, the depth, anything.

Exactly how she wanted it. She clenched around him.

"Fuck," he groaned, taking his lips from hers momentarily. But he still didn't stroke, just continued to kiss her.

"My pace," he said. Then he took her bottom one into his

teeth and nipped and licked it. She clenched again, and he grabbed onto her hips and angled her ass up higher, which felt fantastic, but made her have to lean back on her arms even further, her balance off-kilter. He split her legs more, as he followed her back for more kisses.

Then finally—*finally*—he began to move inside her.

"Yes," she sighed.

His strokes were long and slow and seemed to find every nerve inside of her. "Faster," she whispered and kissed him again. She wanted to wrap her arms around him, to feel those broad shoulders and the strength that came from them, but she knew if she released her arms she'd have to pull off some kind of crazy ass yoga move to keep her balance long enough to snake her arms around him.

He slid deeper inside her and moved his pelvis in some kind of circle or something. Whatever it was sent a shot of electricity through her whole body.

God, she really couldn't believe how her body was responding. She'd thought sex had always been nice and pretty good for her, but now she had to wonder if she'd been fooling herself. She'd always had to work much harder to get to even a fraction of—

"Stop thinking," Petey growled at her. His voice—holy crap—that deep, masculine voice barking orders at her. She was embarrassed at how wet it made her.

"So wet," he whispered in her ear, as if reading her mind. His pace quickened a tiny bit. Not enough for her, but she trusted him now. He knew what she needed, maybe even more than she did.

The hand that had been holding her hip eased in front of him around her thigh, skimming her belly and easing its way down. She tried to open her legs wider, but her heel started to slide from his shoulder. His quick reflexes had it back in place before she could even register what was happening.

"Don't worry, I can fit in there just fine." And to prove his point, he wedged his big hand between her thighs that were only as far apart as the width of his chest.

He found her clit easily and lightly brushed across it.

"Oh, God," she cried out and dropped her head back. "So good."

"I know it is," he said, his pace picking up speed as his finger circled around her. "So fucking good with us." He made another circle, then added his thumb and pinched her clit.

Her head pushed back even further as the waves rushed over her, every muscle in her body clenching and then releasing. The convulsion went through her just as he drove deep, and lights exploded behind her closed eyes. It seemed to go on and on. He gasped and lifted her butt, and then rub or twist again and another jolt would go through her. Just when she started to come down, he said, "Look at me." But she couldn't. She couldn't even lift her head to—

"I said, 'look at me.'" He hadn't raised his voice, but the tone made her lift her heavy head and open her eyes.

He didn't say any more, just took his hand from her and trailed it up her body to the middle of her chest, between her boobs. He pushed. Her arms began to tremble, barely able to hold herself up without him pressing on her. "Let go. Just let go." She did, and he pushed her flat on her back with her legs still up in the air against his chest. He never moved his hand, continuing to hold her down. Pinning her to the table. She closed her eyes, but he pinched a nipple and commanded, "Open your eyes. Keep 'em open. Watch me fuck you."

His words sent another aftershock through her. She began to build again as he started stroking deep and fast. She heard and felt his balls slapping her ass with the force. "Pinch yourself for me," he said as he took his hand from her chest and moved it back to her thigh. She brought her hands up to her breasts and played with them. They felt so tender and achy. Pinching the nipples almost alleviated the pain, but not quite. She tugged on them as he had and looked up at him to see him nodding encouragingly at her as he stroked inside her.

His hands grabbed the back of her thighs and pushed them forward, her legs spreading, calves coming off his chest. He pushed even further, her knees bending and her thighs nearly to her boobs.

He grunted his approval of the deeper position and she showed her approval by squeezing her inner muscles and holding.

"Fuck, that's good," he said in a moan and seemed to snap, slamming himself into her over and over. She tried to keep up with him, to clench on his down stroke, but he was going too fast for her. So delightfully fast. And then she outpaced him and exploded again. Her arms fell to her side, thumping against the table.

Petey drove deep into her one last time, his body shuddering with his release, which seemed to go on and on until he finally slumped down onto her. She lifted her arms—no easy feat—and wrapped them around him, sliding her hands down his back, moist from exertion.

"Wow," was all she could say, inadequate as it was.

But it was more than he could apparently manage, for all he did was grunt and kiss her neck.

They stayed that way for a while. She loved the weight of him on top of her, so big and male.

Eventually he shifted and she realized he'd been standing with the brace and no crutches, and she knew he had quite a bit of force in that stance.

"Petey, your leg," she murmured, nudging him.

"Hurts like a mother," he said as he shifted again.

She pushed on him. It wasn't that she wanted him off of her—because she didn't, not really—but he needed to move that leg, and she needed to come back to her senses.

She wasn't going to beat herself up this time, like she had after Katie's wedding. She'd needed this, needed him. Needed to find out about herself and her suspicions that she wanted to be controlled in bed.

Well, she certainly had that figured out now.

And it wouldn't have happened if she hadn't had the day that she did. A little bit of envy after visiting Katie, tweaked by the visit to her parents' next home. And, oh yeah, dealing with Sherry hinting around about the cabin.

It had all added up to a small wallow of self-pity that could be eased by a professional athlete pounding into you.

He pulled out of her, which sent a shiver of desire through her that he obviously noticed.

"Let's go to bed. But you're going to have to be on top for round two. My leg will barely get me down the hall." He grinned. "But, damn it was worth it."

He pulled up his pants and stepped away from the table. While he hobbled to get his crutches, she slid off the table, walked the few steps to the living room and grabbed a throw from the back of the couch, wrapping it around herself.

"Aww, now that's a shame," he said, watching her as he propped himself up on the crutches. "Come on, I've got to lie down and get this thing off."

She started to speak but kept her mouth shut and followed him to her room. He got himself to the bed and sat on the edge, propping the crutches on the nightstand. He reached for the brace, but she was beside him and brushed his hands away.

"Let me," she said, and bent to loosen the Velcro straps. He started to reach for her, but she got the brace off quickly and moved away, placing it on the floor where he'd be able to reach it in the morning.

He moved back on the bed, then eased his leg up. He propped himself up against the headboard, and looked at her. "You're not coming to bed, are you?"

She shook her head. "It was…it was amazing, Petey."

"Hell yes, it was, and can be again in just a little while. Now come to bed, Al."

"No. And it can't happen again."

"That's what you said last night." It wasn't smug, but more of a gentle reminder that she'd changed her mind once, why not again.

"I know. But it's the truth this time. It was great. And it opened my eyes to some things about me that now make sense. But Petey, you must know there can never really be anything between us."

"No. I don't know that."

She reached out to him, pushed his hair back from his face and then stepped away toward the door.

"Al, seriously, why not?"

She sighed, a sudden sadness taking her over.

"You know why," she whispered and left the room.

Fifteen

When you have to make a choice and don't make it,
that is in itself a choice.

~ William James

Eighteen Years Ago

"THANKS FOR MEETING ME," Alison said to Petey when he slid into the front seat of her car.

He nodded, not quite meeting her eyes. "Sure thing," he said and shut the door of her little Accord. He glanced at her quickly, then stared straight ahead, taking in the view.

She'd called and asked him to meet her at the Quincy Outlook, a scenic viewing area that overlooked both Hancock and Houghton.

Theirs were the only two cars in the lot, but later in the day tourists on their way to Copper Harbor would pull over, admire the view and probably take some pictures. It was a great view year round, but in the fall it could take your breath away.

But Alison could barely see beyond her dashboard. She certainly couldn't enjoy the beauty laid out before them.

"Um…" she started, then stopped. She tried to remember the little speech she'd rehearsed over and over in her mind for the past four days. She looked at him, and her mind went blank. He was so gorgeous. Even in profile. Maybe especially in profile. His black hair still had a little sheen from wetness—he must have just showered. He towered over her, even sitting down, and took up not only the passenger seat, but part of her space, too. His wide shoulders were only inches from her.

Shoulders she'd wrapped her arms around five weeks ago. One night only. Her first. And they hadn't been alone together since. And had barely spoken to each other when in a group since that night in Katie's basement.

She wanted to reach out and run her fingers through his hair as she'd done graduation night. It was so soft, she hadn't touched it nearly enough that night.

"Umm…" she tried again. She wanted to throw her arms around him and burrow into that broad chest that was already so much more a man's than the a boy's.

She'd watched him at the beach when he wasn't looking. She'd been on a towel only a few down from him. Part of the group, and yet now the dynamic had changed. God, how she'd wanted to follow him into the water and wrap her legs around his waist, have him hold her up in the water and feel the slick glide of their skin on each other's. She wanted him to touch her like he had that night. To whisper the words of encouragement and desire that he'd whispered to her then.

"Umm…" She saw his shoulders fall in defeat. He knew. He knew why she'd summoned up her courage, called him and asked to meet.

"Just say it," he said in a whisper. She wasn't sure if he even knew he said it out loud.

"I'm pregnant." His whole body deflated at that. His chin dropped to his chest.

"Fuck."

—⁂—

He tried to rally. He thought he did it pretty quickly, but honestly he had no idea how long it'd been between her dropping the bomb and him swearing. He pulled his body up, bracing like he was about to get checked into the boards, and turning to face Alison.

"What should we do?" he asked. A tiny tremble of what looked like relief shimmered through her tiny body. A body that wasn't going to stay tiny for much longer.

Shit, his dad was going to kill him.

He did some quick calculations—easier to do since Alison still hadn't answered him. They'd done it the night of graduation. He still considered it the best night of his life, even if she'd blown him off afterward. So, she'd have the baby around February. Right in the middle of hockey season. Right around Winter Carnival.

She'd have to stay here, of course. No way could she be in the dorms at State with Lizzie and Katie and her big baby belly. But she could go to Tech for at least the first semester. It wouldn't be a problem for her to get in at this late date—universities had been breaking down her door to offer her academic scholarships. She could have gone to any Ivy League school free of charge, but she'd decided to go to State with her girls.

Kind of like him. He'd been recruited at several schools and been offered athletic scholarships at every one of them but had decided to stay here and play for Tech, even though he wouldn't get the exposure he would have at a larger school. He and his dad had weighed it all out at the dining room table that'd been littered with letters from colleges for most of the year.

Exposure from a larger school versus being the big fish in a small pond. And his parents being able to see him play. He had to admit that one had him in knots, both for and against.

But ultimately he'd decided on Tech. Maybe it was meant to be. With him here, it would make it all easier—they'd have his parents and her parents for help when the baby came. He'd have to call Coach and see about switching from the dorms to married housing. Thankfully they'd both have scholarships. They'd never be able to swing staying in college any other way.

She still wouldn't look at him. She would marry him, wouldn't she? He knew she was embarrassed that they'd slept together and had basically ignored him all summer.

But she couldn't ignore him now.

And yeah, he was scared shitless about the idea of becoming a father so young, but some deep, caveman gene was screaming that now he'd have Alison.

She may be ashamed that Ms. Genius had the hots for Mr. Dumb Jock, but there was no denying how good they'd been together.

It wasn't going to be easy, he wasn't naïve. But damn, he did like the idea of waking up with her every morning.

But first they'd have to tell their parents and then their friends.

Shit, his dad was going to kill him. Well, Lieutenant Dan was just going to have to suck it up.

"I'm not going to keep it," Alison said pulling him out of his imaginary, sure-to-come argument with his father.

"What?"

She shook her head. "No, that's not what I meant." Relief coursed through him, but she was still shaking her head. His gut clenched. "Not I'm not going to keep it. I'm not going to *have* it."

The emotions rolled through his body. Fear—that his parents would find out about it. Irrational he knew, since he'd just been imagining telling them they were going to be grandparents. Shame—that he'd be taking this girl to someplace out of town to…deal with it (shit, he couldn't even mentally think the word). Regret—not about spending the night with Alison, he'd never regret that—but that he'd somehow put them both in this position. Sadness—for the future with Alison he'd just imagined never coming to be. And deep, deep sadness for the child who would not be.

And relief. The sense of relief was overwhelming and it raised the level of shame tenfold.

Could he talk her out of it? He studied her. She was such a strong, proud little thing, but the night they'd been together she'd clung to him, had looked at him with such passion and…

something more.

Did he hold any sway over her? Could he make her keep it? Make her marry him? He'd be off playing hockey, and she'd be stuck at home. He'd imagined her easy acceptance at Tech, but would she be able to keep up with a baby at home?

He was destined for great things on the ice, he knew it. He had a good dose of humility, but he knew deep in his bones that he'd be a hockey star someday. Would having a baby derail that?

How could it not?

Alison was destined for academic greatness. She wanted to be a scientist and was bound to discover the cure for cancer or something else equally amazing. Would she be able to do that with a baby at eighteen?

He pushed the moral dilemma from his brain, too emotionally drained to even contemplate its weight right now. He would grapple with that later.

She finally—*finally*—looked at him. Tears welled in her beautiful brown eyes. Eyes that seemed to take up nearly half of her pixie face. Eyes that held a world of sadness.

His thoughts of trying to sway her in any direction flew from his over-taxed brain. All he wanted now was to take away her pain.

Knowing he could never do that, he vowed to do his best to at least share her pain. He lifted a hand and slowly slid it along her jawline, coming to rest on her soft cheek. His hand was so big that it encompassed nearly the entire side of her face. His fingertips brushed the bottom of her ear. Her hair was so soft against his rough hand.

He bent his head, brought his lips to her forehead and gave her the tiniest of kisses. He then rested his forehead against hers. "How can I help? What can I do?" he whispered.

He saw the teardrops fall. With their heads at this angle, her tears fell straight down. They landed on her bare leg, just below the hem of her khaki shorts. The first one stayed there, a perfect drop upon the brown, tan skin. He wanted to reach down and touch it, smear it, wipe it away, like he wanted to wipe away this day.

But he didn't move. He just held her face in his hand, rested his head against hers, and waited as more tears silently fell. The tears landed on top of each other, eventually causing an overflow that seeped toward her shorts, wetting the fabric at the edge.

He had no sense of how long they sat that way while she cried and he wished he could do something—anything—to help. Finally, she pulled away from him. He wanted to hold on, to ease her back to him, but her intention was clear and strong— she wanted to be away from him. She seemed to want as much distance from him as her tiny car would allow.

It felt just like the first time they'd seen each other after that night, when they'd all been at Katie's. He'd had her for one night. He had her for a few moments now while she cried.

But he'd never really have her. She was too smart for that.

"Would you…take me? Go with me? To Green Bay. I found a place."

"Of course," he said with no hesitation. He'd do whatever she needed him to do. Help ease her pain in any way he could.

He'd worry about *his* pain some other day.

Sixteen

—∾—

Ice hockey is a form of disorderly conduct
in which the score is kept.

~ Doug Larson

THE NEXT MORNING, Alison listened intently to her patient. There was no tendency to daydream, and lord knew she had plenty of material for mind-wandering.

But no, she listened closely to James—not only to what he said, but more importantly to what he didn't.

James had tried to commit suicide two years ago as a senior in high school in Wisconsin. He'd slit his wrists, but his mother—unexpectedly returning home from work with the flu—found him in time.

Now a sophomore at Tech, he'd been seeing Alison, at his parents' urging and encouragement, since his first week in the Copper Country.

In some ways, the Copper Country was a good place for him—calm, peaceful, laid back. In others? Not so much. He was in a high-risk category: male in his early twenties, high intelligence, away from home.

The isolation, the high academic pressure at Tech, and the long winters were all possible triggers for any setbacks with James.

And there had been a couple.

So, no chance to revel in memories of the night before. Which really was just as well.

James made himself comfortable on the couch, sitting in the same corner as he typically did—the one nearest Alison's chair. His hands, always in nervous motion, slid up and down his pants from thigh to knee.

He took a deep breath and then another. Alison waited.

He shrugged, his hands now pulling at the bottom hem of his grey sweater. "I don't know. I guess I don't have much to say today."

"That's okay. Some days I don't have much to say either. How is your roommate?"

"Good. We went to a movie last Saturday night."

"Did you enjoy it?"

"The movie? Or the night out with Bryce?"

"I meant the night, but either."

He went with the movie, describing the action sequences in far more detail than Alison needed, but she let him go. Just having him talk so freely was a good sign from when he'd begun seeing her two years ago.

His IQ was off the charts, but his mind, oh that high-functioning brain, was sometimes his biggest enemy.

She knew what that was like.

"But it was good to hang out with Bryce, too. To go out, and not study for a night." He looked up at her from his lap. "That's good, right?"

She nodded. "That's very good. You need to be able to get away from the books—we talked about that. And you can never have too many friends."

He was nodding, but she could tell that his mind was already off in another direction.

"What are you thinking right now, James?" He took a second too long, and she knew he was debating what to tell her.

"Oh, just that it'd be cool if they made a sequel to that movie."

He wasn't telling her the truth.

Alison continued to ask him questions on how he'd spent the time since their last session. She was trying to lead him somewhere, but she wasn't sure where he needed to go.

His fingers now clasped and unclasped, as if he were trying to warm them, though he'd been inside long enough that any residual cold from the outside would have worn off by now.

He talked about one of his classes he found interesting. It was a diversionary tactic, and usually she'd call him on it and get him back on track. Other times she sensed he wasn't going to get back on track no matter how much she tried to corral his train of thoughts with pointed questions. She let him talk of things that seemed unimportant. She tended to think nothing James said was unimportant, even if he thought that.

As they were wrapping up, she began the assessment of James's current stability that she did every session. She began by softly asking, "James? Have you had any thoughts of suicide since we last met?" Which had been last week. They were at two sessions a week.

"Not really, no."

"That didn't sound definite."

"It's not that I thought about…that. It's just that I've thought about how nice it would be to just fall asleep and never wake up. But not necessarily die or anything. Just…"

"Not wake up."

"Right. Just like one long nap."

Actually, that sounded pretty good to her, too.

"I wouldn't do it, though," he added.

"Do you currently have anything in your dorm room that could be used to hurt yourself? That would include pills."

"No, nothing. And the only pills are the meds Dr. Thompson prescribed."

"And you're taking them?"

His eyes darted away as he nodded. "Mmm-hmm. Yeah."

"It's important to stay on them, James."

"I know," he said, but Alison doubted him.

"If you were to try to kill yourself, do you know how you would do it? Do you currently have a plan?"

"Well, I'd obviously choose a different route," he said, holding up his wrists, the scars from his previous attempt covered by his sweater. He then tried a half-hearted shrug/smile combination.

She wasn't going to let him off the hook with that.

"Do you have a different route chosen, James?"

He looked her in the eye and shook his head just slightly, his body quiet for a moment. "No."

She let out an internal sigh. "So, let's get back to your idea of falling asleep forever."

He went on for a little while describing what sounded to Alison like a lovely passing of time, while also mentally filing it all away to think about later, as she made her notes on the session.

She did some follow-up assessment questions and just barely got them in before James's restlessness got the best of him just as the session was up.

He rose, then moved to the other side of the room and started putting on his outerwear. He struggled with his boots, and Alison resisted the temptation to kneel down and lace him up like a mother would for a small childJames was not a child, and she was not anyone's mother.

After they confirmed she would see him in two days and James left her office, she moved to her desk to make notes in his electronic file. She typed for a good fifteen minutes, trying to objectively transcribe her thoughts on James's mental health.

She looked up James's contact info, then picked up the phone and dialed. When a receptionist answered she identified herself and asked to speak with Dr. Thompson. Scott was a general physician in the area that happened to be the physician to several of her patients. Like most doctors in the area, he took his turn being on-call in the local emergency room. His offices also happened to be in an office park right across from the hospital, which was convenient.

"Alison," he asked when he came on the line. "What can I do for you? Is Petey okay?"

Oh, right, Petey. She pushed all thoughts of the hulking jock out of her head—though the word "jock" made her mentally pause—and said, "Petey's fine. Well, he was still sleeping this morning when I left the house, so I'm assuming he's still fine." She thought about how that sounded and quickly added, "At least, I heard him snoring as I walked by his room."

"That's good. His knee obviously isn't interfering with being able to get good sleep."

It wasn't interfering with other activities either, but she kept that bit of information to herself.

"Actually, I'm calling about James Jurgeson."

"Is he okay?" Scott quickly asked with concern.

"Yes. I mean I think so. He just left a session. I wanted to check with you that he was still on his meds. I mean, as much as you could possibly know."

She heard the typing of a keyboard as Scott answered her. "Let's see. He said he was when I last saw him. But…yes…it says he refilled the prescription two weeks ago, which would have been right on target if he was taking them regularly."

Relief seeped into her. But still, you never knew. "You haven't prescribed any sleep aids, have you?"

When he had first started seeing her, James had given consent for Alison and Scott to discuss his treatment—which they did on a fairly regular basis.

"No. No sleep aids of any kind. Has he been having trouble sleeping? Or are you worrying about something else?"

"Something else. Suicidal thoughts in particular."

"I see. He's not scheduled to come in for another six weeks. Do you think I should get him in here sooner?"

"No, I don't think that's necessary. Not yet, anyway. I'll certainly let you know if that changes."

"Okay. Thanks for keeping me in the loop."

"Of course."

"And Alison?"

"Yes?"

His voice went lower. More personal, less doctor. "Are *you* doing okay?"

"Yes, of course," she quickly answered.

"Really? You're taking care of a lot of people right now. Don't forget to take care of yourself."

"Hey, who's the shrink here?"

He chuckled. "I don't have to be a shrink to know you need a break."

"I've had one," she said, thinking about being flat on her back on the kitchen table, her legs in the air.

The table which she'd vigorously scrubbed this morning before leaving for work.

"That's good, that's good," Scott said. "Make sure you take more of them."

Well, that wasn't going to happen.

"Thanks, Scott. I'll talk to you soon."

"Sounds good," he said and hung up.

Alison set the phone back in the cradle, finished up with James's file and then turned off her computer. She turned her chair so she could look out over the canal.

It had snowed again last night (big surprise!), and the area looked like one white blanket. She watched as two snowmobilers raced down the frozen canal. Checking her watch, she debated calling Lizzie to see if somebody was going to check in on Petey during the day, then decided against it.

She didn't trust herself to talk about Petey's recovery with Lizzie right now. Besides, of course Lizzie—or Petey's mom for that matter—would make sure their precious darling had what he needed.

She wouldn't give it another thought, she told herself. And maybe she wouldn't think about how he was doing right now— the man wasn't going to starve to death with that loaded fridge. But damn, she couldn't seem to stop thinking about what he'd done last night.

To her.

—⁂—

Much as it had sucked to have Darío standing guard as he'd showered yesterday, it was better than having his father here.

Which is what Petey was dealing with today.

Actually, it wasn't that bad, if he was being honest.

They'd gotten through the basics of making sure Petey could get up, showered, and dressed with minimal verbal bloodshed and now sat at the kitchen table sharing coffee and Finnish pastry that his father had brought with him.

Petey sat in the same chair he had last night when Al had come home. The same chair he'd pushed out of his way so he could hold down her small but curvy body and pound himself into her.

The obviously well-scrubbed table reeked of Pine-Sol, and was still slightly damp from whatever deep treatment Alison had performed on it.

It wouldn't be so easy for her to wipe the memory clean—he'd made sure of that.

Except he couldn't erase the memories either. And the one that played the longest and loudest in his mind was of her so casually saying it wouldn't happen again.

And so obviously believing it.

It's just what she'd done so long ago—the two of them as a couple weren't logical and didn't make sense to her, so she never gave it a chance. Never gave them a chance.

And he wasn't innocent in it all, he knew that. There was no way his pride was going to let him keep knocking on the door of a girl who didn't want him for more than a great lay.

And, oh, it had definitely been a great lay.

"More?" Petey's dad said, pulling him out of his Alison reverie.

He looked up and saw that his dad was pointing to his nearly empty coffee cup.

"Please," he said, holding his cup out to his rising father. He took it and his own cup over to the counter where he'd started a fresh pot when he'd arrived.

"While you're over there, could you put one of those bean-baggy things in the microwave for three minutes?"

His father nodded, put the heating pad in the microwave, brought Petey a full cup, then went back to the counter and filled his own. He leaned a hip against the counter and sipped, waiting for the microwave. "The shower and getting dressed make it ache more?" he asked Petey.

No. But standing on it while he fucked Alison on this very table sure did.

"A little bit, not too bad." He took a sip of the strong brew, not meeting his father's stare.

"It's a lot worse than a little bit, isn't it, son?"

He always knew when Petey was lying. He just didn't know what Petey was lying about now. Or if not actually lying, at least not telling the whole truth.

"Yeah, it hurts like a mother this morning. I think I tried to do too much on it yesterday. Maybe you could bring over that bottle of Tylenol and a glass of water, too."

The words were barely out of his mouth before his father was in action. He brought over the Tylenol bottle and found a glass, filled it with water, and put it down in front of Petey.

"Is Alison even helping you at all? Or is she making you do everything for yourself?"

Oh, she was helping him out plenty. And, he guessed, also making him do it himself. He chuckled. "Al's fine. She's been great putting me up. And putting up with me."

His father harrumphed. His parents had never been huge fans of Alison, bristly as she could be.

And of course they'd always hoped that he and Lizzie would one day come home from Detroit and announce that twenty years of best friendship had suddenly blossomed into romantic love, and they'd be getting married.

Every parent wanted their son to marry a Lizzie.

But this son wanted Alison.

He nearly choked on the Tylenol as he clarified his own internal thoughts. To fuck. To make all of her sexual fantasies come true. To finally get this itch he'd had for her out of his system.

But to marry? Well, no, that would be disastrous. The two of them forever in harmony?

Not going to happen.

No way did he want to spend every day in a constant battle of the minds that he was destined to lose.

After basically spending his whole life in one long physical brawl on the ice, he wanted to spend his Chapter Two in a mellow, peaceful existence.

There'd be no peace with Alison.

Holy shit, had she figured that out eighteen years ago?

Of course she had, it was just the dumb jock who took decades to figure out something so easy to see.

Damn, he really wished he'd gotten the painkillers after all.

He got the Tylenol—five of them—down finally. "Besides," he said, "she's gone most of the time for work and dealing with her parents. Between you and Mom, Lizzie and Katie, and even Darío, I'm more than covered without Alison."

He had a million puns in his mind about covering Alison, but he let them all slide by. This was no time to get a hard-on thinking about her.

"Well, as soon as you're able to do stairs you can come home until your renters leave at the end of the semester."

Well, shit, how could he not have thought beyond Alison's house? It would be three months until his house was available.

"I figured I'd go back to Detroit as soon as I could travel," he said, making up the option on the spot.

"Why?"

"That's where I live."

His father waved a hand, dismissing Petey's words. "You

don't live there. You have a condo there to throw your stuff during the season. You live at rinks during the season. You *live* here."

He couldn't argue with that.

"At the very least, I need to go back and tie stuff up. Get my shit together. I suppose put the condo on the market."

There was a question in his voice. "Although in this market, I might just want to hang on to it for a while. Lizzie hung on to hers."

"You said she spends time down there each month for business."

"Yeah, that's true." A sudden shadow seemed to envelope him. Holy shit—what the hell was he going to do for the rest of his life?

He was set financially because he'd made good investments. Though he'd lost his share in some of the recent economic crises, he was diversified enough, and young enough, to be able to ride it out, and his portfolio bounced back.

But there was no way he could just sit around and make investments for the rest of his life. He'd go mental.

Maybe he would hand out buckets of balls to kids after all.

"How do you think an indoor driving range would go over here?" he asked his father, then immediately regretted it.

His father narrowed his eyes at him. "Why?"

Petey tried to be nonchalant in both the shrug he gave and his tone as he said, "Just an idea Darío had. It seemed like a good one."

His father's posture relaxed. "Oh. Darío. Yeah, that would make sense. He'd have somewhere to practice. I think it's a great idea." He paused, took a sip of coffee and then added, "For Darío to do."

He knew he shouldn't ask this, knew he'd regret it, but still he said, "Dad, what do you think I'd be good at for a second career?"

"Why would you even think you'd need a second career? I thought you said you were fine financially?"

"I did. I am." Early on, Petey's dad had taken control of his finances. When Petey was twenty-eight, he'd cut his father out of that part of his business. They'd had a doozy of a fight over that and had even gone several months without speaking. It had eventually blown over, but they were both careful not to bring up Petey's money.

He'd offered to buy his parents a home on the water, a second home in Florida for when they retired or any number of things, but they'd always declined.

His dad didn't want his money. He just wanted to control Petey's life.

"Son, we've talked about this. Broadcasting is the next logical step for you, if you want to keep working. So, if you want to get rid of the Detroit condo, that's fine. You can just fly out of here for games. But maybe you should hang on to it. It'd be a much more convenient hub."

Petey thought this particular path had been axed a long time ago. It certainly had been for him. "Dad, I'd make a terrible broadcaster."

His father looked shocked. "What do you mean? You'd be great. Nobody knows the game better, and you know all the current players. Your analysis of them is always spot-on."

"Yeah, and like a mine field loaded with F-bombs."

His father gave another wave of dismissal, a movement Petey knew well. "They help you with all that stuff."

"Exactly! They'll make me less me so I'll be presentable for the public." He leaned forward, arms on the table. His hamstring strained from the brace and last night's exertion, but the knee was okay.

"Dad, I don't want to be in broadcasting." He said it in the no-nonsense voice that he'd developed for conversations just like this.

It was the voice he'd used on Alison last night to make her come apart.

"You've got time to think about all this. No need to decide

anything right now. Just get your knee back in shape."

His father backing off could have been concern over his health and knee, but Petey wanted to squash any thoughts his father might be harboring. "I was serious the other night before I fell, and I still mean it. I'm done playing, Dad. The only difference now is the timeline."

His father looked away from him, drinking his coffee and staring out the window where the snow softly fell.

He didn't answer Petey, but he didn't argue with him either.

In Petey's eyes, that was a success.

Seventeen

—⚇⚇—

We are never so defenseless against suffering as when we love.
~ *Sigmund Freud*

Eighteen years ago

"**WHAT DO YOU KNOW** about this place?" Petey asked Alison as they drove to Green Bay.

"I made some calls to doctors in the area, and this place's name came up a few times."

"How'd you get the numbers?"

"I spent a long time in a phone booth in Chassell one day."

"Why Chassell?"

"I didn't want anyone to see me and wonder why I wasn't using my home phone."

That must have been why she had him meet her in the parking lot of the casino in Baraga, a half hour from their hometowns. She'd left her car there and joined him in his truck, overnight bag in hand.

As if reading his thoughts, she said, "No one will notice if I leave my car in the casino lot overnight."

She was the smart one, no doubt about that.

She didn't say another word for an hour.

"You know," he finally said, "I never really said—that day in your car—how sorry I am. All I can think of was I stayed inside you too long, and when I pulled out, the condom—" She held up a hand to stop him, though she continued to look out the passenger window. All he could see was her neck and ear.

"I've thought about it," she said. Of course she had. "And that's probably what happened. And I'm the one who didn't want you to...who wanted you to stay..." She turned even further away from him. "It's not your fault," she said so quietly he barely heard her.

"It's not yours, either," he said, but she didn't answer. "Al? You know that, right? We were careful."

"Not careful enough," she said with a deadness in her voice that chilled him.

He wanted to say so much. To tell her that she could still change her mind. Just one word from her and he'd turn the truck around and drive straight to Houghton City Hall and get a marriage license. It would be hard—really hard—and it wasn't how he wanted his life to play out, but he'd do it if that was what she wanted.

But no, she'd told him what she wanted. And he had to respect that.

So he kept his mouth shut and drove.

"Are you hungry?" he asked as they neared Iron Mountain. They'd been on the road for two hours, with two more to go before they reached Green Bay.

"Yes," she answered. "But I don't know if I'm not supposed to eat. I forgot to ask when I made the appointment."

"Didn't they tell you?" She didn't answer him. "Al?"

He glanced over at her. Her shoulders silently shook. Well, shit. He pulled in to the parking lot of some insurance company on the Iron Mountain main drag. Cutting the engine once he parked, he turned to her. "Al? Talk to me."

She shook her head, still not looking at him. He put a hand on her shoulder and gently tugged. Slowly she turned toward him. Her face was stained with tears that ripped his heart out.

"Al," he whispered, trying to gather her to him. She resisted, scrambling back in the seat, away from him.

"I know it's the right choice. For me. Right now. I know it's the thing to do..." There was a slight upward inflection to her voice at the end. Was she questioning it? Questioning him?

Now. Now was the moment he should say what he was thinking. Tell her he was going to turn the truck around. Dry her tears and tell her that they wouldn't have to go through with it.

But should he? *Could* he?

Wasn't this ultimately her choice to make? Yes, the child was his and he was involved, but could he make this choice for her?

He kept quiet.

After a while she swiped her hands over her face, sat up straighter and said, "They probably did tell me whether I could eat or not before, but I didn't catch it. Let's err on the side of caution and I won't eat. I don't want to get there and have the whole thing delayed by a day."

He started up the truck. "But you can run through a drive-thru for something for you. I don't care," she said.

"I'm good," he said and put the truck in gear. No way in hell was he going to scarf down a Whopper while she sat hungry and crying beside him.

She shifted in her seat then, and a flash of red against her white shorts caught his eye.

"Al?" he said, pointing toward her crotch and the red stain, which seemed to be growing before his eyes.

She looked down at herself and then quickly back at him, her eyes wide with fear. "I've been having cramps for the last hour, but I just figured they were, you know, cramps."

"But you shouldn't be having cramps, should you? I mean, not period cramps anyway?"

It was the only time he'd seen her look anything but brilliant. In fact, she looked downright stupid as she put the logic together.

God, they were so young and stupid. How had he thought for even a moment that they'd be able to handle a baby.

And yet, people did it all the time. His parents had.

"No, you're right. I'm not—" She doubled over, holding her stomach. "Holy crap, that hurts," she said, breathing seemingly hard for her.

Petey turned the truck around and pulled out of the parking lot back onto the main drive. He drove a couple of blocks looking for one of those blue "H" signs that would lead them to a hospital, or possibly someone walking along the street that they could ask for directions.

He saw a sign first and followed the direction it pointed. He made a couple turns while he murmured, "It's okay, it's okay," to Alison. Finally, he pulled up at the emergency entrance to the hospital.

He parked in front, and as he was walking around the front of the truck, a nurse came through the door, looking at him expectantly.

"My...she's pregnant," he said as he opened Al's door. The nurse seemed to be expecting a woman about to give birth. She gave Petey a look as she moved toward a non-showing Alison. "She's six weeks along and she started bleeding. She said she started cramping a couple of hours ago."

The nurse nodded, took a few steps back through the door and called out to someone. She then returned to Alison and took her hand. "Just relax, honey. We'll take good care of you and your baby."

The look of confusion on Alison's face wrenched Petey apart. "Yes," Alison finally said, clutching at the nurse. "Take care of the baby if you can. Save it if..." She looked at Petey and he nodded his encouragement and stepped toward her. But he was halted by a man and a woman, both in scrubs, coming out of the door pushing a wheelchair.

"I need for you to get out of the way right now," the nurse gently told him. "What's your name, honey?" she said to Alison.

"Alison," she croaked out.

"Alison, I need for you to try to stay calm. We're going to get you in this chair and take you inside, okay?"

Alison nodded, her eyes huge with fear, looking at Petey for...what?

"It's going to be okay," he said as they helped her out of the truck and into the chair. He wanted to touch her, hold her hand...something to let her know he was with her.

He didn't get the chance. They were wheeling her into the hospital before he could get close enough. The first nurse stopped him as he tried to follow. "I need you to move your truck. We have to have this space available for the ambulances and emergencies. You can park over there." She pointed to a lot a hundred yards away. "Then come back." What? Like he was going to leave her? "We'll need to get some information from you about Alison."

She was gone before he could respond, but he still nodded his head in acceptance. He ran around to his side of the truck and jumped in. He didn't look at the empty passenger seat for fear of seeing Alison's blood. After he parked the truck, he sprinted back to the emergency entrance and to Alison.

Hoping that it was going to be okay. Hoping that Alison was going to be okay. Beyond that, he wasn't sure what else to hope for.

—⚊⚊—

Alison had never been so scared in her life. And she'd had some scary days lately. The first was when she realized she had skipped a period. The second had been her drive to Calumet to buy a home pregnancy test from an out-of-town drugstore.

And, of course, waiting for the line to turn blue after she'd peed on the stick.

But those all paled as the medical staff wheeled her into an examination room and began asking her questions as a nurse helped her out of her clothes and into a gown.

She had wanted the drive to Green Bay. Four more hours to really decide if this was a choice she could make. Petey seemed willing to go along with whatever she decided. She knew she should have found that incredibly supportive, but it actually just pissed her off.

She was eighteen, scared to death, and had to make a choice that would affect several lives.

But now it seemed that the choice might be taken from her. The staff had her prepped and lying down and a female doctor came in and examined Alison.

"You say you're six weeks along?"

Alison nodded, not trusting her voice to speak. It seemed to take forever, but probably was only a few minutes before the doctor pulled away from her and removed her gloves.

"I'm sorry, but it appears you've suffered a miscarriage. You'll continue to have cramping for a while, but the worst is over."

"But it isn't even that bad. It doesn't feel any different from a regular period."

The doctor was nodding with Alison while she wrote in a chart. "That's often the case with early pregnancies. Many times women don't even know they're pregnant."

She wrote down a few more things, put the chart back at the end of the bed, and then came to Alison's side and touched her arm. "Sometimes this is just nature's way. But there's no reason why you can't have more children." The doctor paused, then added. "When you're ready."

It was probably something she said to every woman who miscarried, but Alison's face turned red with embarrassment.

"Do you live in the area? Close by?"

"No. We were just driving through on our way to Green Bay."

"If at all possible, I suggest that you not travel any more today. I'm going to keep you here another hour or two to make sure the bleeding is under control—which I expect to be the case. But you need rest, and to be in bed for the rest of the day."

Alison nodded her understanding. They'd planned on staying in Green Bay tonight anyway...after. They'd just stay in Iron Mountain instead.

"I'll stop by and check on you in an hour or so. Try to relax if you can," the doctor said, and left the curtained-off area.

The nurse who had come out to Petey's truck poked her head in and said, "Your friend is out here and would like to see you if you're up to it."

No, she wasn't up to facing Petey. But things had to be taken care of. "That's fine," she told the nurse.

Petey came in a moment later. His face was completely white, and he looked liked he'd aged ten years in the last hour.

She knew the feeling.

Relief flooded over his features as he saw her. "I'm okay," she repeated. He started toward her, then seemed to think better of it and stopped at the foot of her bed.

"They said you were, but I didn't…I needed…" He ran his hand through his dark hair, taking a deep breath and then letting it out. "Jesus, Al, I was so scared." His voice wavered, and she held a hand out to him. He quickly moved to her side and took her outstretched hand in his.

"Me too," she whispered. And then the tears came again.

"It's okay, it's okay," he said over and over as one of his hands held hers, and the other stroked her hair.

"I lost it. It's gone," she told him, though he most likely knew or had figured it out.

"I know," he answered in a soft voice. He squeezed her hand.

"I wish…" But he didn't finish the sentence and Alison knew how he felt. She wasn't sure what she wished for either.

So he just stood there and held her hand and stroked her hair. And she said nothing.

There was so much for them to say, yet neither of them had the maturity to find the right words. But they instinctively knew it was better to say nothing than the wrong words.

Finally Alison said, "They said I shouldn't travel today. That I should rest. So, can you find a motel room for us here? And call the place in Green Bay and tell them we won't…"

"I'll take care of it," he said. He squeezed her hand, placed it on the bed and then took a step back away from the bed.

"The number of the place is in my overnight bag in an address book. I guess you should probably bring the whole bag. I'm going to need the sweatpants I packed."

He nodded and started to leave the area. At the curtain he stopped, turned around and then walked back to Alison's side. He bent down to kiss her forehead and then turned his head to her ear. She couldn't see his face, but she heard his whispered words.

"I desperately want to say the right thing to you, but I know I'll probably fuck it up. Please know I never want to see you hurt like this. I don't know if this was God intervening or nature, or dumb luck or what. But I'm sorry you have to be going through any of it."

He kissed her ear and silently left the room.

Alison kept her eyes shut, not watching him leave.

Eighteen

—⚮—

Everything that irritates us about others can lead us
to an understanding of ourselves.

~ Carl Gustav Jung

AVOIDING PETEY THAT NIGHT was fairly easy. She stayed at
the hospital with her father later than normal, and by the time she
got home Petey was asleep.

She felt both relief and, yeah, okay, a little bit of annoyance.
Chase her, my ass!

She got ready for bed quietly, not quite willing to wake the
sleeping giant. Crawling into bed, she tried to turn her mind
off from all the things swirling around. Her parents' upcoming
move, her sisters possibly making trouble about her cottage, and
her patients.

Nothing helped, and she considered—not seriously, but
still—getting up and crawling in next to Petey.

She didn't want to wake him up or anything. She just wanted
to back into some spooning action.

The one time that they actually spent the night in a bed
together was the blurry night of Katie's wedding. Parts of that
night had been coming back to her in lovely snippets, but she
obviously remembered waking up next to him. And for that
moment before she realized who he was—and all the history they

shared came screaming back to her—she had felt so safe and at peace being wrapped in a Petey blanket.

Eventually her mind must have shut down from exhaustion. When she awoke, she was stunned to see it was past ten. She seldom even set an alarm, as her body would always wake her up before one would go off. Thank goodness she didn't have patients today. She would have missed her first appointment.

So, how to continue with her cowardice and sneak out of the house without Petey seeing her? She listened for sounds of either a sleeping Petey or one thumping through the house. Nothing.

Then she heard the garage door opening. The idiot wasn't going to try driving, was he? With a brace on his right leg? In her little car?

She jumped out of bed and threw a robe over her flannel pajama bottoms and thermal Henley she slept in. She slid her feet into her sheep's wool slippers and left the room. A quick glance as she passed her room confirmed that Petey was out of bed.

She went through the great room, barely glancing into the living area, just enough to make sure he wasn't on the couch. The kitchen was untouched, with no coffee in the maker and no cup in the sink. Nearing the entryway to the garage, she did see his shoes were gone. Rather, one was gone. The right shoe was sitting all by its lonely self.

Damn him. He had better not do anything that set his recovery back.

On the other hand, if he was recovered enough to drive, he could damn well climb the stairs at his parents' house.

She opened the door to the garage expecting to find it empty with the door shut, but no, her Subaru sat in its space and the garage door was up.

Petey stood against the back wall, waving hand directions to a pickup truck that was backing into the second spot in her two-car garage.

Not just any pickup, but Petey's red Ford. A truck that should have been in Detroit.

The truck made it in and stopped when Petey held up his hand. The engine was cut and Finn stepped out. Just then Lizzie pulled into the driveway in her Navigator.

"What's going on?" Alison asked, startling Petey. He must not have heard her open the door over the noisy truck.

"Lizzie had one of her interns drive my truck and a bunch of my stuff up," he said.

"Why?"

"So I had more than my jeans and these track pants that I'm so frickin' sick of I could scream."

"A quick trip to Shopko would fix that."

He made his way over to her. He was walking with only one crutch, which he used more for balance than support.

"Yeah, but this is better. It's my stuff, and, more importantly, my truck. I should be able to drive in a few days if the doc okays it. And I can't be stuck asking my mom and dad to borrow their car."

She noticed he didn't include her in that statement. He was probably just as anxious to get out of her house as she was to have him gone. For her, it was to reduce temptation. She didn't want to think about his motivation.

Lizzie got out of her car and went to the backseat where she unbuckled Sam from his car seat base. Finn came over to her and took Sam in his carrier from Lizzie, who then reached in and grabbed a diaper bag.

"I'll put on coffee," Alison said, and ducked back into the house.

They all came in, and Lizzie and Finn rid themselves of their winter garb.

"Oh, I forgot the coffee cake," Lizzie said and started to turn back, but Finn handed her Sam, said he'd go get it, and went back through the garage.

"Best perk of being married, bar none," Lizzie said. "The bringing in of groceries."

"God, please no more groceries," Alison groaned. "There's

no room in the fridge as it is."

"There's room now," Petey remarked as he went to the cupboard and got out four mugs and brought them to the table. "I cleaned up the lasagna last night." He came back by her and looked at her as he added, "It wasn't nearly as good as the first night." He winked at her. "But it was still pretty good."

"We didn't bring more groceries. Clea made a coffee cake, and we brought some milk to wash it down, that's all."

"Oooh, Clea's coffee cake," Alison said. She'd had Finn's grandmother's specialty on a couple of occasions at Lizzie and Finn's.

The coffee was nearly done. She started to get out plates and forks, but Petey had beaten her to it.

"You should sit down," she told him.

"I need to be on it a little more today," he said. "I was on my ass all day yesterday. No exercise at all. No exertion of any kind."

She shot him a look while Lizzie got Sam out of his carrier and unwrapped the baby from his many layers of warmth.

Petey did sit down then, motioning to Lizzie to bring Sam to him.

"Okay. Give me that kid. I didn't get to hold him that day in the hospital."

Lizzie handed Sam to Petey, nervously holding her hands out lest Petey drop the baby. "I've got him, Lizard," Petey told her, and the new mother took a step back. A reluctant step back, it seemed to Alison.

"Hey, you're not such a big guy at all," Petey said to Sam, who just stared back at Petey in awe. "How can a guy with the big name of Samuel Ezekiel Robbins be such a little peanut?" His voice was soft and low, with a lilting quality.

Finn came back in and handed the still-warm pan and the gallon of milk to Alison, who placed them on the table while Finn took off his boots.

Lizzie and Finn sat at the table and watched Petey hold their son, broad smiles on their faces. Alison grabbed the coffee pot, brought it to the table, and sat with the rest of her friends.

"And pretty soon we'll get you on skates," Petey cooed to Sam.

"Oh, no," Lizzie said. "No son of mine is going to be a hockey player. A hockey-playing stepson is bad enough."

"Don't forget a stepdaughter."

"Seriously?" Petey said, looking up from the baby to Finn, who was nodding.

"Annie started skating this year. She's not ready for hockey yet, but she says she wants to play next year."

"Awesome," Petey said. "As soon as I'm able, I'll take her to the rink for a few laps on the ice."

"She'd love that," Lizzie and Finn said at the same time.

Petey had bonded with Finn's kids two summers ago when Lizzie had planned a fundraiser to cover Finn's daughter's medical expenses for lumbar fusion surgery.

"Wow, hockey. Skating even. That's amazing," Petey said, shaking his head. Alison agreed with him. Annie's recovery had been nothing short of a miracle.

"Hockey will be a long shot. We don't want any chance of injury, but we decided to wait and see what the doctors think next year," Lizzie said.

"And just why wouldn't you want Sam—and Stevie and Annie for that matter—to be hockey players?" Petey chided Lizzie. "Hockey players were your first clients when you put up your own shingle."

"Yes, I know, and I'm grateful to them. I love them as clients—lord knows they need PR help. But I know them a little too well to want that life for my boys." She looked at Finn and smiled. "And for my girl." Lizzie and Annie had started out pretty rocky, but were solid now.

The smile she gave Finn was small and intimate, and returned in kind. Alison felt like an intruder, so she turned her attention to Petey, who was holding Sam to his chest now, whispering in his ear. "What are you telling him?" Alison asked and then wished she hadn't. She covered it with, "Teaching him the F-bomb already? Sharing with him the maximum way to enjoy a good chew?"

Petey looked over at her. She was expecting some kind of comeback about her lack of maternal skills, but all she saw was hurt in his eyes.

Well, crap.

"Actually, I was telling Sam here what a lucky boy he is."

She had nothing to say to that, but Lizzie quickly jumped in with, "No. We're the lucky ones." She looked at her husband again, and he slid a hand along the table to Lizzie's.

They had overcome a lot to be together, and Alison was proud of her friend for putting her fears behind her and reaching for happiness. Right now, however, she wanted this freakin' marvel of familial bliss out of her house.

She took another glance at Petey and Sam as she sipped her coffee. The tiny baby looked miniscule in the giant's paws. Petey leaned his head down and smelled Sam's head and smiled. A deep pain shot through Alison.

Yeah. Wasn't it time for Lizzie and Finn to hit the road?

Nineteen

—ɯ—

I went to a fight the other night and a hockey game broke out.
~ *Rodney Dangerfield*

Eighteen years ago

ALISON HEARD PETEY COME INTO the motel room but pretended she was asleep. It wasn't hard to do because the pills they'd given her at the hospital had knocked her out for most of the day. It had to be nearly eight o'clock, but she was facing away from the nightstand and the clock.

Petey quietly moved around the room. She heard the rustle of a paper bag. Good, he'd gone out to get some food. He must have been absolutely famished by now. The thought of food for her, on the other hand, turned her stomach.

This is what she'd imagined this night would be—her resting in a motel room, Petey available if she needed him.

But it was Iron Mountain, not Green Bay. And the ultimate choice had not been hers but had been thrust upon her.

She tried to be honest with herself and poked around her raw feelings for a little relief that she hadn't had to make the choice.

It was there.

But so was the relief that she wouldn't have to tell her parents she was pregnant after all.

She'd agonized over telling them originally, and of course Lizzie and Katie, but had decided not to. For one thing, she was deeply, deeply ashamed of what she'd let happen.

She was the smart one, the one who should have known better than to let this happen.

And her future. Degree, advanced degree, research, then something amazing like curing cancer.

Technically it could still be done, but it wasn't as realistic with a baby at eighteen.

Ultimately, she didn't want her parents to be disappointed in her. They were so proud of her academic achievements and of the full-ride Ivy League offers.

She did not want to tell them until she'd decided with absolute certainty that she'd have the baby.

And that's when she knew she probably would have changed her mind in Green Bay.

No you wouldn't have. You're just telling yourself that now to absolve yourself from the guilt of your decision.

Not able to stand the war her thoughts were waging, she turned over and opened her eyes. Petey sat at the little table in the room, watching her. He started to get up when he saw her look at him but then sat back down.

When she saw the unopened bags from McDonald's she said, "Go ahead and eat. I don't want anything yet."

He hesitated, so she added, "Just save me something for a little later, but go ahead and eat while it's still warm."

He nodded and started pulling burgers and fries out of the bags. She pointed to one of the large beverages. "Is that a shake?"

He had it in his hand and was bringing it to her half a second later.

"Chocolate," he said. Her favorite. Did he know that or was it just a happy coincidence?

It was cool and smooth and felt good going down her throat, which had been made raw from crying throughout the day.

"Thanks," she whispered.

It seemed like he wanted to stay beside her, but couldn't make up his mind.

"Go ahead and eat," she said, motioning to the food on the table and making his choice for him.

And didn't that just seem to be the theme of their ill-fated, short-lived romance.

A sudden hatred directed at Petey swelled up in her. She knew it was irrational, but the feelings continued to rise like an imaginary tide coming in, and she couldn't move out of its way. It rose up in her body, chilling her and stifling all the feelings she'd had for him for the past year.

He could have pulled out of her right away, rather than waiting until he was half hard and the condom was sliding off.

No matter that she'd held him to her and told him to stay, loving the weight of him on top of her.

He could have demanded she keep the child.

No matter that she'd told him she wasn't going to keep it moments after she'd told him about the pregnancy in the first place, not asking for his opinion or advice.

He could have told her that he loved her and wanted to marry her.

No matter that it wasn't true.

He could have done something instead of letting her make all the hard decisions.

No matter that she would have hated him for trying to take control.

Oh, but part of her would have liked it—handing the control over.

God, what a tangled, jumbled mass of contradictions the human mind was.

His eyes sought hers while he ate his dinner, but she'd look away when they met. She sipped the shake dry, then turned over and went back to sleep, willing the darkness to come and quiet her mind.

—∞—

Petey watched as she slept on. He quietly cleaned up his wrappers, her empty cup, and the other garbage and threw it away. He put the food he'd saved for Alison back in the bag and put it on the side of the table. It'd probably be pretty gross by the time she woke up, but if she were hungry, at least there'd be something here for her.

Or maybe she'd sleep through the night and be ready for some breakfast when she woke up.

They had planned on driving back home from Green Bay in the morning They'd both given different cover stories to their parents about being gone overnight. And it'd taken surprisingly little juggling to make sure their group of friends wasn't aware that they both were out of town on the same night.

Summer jobs had everybody on different schedules anyway, so being out of the loop for two days and one night wasn't going to throw anybody into suspicion mode.

He'd paid the hospital in cash. Cash he'd brought for Green Bay. They'd pooled their graduation money together and had eked out just enough to cover the trip and the…procedure.

They'd drive home tomorrow, and the result would be the same as if they'd made it all the way to Green Bay.

Wouldn't it?

He wasn't sure, but it wasn't something he thought he could talk to her about.

He kicked off his shoes but stayed dressed in case she needed him in the night or needed him to run out for something. Or, and he hated to even think it, if she needed to go back to the hospital.

He crawled under the covers and lay on his side so that he could watch Alison breathe.

At some point he must have fallen asleep because it was eight in the morning when he woke up. A sliver of light shone through where he hadn't shut the drapes the entire way.

He looked over his shoulder to see if Alison still slept or if the light had awakened her, too.

Her bed was empty and she sat fully dressed at the table.

"How do you feel?" he asked her.

"Fine," she answered. "We can get going whenever you're ready."

"There's no rush. We weren't due to be home for a while."

She nodded her head, as if agreeing with him, but then said, "I want to go home."

He pushed the covers off and got out of bed. Grabbing his duffle bag, he passed her on his way to the bathroom. He reached out to touch the top of her head, but she moved away from him.

She hated him. He saw it forming last night, could almost see the moment her mind shut him down as she'd drunk her shake.

He'd held out hope that it was just the physical pain and the drugs, but it was still there this morning.

She definitely hated him.

And he couldn't really blame her.

He dressed as quickly as he could, skipping a shower, though he would have dearly loved to wash away the past twenty-four hours.

He carried their bags to his truck. While he'd been waiting for her to be released from the hospital, he'd gone to a store, bought some cleaning solution, and scrubbed the ever-living shit out of his seat, banishing Alison's blood.

He checked it now to make sure it was dry before Alison sat on it. Thankfully it was. He went back to the room to get her, and they left the motel. He went through the McDonald's drive-thru for breakfast, which he devoured and she picked at until Crystal Falls when she finally just put it back in the bag and set it on the floor by her feet.

They hadn't talked a ton yesterday on their way south, but compared to today they'd been downright chatty.

The only thing she said the entire two-hour drive was, "Do you know what degree you need to be a psychologist?"

When he said he didn't, she kind of shook her head, in an "Of course you don't, what was I thinking even asking you" kind of way.

Which made him feel even more like shit.

When he pulled up next to her car in the casino lot, she tried to grab her bag and jump out before he barely had the truck in park.

He took her bag from her grip, got out of his side and walked around to her side to help her out, but she was already to her car and putting the key in the lock.

"Just throw it in the back seat," she said to him after getting the doors unlocked and opening hers.

He did, then moved to the driver's door and stood so she couldn't close it on him, as she so clearly wanted to do.

"You'll call me if you don't feel good, right?"

She wouldn't even look up at him, but nodded.

There was so much more he wanted to say, but he didn't know how to start. Finally he stepped away and she quickly shut the door, started up the car and drove away.

He didn't see her again for nearly a year.

Twenty

—ᴍ—

If the only tool you have is a hammer, you tend to see every problem as a nail.

- Abraham Maslow

AFTER A VERY LONG SHOWER, Petey finished toweling off in Alison's room and rummaged through his duffle bag for a new pair of sweats.

It felt good to have some of his things here. He and Finn had left most of the stuff Lizzie had directed his cleaning lady to pack up right in the truck, only bringing in a few things for now.

It didn't seem as though he was going to get an extended-stay invite from Al, so Petey had Finn bring in just the one large duffle that he took on the road with him and always had packed.

He sat on the bed and examined his knee. Just three tiny scars since they went in arthroscopically. It made healing that much easier, and he'd always been a quick healer anyway. It was one of the reasons he'd made it this long in the league.

He tentatively bent the knee and was happy with the result.

"Petey," he heard Alison call. "I'm back."

"In here," he said loudly.

She had seemed to rush Finn and Lizzie out of here this morning, so he'd had a glimmer of hope that maybe she wanted to talk. Or do other things for which they needed privacy.

But no. Shortly after their friends left with their little bundle of joy, Alison announced she was going to her mom's to help Sherry with the packing of her parents' things and left him alone. He'd crawled back into bed and slept most of the day away—which, damn, felt really good.

And even though Alison hadn't told him when she'd be back, Petey had turned down his mom's offer to come over with dinner, saying he was tired and needed to rest. (Because what mother is going to say no to that?)

"I brought pizza from the Commodore if you're—" The words died as Alison entered his room. Her room. "Oh. Sorry. I didn't realize you were...that you'd be...."

He was naked, yes, but his towel was draped over his lap as he sat on the side of the bed.

"You've seen me naked before. Recently, as I recall," he said as he continued to bend his knee.

She didn't say anything to that, but she didn't leave the room, either. Which was nice.

He gently rubbed his knee, and—okay, he wasn't proud of it—he winced as he did so, even though the pain was negligible at best.

"Bad?" she asked, walking into the room.

"Not too bad, no," he said. "What'd you do today? Pack the whole time?"

She looked at the chair and he could tell she was measuring whether she should sit or not. Whether she should stay.

"Sherry say anything stupid today?"

She chuckled and crossed the room. Settling into the chair, she took the throw from its back and tossed it over her jeans-clad legs. It seemed to be a familiar motion to her and he suspected it was something she did most nights when she came home. And if he wasn't so content being here, he'd apologize to her for commandeering her happy place.

But he was content being in Alison's space, with her. And for more than just the hope of getting her back on, well, her back.

"She wasn't too bad," Alison answered. He shifted on the bed, sitting back against the headboard, lifting his legs onto the mattress carefully—and obviously—keeping a hand on his bum knee.

She nodded her head to his leg. "Are you sure it's not too bad?"

"Nah," he said. "Nothing that standing at a table with you laid out in front of me wouldn't cure. That's my kind of therapy."

She chuckled and threw one of the small pillows from her chair at him.

Ah, good, the playful Al was here tonight. You never really knew with her. He wouldn't call her moody, just someone with many sides to her.

Sometimes it fascinated him. Sometimes it pissed him off. And most time he felt that trying to wander around her minefield of a mind was worth it.

He was feeling that way more and more, and it kind of scared the shit out of him. The thought of a physical future with Al greatly appealed to him. A future of constantly wondering which Al was going to come home? Not so much.

But this Al? The one who took his jokes as intended and volleyed back? Yeah, she was the one for him.

Especially if she'd take off those damn clothes.

She told him about her day and he told her about his, summed up with two words—marathon nap.

"Hey," he said when there was a comfortable silence. "Why were you giving Finn and Lizzie the bum's rush this morning?"

To her credit, she didn't deny her actions. She stared out the window for a long time, watching the snow fall. He knew she was gauging how honest to be. But with him, or herself?

Finally she turned to him and said, "It was seeing you holding Sam. It was very hard for me."

A niggling thought at the back of his mind told him he shouldn't be surprised—but he kind of was. "Oh." There wasn't much he could say beyond that. "I'm sorry," he added.

He didn't think he'd said those words to her since she'd hustled out of his truck in the casino parking lot all those years ago. He'd said them so many times before and during their ill-fated trip and had gotten nothing back from her. So he'd stopped.

She looked at him for a long time. "I know," she whispered. "I know you're sorry. I *knew* you were sorry."

Jesus. Were they finally going to talk about this? Eighteen years of trying to break down her walls and she was ready to try when he was draped in a fucking towel?

He sat very still, willing her to go on. Not wanting to scare her off, he stayed on the bed when he would've loved to be closer to her. Even just to hold her hand.

"Do you ever think about it? I mean, not about what happened, but what if I hadn't...."

He waited, but she didn't finish the sentence. She didn't need to. "Yes," he said. "I did a lot more the first few years. Sometimes with a sigh of relief, you know?"

He held his breath, figuring maybe she'd think him a callous bastard—not that she'd be wrong.

"Me too," she said, letting out a sigh, as if trying to expel eighteen years of heaviness. "Especially that first year at State. All I could think of was I could have missed it all. I would have been at home with my parents instead of in the dorms with Kat and Lizard.

"And then I'd feel like crap for being so happy. But I was." She looked away, back out the window. "I was really happy there. Except for the times when I'd think about it. So I started thinking about it less and less."

"Self-preservation. Nothing wrong with that."

"No, I suppose not. It doesn't matter now anyway." She half raised a hand in a wave of dismissal, but it was a crappy effort.

"It *does* matter. It always mattered," he said.

She didn't look him, but she did nod her head—not too noticeably, but it was there.

"And then," she continued, "when other friends of ours

started having babies in their late twenties, it all came back to me."

"Of course it did," he said softly, not wanting her to stop but wanting her to know he understood. And he did—understand. Oh, he hadn't had the depth of regret she surely had through the years, but there were times when it would sneak up on him and he'd wonder about the what-if of it all.

"I got lucky in that Katie couldn't get pregnant and Lizzie was never much interested in kids. So I didn't have babies in my life all that much. Although I know Katie didn't feel so lucky during those years."

"No, she didn't."

"That was hard. Listening to her cry and cry because she couldn't have a child, and I had…."

"But you didn't, Al. You didn't."

"And, God, that's been its own kind of torture, you know?"

Oh yeah, he knew. He'd played that game a thousand times—would he have stopped her? "Yeah. I had a lot of the same thoughts. Some parallel-universe shit goes through my mind at weird times. That fall you were at State and thinking about how you'd have been at home?" She nodded. "I had the same flashes that first year at Tech. I'd drive by the married housing area on campus and think about how easily I could have been living there with you. How you'd take classes that first semester while you were still able to.

"When we'd party after a hockey game, I'd think about how I would have skipped it and gone home to be with you and the baby. And then I'd—" He stopped at her expression which had changed from melancholy to confusion. "What?"

She was shaking her head. "What do you mean married housing? And that you'd come home to us after games?"

He shifted on the bed. Feeling the need for protection, he pulled the sheet up, over the towel. "If you'd kept the baby. We would have gotten married."

"When did you decide that?"

He sat up straighter. No time to be a pussy. "About ten seconds after you told me you were pregnant."

Her shoulders slumped, and she leaned back further into the oversized chair. "Why didn't you say something? Anything?"

"Because. About *fifteen* seconds after you told me you were pregnant you told me what you'd already decided."

She wrapped herself in the blanket—apparently he wasn't the only one who needed the protection provided by linens—and stared out the window. "I never really asked you what you wanted to do, did I?"

"No," he said, maybe a little too quickly. But it had to be said. If only he'd had the maturity at nineteen to say it then.

But really, would anything be different?

They'd never know.

He could live with that much easier than the logical Alison could—a woman who chose to study why people did the things they did. A woman who deeply believed in the cause and effect of the human psyche.

He'd kind of had the "shit happens" philosophy most of his life.

"I'm sorry, Petey," she said. The words did not flow easily from her, that was for sure. She cleared her throat and added, "For never letting you have a say."

He could have pinned her on that one, made her feel like shit like he had for so long. And he probably would have a year ago. Maybe even as recently as their last hook-up at Katie's wedding.

But he'd done a lot of thinking since last fall when faced with a body that was calling it quits on professional hockey. And even more this past week when the towel had been definitively thrown in on his career.

"It's okay, Al," he said softly. That got her. Her head snapped up to look at him. Those brown eyes widened with surprise, then narrowed with wariness. She was waiting for his knockout punch. "Really. Part of me is grateful you didn't give me a choice. I saw the weight of it on you— I didn't want that. I couldn't handle that."

She still looked a little wary, her head tilting as if measuring his words.

"The other part of me could feel self-righteous about you shutting me out. And believe me, I did hold it against you many times."

"I know you did. And I didn't blame you."

"Didn't stop you from ripping me a new one every chance you got."

She smiled, the storm past. "Oh, you gave as good as you got, buddy."

"Would you have had as much fun if I hadn't?"

Her smile broadened. God, she was cute when she smiled ear-to-ear like that.

"Not hardly."

They both laughed and then the phone rang, startling them both. It was a cordless and the cradle was sitting on the nightstand next to him. He could have easily tossed it to her, but instead he picked it out of the cradle and held it out so she had to come over and get it.

And be right next to him.

Within touch.

Twenty-One
—ɯ—

Street hockey is great for kids.
It's energetic, competitive, and skillful.
And best of all it keeps them off the street.

- Author Unknown

ALISON KNEW SHE SHOULD have just reached out for the phone. Instead, she got out of the chair and made her away around the bed to Petey's side, taking the phone from his hand.

"Hello?" she said as she noticed his hair was still a little wet from his shower. It curled at the ends, just barely grazing his shoulder. If she just reached out she'd be able to run her fingers through—

"Alison? It's Darío."

Why would Darío be calling her so late? Did—"Katie? Is she okay?" Terror rushed through her at the thought of something happening to Katie's baby.

"She's fine. They just wheeled her away."

"She's in labor?"

"Yes. She's been having contractions since noon, but they've just gotten to the point where the doctor had us come in."

"So, you're at the hospital?" Her voice caught. Katie had wanted a baby for so long, and it looked like she'd soon be able to hold hers in her arms. Petey's hand clasped hers and squeezed. She slid hers more firmly into his, loving the way his swallowed hers up. "I'll be right there," she said to Darío.

"No. That's why she wanted me to call. We're going to be here a long time. Her family's on the way now. She wanted you and Lizzie to come later. Tomorrow. She said she'd need you two to run...."

"Interference?"

"*Sí*. Interference. She said she might have had enough of her family by then."

Alison laughed. Katie had a big family who would be camping out at the hospital and no doubt driving her crazy.

"Okay. I'll be there first thing in the morning. But you'll call if something...." God, she couldn't even think it.

"I'll be in the delivery room. But I'll have one of her brothers call you if there's news."

"Okay. Thanks."

"Bye, Alison."

"Bye. Oh, and Darío?"

"Yes?"

"Congratulations!"

The line was quiet for a moment, and he said in a thick voice, "*Gracias*, Alison." Then he was gone. To his wife and their soon-to-arrive baby.

She set the phone back in the cradle with one hand. Petey gently tugged on her other and she sat on the bed, her butt near his hip, her back to him. He released her hand and snaked his arm around her waist. He scooted forward a little and rested his chin on the top of her head.

"You know what this means?" he said.

"What?"

"Well, you know what happened the night Lizzie went into labor."

She smiled, even though he couldn't see. Maybe *because* he couldn't see. "You think every time one of my besties goes into labor I'm going to sleep with you?"

"I'd say right now it's about a fifty-fifty shot." He rocked his chest against her back, then kissed her neck.

"I feel like I've done nothing this week but say no to you one night and yes the next."

"That sounds about right."

"That's not the kind of person I'd like to think I am."

"Complicated?"

She looked over her shoulder at him, as his blue eyes studied her. "Wishy-washy," she said. Then she added, "You think I'm complicated?"

"Are you shitting me?"

"No. I'm not. I think of myself as a pretty rational, logical person. I think most people do."

"I'm not most people." She opened her mouth to smash the lob he'd just tossed her but he quickly added, "At least, I'm not most people where you're concerned."

"True enough." She turned back around and he began to nuzzle her neck. She tilted her head, giving him better access.

"Just so we're clear, this is the last time."

"Uh-huh," he said, then ran his tongue up her nape. "Have I ever told you how fucking sexy the back of your neck is?"

"That would be no," she said on a sigh.

"Climb up on the bed. Climb up on me," he whispered in her ear, then nipped her earlobe. While his arm continued to hold her to him, his other hand inched its way under her sweater and up her back. She figured he'd stop at her bra clasp, but no, he slid all the way to her shoulders, where he gently massaged her tense muscles.

"It's been kind of a crazy year for you, Al. And I know I make you crazy, too. And I don't mean the monkey-sex kind of crazy."

She rolled her neck, relaxing into his touch. In the front, he burrowed his hand under her sweater and rested his fingers just slightly inside the waistband of her jeans.

"I don't think of you as wishy-washy, or a tease, or anything like that. I think of you as a woman who occasionally listens to her body over her head. And as the recipient of that lapse in judgment, I can only say…right on."

She laughed—a big boisterous guffaw. Then she yelped as he slid her body over his so that she was in his lap.

"This seems familiar," she said, thinking of his first night in her house. In this bed. God, had that only been a few days ago?

She wrapped her arm around his neck and inched up a little so that her face was deliciously even with his mouth.

"Kiss me," he whispered. She leaned closer, but he pulled back a few inches and whispered it again. Fire rushed through her at the thought of playing games with Petey.

She knew some people thought of him as a dumb jock, and she'd called him exactly that on many occasions. But the truth was in this—in sex play—he was definitely her intellectual superiorWhich was fine with her.

She zeroed in for his mouth and this time he didn't pull away. Such a soft mouth for such a hard man.

And growing harder.

She wiggled her ass on top of him and he groaned. As their tongues played, he grabbed her waist and started to turn her, to lay her down, then stopped.

"Damn, I won't be able to get deep that way. I still don't have the leg strength for good ol' missionary."

Embarrassed, she buried her head into his neck, nuzzling him, breathing in his male scent and tasting him with her tongue.

"Yeah, that's good." His hands moved up from her waist, taking her sweater with them. "Let me get this off you. Yeah." When she raised her head and then her arms, he whisked her sweater off and tossed it to the floor. He dropped his hands and leaned back against the headboard, putting way too much space between them. But oh, what a lovely view of that massive chest. She reached out to touch him, but he brushed her aside. "Take off your bra," he said.

In *that* voice.

She shifted again, her arousal spiking at his tone. And at that grin that spread across his rugged face.

"The bra, Al. Lose it."

She reached around and unclasped it. No teasing show with it this time. She wanted it gone so she could rub her aching nipples against that gloriously hairy chest. She slung it away and moved closer, but he put a hand on the base of her throat, stopping her progress.

She whimpered.

He chuckled.

"I want the jeans off. And as much as I'd love to see you wiggle out of them again, I'm so fucking hard I can't wait. Stand up, get them off, and get back on me."

She did as he said, sliding off him, undoing the clasp and fly of her jeans, and yanking them off. She put her hands in the waistband of her red panties and looked at him questioningly.

"They sure are pretty. But yep, get them the hell off that pussy."

Who knew she, brainy Alison, could get so turned on by dirty talk? It both surprised and titillated her.

And spurred her on to strip the panties down her legs and off. She stepped to the bed and put a knee up. "Your leg?" she asked.

"Is fine. But you're going to have to do most of the work this time."

She bit her lip.

"Don't worry, Al, I'll tell you exactly what to do."

She warmed even more at his words. He gave her exactly what she needed in bed. It felt like she was just discovering herself sexually at thirty-six.

And she liked who she'd discovered.

Before she climbed onto the bed, she peeled the pink sheet off of him in a slow reveal, disappointed to find the towel she'd forgotten was there. She reached for it but stopped when he said, "Leave it. At least for now. It's good friction."

She couldn't quite identify the sound that came out of

her at the thought of all that friction—sort of a half moan, half sigh. She climbed on the bed, being careful of his knee when she swung a leg over him. He clasped her waist and dragged her up his chest, fitting her neatly against him, her knees bent along his hips. She grabbed his wide shoulders. In a flash his hands were gone from her waist and nestled deep in her short hair, pulling her head toward him as his mouth found hers in a heated kiss. She wrapped her arms around him, burying one hand into that silken black hair, her other skimming across his broad back. His tongue probed her mouth as he deeply kissed her. He held her head tightly in his hands. He only broke away long enough to grunt, "Rub yourself on me." Then he was once again covering her mouth, sipping from her, licking her lips.

Devouring her.

She started moving forward and back against him. The cotton of the towel covering his hard erection chafed her in all the right places.

"Yeah. That's it. A little faster." His mouth moved down her cheek, her chin and to her neck where he began to suck. "Let's mark you up," he said in her ear. "Let's put my mark on your pretty skin. Do you want that, Al?"

She couldn't answer but only rubbed faster. Until he put his hands on her waist, stopping her.

"Answer me," he said in his command voice. She opened her eyes and looked at him through a haze of lust. His blue eyes bore into her. "Do you want my mark on you? Do you want me to brand you as mine?"

She nodded.

"Say it," he barked, squeezing her waist.

"Yes. Make me yours," she whispered.

He growled his approval and his mouth was back on her neck as his hands prodded her hips into movement.

She hugged him closer and rose up on her knees, needing to feel his flesh beneath her. Reading her mind, one of his hands ripped the towel out from under her and she sat back down on his wonderful hardness. They both moaned in satisfaction—and he wasn't even inside her yet.

"Take me in your hand," he said and then returned to sucking on her neck. She reached between their bodies, grasped his thick cock, and started stroking.

He hissed. "No. Shit, I'm too close. Just get me...yeah... that's it." She shifted up and then eased down on him, her muscles stretching to take him all in. She arched back, taking him deeper. He leaned forward and took a nipple into his mouth. His tongue twirled before he sucked on her. She held his head to her and began to ride him.

"Yes. That's it. Ride me. Ride me hard," he said, then moved to her other breast and sucked. His arm wrapped around her and settled across her ass, his hand on the indent of her hip. He pulled back from her chest and took her face in his hand, forcing her to look at him.

"Faster now, baby. That's it—see how deep you can take me." His words drove her frantic pace. His thumb dug into the top of her ass, his fingers grasping the curve of her hip. She tried to kiss him, to bury her head in his neck, but he held her still, demanding she look at him. She braced one hand on his shoulder, the other on his pec and picked up her pace.

"Do it. Take it. Take what you need, Al." His voice was commanding even though in essence he was giving her the power. Her knees ached with her rapid motion.

"I...I can't...get there," she moaned, trying to release his grip on her, thrashing her head.

But he didn't let go. In fact, his grip tightened as his other hand slid back around to her front and down into her curls. "I've got ya. Just keep riding. I'll get you there." He found her so quickly, seemed to know exactly the right pressure to apply. His thumb circled her clit and then pressed just as she came down hard on him.

This time when she reared her head back he let go and moved his hand to clasp her shoulder as she shuddered in her climax.

"Keep going, keep going," he urged. It went on and on, wracking her body with spasms and lights that flashed in her head.

Just as she was coming down, his grip on her shoulder tightened, his other hand grabbed her hip, and he pumped her up and down on himself as he came.

They breathed heavily through the aftershocks and their arms easily wove around the other, hugging tightly.

They stayed entwined—sated. When she finally made to move, he held her tight and whispered, "Stay with me."

She nodded into his chest, not trusting her voice.

As gracefully as she could, careful to slide to his left side and away from his bad knee, she moved off of him. He kept an arm around her as he slouched down out of his sitting position and onto his back. She curled up next to him, her hand and head on his chest.

For all they'd been through, they'd never had a moment like this—peaceful intimacy.

"This is nice," he said, reading her mind.

"Yes," she agreed and burrowed into his side. She kissed his chest and was rewarded by a tightening of his arm around her.

Her neck tingled and she chuckled.

"What?" he asked, nudging her.

"I was just thinking that it's a good thing it's turtleneck season, 'cause I'll bet I'm going to have one hell of a hickey come morning."

"I can guarantee that," he said with a shit-eating grin on his face.

"Why do you suppose I get so turned on by the caveman thing?"

He raised his other hand and covered his face. "Jesus, Al, do you have to analyze everything? Can't we even have a little afterglow before you have to pick it apart and examine it?" There was teasing in his voice, but she knew he meant it.

And she knew that he was right.

"Sorry. Sorry." She kissed his chest again and licked his

nipple. She loved the groan that came out of him and licked again. "I just find it fascinating. I mean, there's no way in hell I'd ever let you control me out of bed."

"Believe me, I'd never try. I may be a dumb jock, but I'm not stupid. I only know there's no right or wrong way to get turned on. What does it for you—does it for you. To try to understand it can only kill it."

She laid her head back down on his chest as she smiled.

For a dumb jock, he could be kind of smart.

Twenty-Two

I don't sing because I am happy; I am happy because I sing.

~ *William James*

WONDER OF WONDERS, she was still in his arms when Petey awoke the next morning. Not quite morning, but the hours just before. The only other time they'd spent the night together—after Katie's wedding—she'd snuck out him while he slept.

Depriving them both of the morning hard-on he'd awakened with, just like he was sporting this morning.

But today she was soft and warm and right next to him. Her back to his front, they made a lovely spoon. He slid his hand from where it rested on her hip up to cup a breast. He molded and fondled and the tip of her nipple hardened in his fingers. She moaned and rocked her ass into his erection. He nuzzled her neck as he played with her tits. She was obviously awake, but he didn't speak, not wanting to break the mood. But would she get as hot—as worked up—without him telling her what to do? Without his demands and control?

His hand slid off her breast and she let out a whimper, which he tried to calm with a soft "Shhh," and kisses on her neck. He trailed his fingers down her petite body, over the curve of her hip, down to her stomach, gently circling her belly button. Her hips started to roll and her own hand came up to her tits and continued what he'd started. "Yes," he encouragingly whispered.

He moved down further, into her curls, fingers spreading her. So. She didn't need the commanding voice and stern direction to get wet. His fingers glided in her moisture, slick and hot. He slid one finger inside her and she clenched around him. He nipped her neck and then kissed the same spot. Even in the pre-dawn hazy light, he could see the mark he gave her last night. He licked it just as he added a second finger and she sighed, her body pliant and relaxed. He removed himself from her warm pussy and slid his hand down and around to cup her thigh, which he lifted just enough to be able to slide his hard cock deep inside her.

"Ahh," she said, echoing his own thoughts. There was a stillness to them. No frantic pace, no commands, just the two of them joined together.

He couldn't ever remember feeling more…at peace. He rocked into her slowly, the stroke deep but gentle. His fingers returned to her center, finding her clit, hard and in need of some attention. Which he gave as he slowly ground his hips with each surge forward. Her hand left her tits and reached back for his arm, which she held on to as he wiggled her clit and she came apart. She didn't cry out this time, or moan in delight. She rode her wave in silence, her little body shuddering on the outside, her pussy spasming around him. He followed soon after, emptying himself into her. The thought briefly went through his head that it was too bad she was on the pill. He waited for sense to prevail, to be horrified at his momentary lapse in judgment, but it never came. Instead, he found himself warming to the idea.

He nuzzled her neck again, rocked into her one more time. He moved his hand up her belly and held her anchored to him, her hand still on his forearm.

"We can do this, Al," he whispered in her ear. He was suddenly drowsy again, his lids growing heavy, his thoughts muddling. But he wanted to say this, felt he had to get it out. "We can finally do this. Give us a real shot." He kissed her neck one more time and then burrowed his face into her sexy nape as sleep overtook him. "Get it right this time. Make it count."

He barely registered her body tensing as he drifted off.

—❦—

"What's that on your neck?" Lizzie asked Alison when she came into the waiting area at the hospital where Alison had been sitting.

"What? Where?" Her hand flew to the spot where Petey had left his mark, only to feel the two layers of clothing—turtleneck and high-necked sweater—that she'd put on this morning to hide the hickey.

A hickey! At thirty-six!

"No. Here," Lizzie said, reaching for her other side and then pulling back with a piece of red fuzz, which she flicked off her fingers. "It must be from your scarf. It looked like blood when I first saw you."

"Nope. No blood for me." Though she felt like she'd been bloodied—at least emotionally.

We can finally do this.

His words had been running like a loop in her mind ever since she'd crawled out of bed. She'd done so quietly, not wanting to wake him after he'd fallen back to sleep. The entire time it took her to shower and get dressed, she'd expected him to awaken and join her, but he hadn't, so she'd quickly left the house and come to the hospital. Katie and Darío were in the delivery room, the baby on its way after a night of labor, or so Katie's mom told her.

Alison had gone up to see her father to kill time, but he'd been sleeping, so she'd gotten herself a cup of coffee and returned to the waiting area where she'd made small talk with Katie's family until Lizzie'd shown up.

Lizzie passed out a bunch of coffees that she'd bought from the gourmet place in Houghton.

She gave Alison one, which she gratefully took, having polished hers off a while ago.

"How long have you been here?" Lizzie asked her.

"A few hours, I guess. I figured if there was no news with

KitKat I could see my father, but he's still asleep."

Lizzie sat down next to her on the little upholstered loveseat Alison had been sitting on and put an arm around her.

"Poor Al. You've been in this place so much lately. Too much."

She nodded, then put her head on Lizzie's taller shoulder. "I'm tired, Lizard. Really tired."

"Of course you are. I can't believe you're holding it together so well with all the back and forth you've been doing these past months. And to top it all off, you have to come home to Petey, with the way you two push each other's buttons."

"Yeah," she said noncommittally. She didn't want to give away just exactly what buttons of hers Petey had been pushing. And pulling. And sucking.

"You know, I owe you an apology for that. It just seemed like a great solution that day in the hospital, but it totally put you on the spot."

Of course, she had no idea of their history. She was talking about just the nuisance of having a buddy you occasionally verbally sparred with in your home.

"It's fine. It's worked out okay." She meant it. And it went well beyond having the best sex of her life. Last night had been cleansing for them both, and she felt that they could finally put some of their shit behind them and let it stay there.

Make a go of it.

But that? What he'd said this morning as he had held her close? She just didn't see how they could have any kind of future beyond a few more nights of great sex before he was able to move into his parents' house.

She wanted to get married, wanted to have a baby—there was no reason physically why that couldn't be possible. And she just couldn't see that happening with Petey. They were too different, too combustible, and had way too much history.

She wanted a nice, quiet life with a husband who loved her, a child—or two—to raise, and the chance to help her patients with their lives.

And yes, perhaps her sex life might be as boring as it had been with the men she'd dated who were perfect for her on paper. But there was more to making a great life than passion and complete compatibility in bed.

She took a sip of the coffee and continued to rest her head on Lizzie's shoulder. Lizzie put her hand on Alison's head and patted her.

She tried to think what she'd say to a patient who said to her what Alison had just said to herself—that she'd trade passion and great sex for a nice quiet life with someone who may not meet her needs in bed.

She'd probably try to lead her patient in discovering why she didn't feel she could have peace and stability with someone to whom she was attracted.

Or perhaps she'd steer her toward the realization that passion and great sex ebbed and flowed in a long-term relationship and that there were ways to spice up one's sex life. But compatibility and respect were sound foundations of any relationship.

Shit. Maybe she'd just tell this phantom patient to squeeze every inch she could out the great sex guy and move on.

Physician, heal thyself.

She was interrupted from her sub-par self-analysis by Darío coming into the lounge area and their collective group rising to their feet.

"Everything's fine. She did great. She's exhausted, but good." His eyes glazed over and his Spanish accent was thick as he added, "My *gata*, she is amazing."

Alison sagged with relief.

"And the baby?" Lizzie and Katie's mother asked at the same time.

Oh, the smile that came over Darío's tired face. It caused everyone in the room to light up as well and Alison's heart to clench in envy.

"She. *She* is beautiful. And healthy."

Katie's mother started crying and her father patted her back. Alison and Lizzie put their arms around each other's waists. "Seven pound, three ounces. Twenty inches long." He paused and smiled even more. "And her mama's good looks."

They all laughed, some through tears.

"Have you named her yet?" Lizzie asked.

"*Sí.* Sofia Peach Luna."

"After your mother," Lizzie said, and Darío nodded.

"*Sí.* And I need to call her." He was starting to pull his phone out of his pocket when Katie's mom rushed to him and gave him a big hug, which he quickly returned. Katie's father shook Darío's hand, then the whole family gathered around for hugs and hand shakes.

"Can we see her now?" Katie's mother asked.

"Yes. But they said for only a few minutes. She's feeding Peaches now, and then she really needs to get some rest. It was a very long night."

Her parents nodded and then rushed from the room, the rest of the family trailing after them.

Darío came over to her and Lizzie. "She wanted you two to come back later, if that's okay with you. She wanted to get the family out of the way. But she definitely wants to see you both."

"We'll come back this afternoon, right Al?"

Alison looked at her watch. She had patients starting in a half hour.

"Yeah. That actually works better. I won't have to cancel any appointments. I can be back around two."

"That'd be great," Darío said. He gave them both a quick hug and then hurried out of the room, his phone once again raised in his hand.

"Well," Lizzie said in a teasing voice. "Two down, one to go, as far as joining the ranks of motherhood." She tweaked Alison's shoulder then started to walk out of the room. "I'm going home for a while and relieve Finn from Sam duty. I'll see you later?"

Alison nodded and watched her friend leave the room to go

home to her husband and children.

A husband she had nothing in common with, had incredible sex with (according to Lizzie's giggling confessions over drinks at the Commodore), and with whom she was living a life of peace and stability.

If you could count 2am feedings, a daughter with ongoing health concerns, and a son entrenched in his teenage years as peaceful.

And Alison was sure that Lizzie did.

Twenty-Three

—∞—

Hockey players wear numbers because you can't always identify
the body with dental records.

- Anonymous

SHE JUST BEAT HER FIRST PATIENT to her office. Beverly was
a woman going through a divorce after thirty years of marriage.
She listened as her patient raged on about the injustice of "doing
her time" only to have her husband leave now. Alison tried to lead
her to more constructive insights, but it wasn't happening today.
Bev needed to vent.

Alison got that and let her go on. She did give her some things
to think about for the next week and even a relaxation exercise
to tryShe could have recommended hot sex with a professional
hockey player to help take the edge off, but she wasn't about to
share her "release" secret.

Her next patient was Brian, a middle-aged man who was
struggling with his first bout of SAD. It was a good session, and
she felt encouraged when he left. That was why she did what she
did. For the small victory of seeing someone walk out feeling
better about life than when they'd walked in.

James was late for his session, which wasn't unusual, so she
updated Bev's and Brian's files. She made herself another cup of
coffee, sat at her desk, and stared out the window at the falling

snow. They were on track to match the record snowfall for the area.

When James was over half an hour late she felt a little sliver of alarm. She pulled up his file on her computer to get his phone number and called him. The call went straight to voicemail. She reminded him of their appointment and asked that he call her to reschedule and to let her know he was okay. Not strict procedure for a therapist, but she felt there was a need for the call where James was concerned.

She debated calling his parents to see if they'd talked to him in the past two days, but she didn't want to alarm them.

James was troubled, yes, and battled severe depression. But he was also a college kid who sometimes slept in and missed class or appointments.

Where was the balance?

She waited a full hour past his scheduled time, then decided to pack it in and head back to the hospital. First she called her mother's place and talked to Sherry about details of the movers coming in a few days to transport what would fit into the assisted-living apartment. Things had started off rocky with Sherry, and Alison had to admit she was a little peeved that her sister had only swooped in at the last minute when Alison could have used help many times in the past year. But she was grateful for the assistance now, and it had considerably eased the load.

She tried James's number once more, left another message, and bundled up and made her way back to the hospital.

She went to her father's room first since it was her normal visiting time and routine seemed to help him.

"Hi, Daddy," she said when she entered his room. She divested herself of her coat and scarf and threw them onto the chair in the corner. Then she crossed to his bed and gave her father a kiss on the cheek.

"We were just talking about you," he said, taking Alison's hand, patting it in both of his.

She looked around at the empty room. "We?"

With confusion in his eyes, her father looked to the side chair where no one sat, to the door and then back to Alison. "Umm...yes. We were just...." He looked to her for assistance.

"What were you saying about me?" she said in a teasing voice, trying to take the emphasis away from the fact that he was probably remembering a conversation he'd had decades ago.

"Oh, I don't think I should say," he responded, playfulness in his voice. It'd been a long time since she'd heard that tone coming from him.

"Why? You weren't talking about how brilliant your daughter is?"

He chuckled. "Well, partly. And of course you are, my whiz kid." He'd called her that as a child when it became obvious that she was an early developer on the intelligence scale.

Didn't keep her from acting like an idiot lately.

"But being brilliant doesn't mean you're always smart."

A chill ran up her spine. It was a thought she'd had many times, but she never realized others had it about her.

"What do you mean?" she said as lightly as she could.

Her father waved a frail hand. "Oh, you know. How somebody can be so smart, and can see the things in others that keep them from having a better life—like you do with your patients. And yet can't seem to figure out her own issues."

Issues? That did not sound like father-speak.

"Daddy, was somebody really here?"

"I told you that."

"Who?"

"Jimmy. He's shipping out tomorrow, you know. And he's just crazy about you, Sally."

Back to the '50s. Well, at least it was Sally and her issues that her father had been discussing with Jimmy.

Still....

She stayed with her father through his afternoon meal. He never came back to Alison and present day—if he'd ever even been there at all.

As her visit wound down, she texted Lizzie to see when she'd be coming back to the hospital.

"Just left Kat's room. She's sleeping. Baby's back in nursery. Heading home. Will be back after Sam goes down tonight."

Not wanting to disturb Katie, she figured she'd just come back for her evening visit with her father a little earlier so she could see her friend.

She thought about texting Petey to see if he wanted her to bring anything home for dinner, but decided not to.

His words this morning after they'd had sex were still unsettling to her.

And the sex…it'd been so different. Slow and tender and yet still so…right.

She pocketed her phone without texting him and headed for the elevators. When she entered, her hand hovered at the button. Instead of choosing to go down to the ground floor and the exit, she chose the up button, to the nursery.

Once the elevator opened, she stepped out and followed the signs to the nursery viewing area, where she had to sign in at the nurse's station. Not many baby snatchers in the Copper Country, but you couldn't be too careful.

She rounded the corner and saw Darío and Petey standing at the viewing window. Petey was leaning on his crutches, making his head even with the much shorter Darío.

She stood where she was. Their backs were to her, unaware of her presence.

"She's beautiful, man," Petey said and clasped a hand on Darío's shoulder. She couldn't hear the new daddy's response but Petey patted him on the back a few times and then brought his hand back to the crutch.

"I knew she was coming. Obviously. But until I saw her, you know? I don't think it really…"

Alison had read a study once about men and women and their acceptance of parenthood. It concluded that women felt they became mothers the moment they realized they were pregnant.

Men, on the other hand, felt they became fathers the first time they saw their child.

It seemed Darío confirmed the study's results.

"Yeah. Well. Is anybody *really* prepared to become a father?" Petey said.

Darío shook his head. "I wasn't. A year ago I hadn't even met my *gata*, and now here I am."

There was a deep happiness—almost awe—in his voice.

Yes, Sofia Peach Luna hadn't been planned, but she was definitely wanted.

She must have made some sort of noise because Petey looked over his shoulder at her. He smiled at her. Not his trademark grin, but a genuine smile. "Come and take a look at baby Peaches, Al."

Darío turned at Petey's words and smiled at Alison as she walked toward the men. He moved aside so that she ended up standing between them. Her eyes scanned the row of babies in the nursery window. There were three, but only one was wrapped in a pink blanket.

"Oh my God, is that a bunch of black hair showing from under her cap?"

Darío nodded, looking both proud and embarrassed. "*Sí.* She *is* half Spanish, you know."

Alison laughed. Peaches was definitely going to stand out amongst her cousins when Katie's Nordic-looking family got together.

"I'm going to run home while Katie's sleeping and get some things she asked for," Darío said. "Will I see you when I get back?"

Alison nodded. "I was going to stick around for a while." They all said their goodbyes and Darío reluctantly left his perch in front of his new baby girl.

When it was just the two of them in front of the window, she turned to Petey. "How'd you get here anyway? And should you even be here?" She motioned to his leg, which was held firm and straight by the brace.

"My dad picked me up and brought me here during his

lunch hour. And yes, the doctors said it was okay to start moving around more, as long as it felt good."

"And does it?"

Now he pulled out the grin. "Oh, yeah. I'd say I haven't felt this good in an awfully long time."

"The knee, dickhead. How's the knee feel?"

"Oh. That's good too," he teased.

She rolled her eyes and turned back to the window. Katie's baby was breathtakingly beautiful. Emotions bubbled through Alison. Happiness for her friend. Joy at the birth of this healthy baby. And yet there was pain. Deep and cutting, it flowed through Alison like a poison entering her bloodstream.

Peaches chose that moment to open her eyes and look around. She seemed to be staring straight at them.

"She may have her daddy's hair, but she's got her mama's blue eyes," Petey said.

"All babies' eyes are blue when they're first born," Alison told him.

"Is that right? Hmmm. So we'll just have to wait and see what gene pool wins out with Peaches. Spanish or Finnish."

"If that hair is any indication, I'd say her Spanish side is leading."

They both chuckled, then fell silent. The weight in Alison's chest eased a little, but it was still there.

"We'd be in the same situation. Brown eyes and blue eyes. Though I…."

She didn't hear him finish. Her body tensed up and the breath seemed to leave her body.

She'd thought of what their baby would look like hundreds of times. But always with regret.

And always in the past tense.

But it didn't sound like he was talking in the past tense—about the baby they'd lost. It sounded like he was talking about a future.

Together.

Yes, she wanted children and knew her clock was ticking, but to have Petey's child now? After all they'd been through?

Her phone went off and she was grateful for the distraction from her thoughts.

The caller ID came up as the hospital and she had a moment of fear about her father, who'd been fine just a few moments ago. "Hello?"

"Alison? This is Scott Thompson."

Relief went through her. Scott wasn't her father's doctor—he wouldn't be calling her about him. So why—

"James?"

"Yes, I'm afraid so. Someone found him in his dorm room and called 911. He's just come in through the emergency room."

"He's alive?" She started to leave, but Petey put a hand on her shoulder, a question in his eyes.

She shook her head at him, but wasn't sure why. Letting him know it wasn't anyone he knew, she supposed.

"Yes. It looks like some kind of overdose. We're pumping his stomach now. I thought you'd want to know."

"I do. Thanks for calling me. I'm actually in the hospital now. I'll be right down."

"Okay. I'll see you soon."

She disconnected and brushed Petey's hand from her shoulder. "I have to go to the emergency room. One of my patients is there."

"I'll go with you."

"No," she said abruptly. She didn't want Petey in her real world. He was a nice diversion when she'd come home this past week. And he was fun to volley barbs with in the summers.

But this was her reality. Hospitals. Patients who depended on her. Parents who needed her help.

Not a gorgeous jock who been a part of the greatest pain she'd ever known—even if they'd just been dumb kids at the time.

And who had also made her face some hard truths about herself and sex.

"I don't know what I'll find there. If I'm there as his therapist it wouldn't be professional to have you with me."

"What? Therapists aren't allowed to have boyfriends?"

She took a step backward at his words, almost like she'd been slapped.

Boyfriend? Seriously? This was all getting way too...real.

"I need to go. Alone."

"Okay," he looked put out but didn't try to stop her. "I'll see you later in Kat's room?"

She nodded, but didn't commit.

When she reached the emergency room Scott was just leaving a curtained-off area that she assumed James was in.

"He's stable," was the first thing he said to her.

"Thank God."

"I told him you were on your way and asked if he wanted to see you." She started walking toward the area, but Scott placed a hand on her arm. "I'm sorry, Alison. He doesn't want to see you."

Intellectually she understood it. James was in pain and most likely deeply embarrassed as well. But she also felt a deep hurt and a sense of failure—something she'd never felt in her professional life.

"How about his parents? Will he let you call them?"

Scott nodded. "Yes. He said he'd like you to call them. But he..."

She was nodding. "That's fine. I'll call them. Do you have their number in his file somewhere? I have it, but it's back in my office."

"Why don't you use my office? I'll call up and tell Nancy you'll be coming and that she should get James's parents number out for you."

"Okay. What can I tell them about his condition?"

"He's told me you can tell them everything. He took an overdose of sleeping aids that he'd been buying online and apparently hoarding."

"Oh, James," she whispered.

Scott put a hand on her shoulder. "He had been ordering them for a few years. Long before you began treating him. He said he'd lied to you. I think that's why he can't face you—he's ashamed."

He was trying to make her feel better, but it didn't work.

"You know where my office is?" Scott said, wanting to return to his patient.

Her patient.

She nodded and numbly walked toward the elevator. On her way to make the hardest phone call of her life.

When the elevator opened, Petey swung his way out. "Everything okay?" he asked.

She shook her head, not trusting her voice.

"Is there anything I can do?" She shook her head again.

"Are you on your way to Kat's room?"

"No. I have something I have to do first. In fact, I'm not sure I'll even get there."

"Okay. Are you sure—"

"You sure your knee is doing okay?"

He looked at her with puzzlement but nodded. "Yeah, pretty good. It's held up well today."

"Good. Then you can manage the stairs at your folks' place. I'd like you gone by the time I get home tonight." She stepped into the elevator and turned around to press the button, not looking at him as the doors closed.

—∽—

He'd lost her.

It'd started this morning when he couldn't keep his fucking trap shut in bed and had spouted his feelings about them finally being able to give it a shot. He'd felt her body tense up but had hoped it was just his imagination.

And then up at the nursery. They'd had a moment there, and then he'd had to go and wreck it by thinking out loud about the genetics of their child. He'd been talking about a hypothetical future child—which had scared the shit out of him as he said it.

But even as he warmed to the idea of the future, she went back to the past.

And even though they'd had a mini-breakthrough last night, it was evident that she didn't truly forgive him.

Or herself.

Especially herself.

And if she didn't, there was no way she'd ever let him in, truly give them a chance.

And now? With whatever had happened down here with her patient? It had apparently been her last straw. But to kick him out? When they were so close to...well, he wasn't exactly sure, but he knew he sure as shit wanted to give it a shot.

Which would be hard to do from his parents' house and not Alison's bedroom.

He pulled his phone from his jacket pocket and pushed some buttons. "Dad?" he said when his father answered. "Do you think you could get Mom and then pick me back up at the hospital? I need to pick up my stuff at Alison's and need one of you to drive my truck and me to your place."

Twenty-Four

—∞—

The most terrifying thing is to accept oneself completely.
~ Carl Gustav Jung

HE WAS GONE WHEN ALISON got home later that night. She wasn't sure how she felt about that, but it didn't really matter. He'd done what she'd asked. Didn't even argue with her about it.

She'd had an excruciating conversation with James's parents, who were even then driving from Appleton to the Copper Country to be with their troubled son.

Alison then went back to her office and examined James's file, her handwritten notes, her digital dictation—anything and everything. She perused the notes and listened to her recordings trying to find something that maybe she'd missed. Something that if she'd been a better therapist would have helped James sooner.

Nothing came to her. Intellectually she knew that when dealing with the human mind and mental illness, sometimes there was no help. It was a lesson taught over and over in school and in training, but it had never really sunk in.

The logical side of her got it. The emotional, human side still struggled. She knew her empathy made her a better therapist, but God, it hurt sometimes.

After hours in her office, she went back to the hospital and checked on James—who still wouldn't see her. She spent an hour with her father, who was still calling her Sally.

She knew she should stop in and see Kat, but she just couldn't. She'd be expected to be joyful and happy for her friend—and of course she was—but there was no way she'd be able to fake it tonight. She almost swung by the nursery to see Peaches again, but knew that would only fray her raw nerves even more.

Finally she just went home, half hoping to see that huge red truck taking up most of her garage. But no, her garage was empty, and she parked her Subaru smack dab in the middle.

She looked in her room and saw that the bed had been stripped of the pink sheets and new, clean sheets had been put on her bed. She found the pink sheets in a bundle on top of the washer in her utility room. Did he do that himself or did whoever came to get him do it? His mother? Lizzie? It was the kind of thoughtful thing one of those two women would think of—preparing her bed so she could sleep in her own room once again.

But she didn't want to. Instead, she went to the guest room and spent the night there.

It was a long time before sleep claimed her.

—⁄∿∿—

The first night in his parents' home, Petey ended up sleeping on the couch. He knew the stairs wouldn't really be a problem, but it just seemed like too much work. His mother brought him some bedding and made up the couch for him.

It hadn't been too bad.

And it wasn't pink.

The second night he took the couch again, but on the third, he hopped up the stairs and spent the night in his old bedroom, virtually unchanged since he'd left for the dorms at Tech. His parents had left his trophies, ribbons, and posters up on the walls. They'd even added his poster from his third year with the Red Wings when his reputation as an enforcer started to take hold.

What were once accolades of his achievements adorning the walls and shelves now seemed like harsh reminders that he was unemployed.

The next night he spent back on the couch again.

He kept waiting for Alison to call, or text, or email, or something. Surely she'd seen the note he'd left her by now. He could only surmise that the words that he'd spent that whole shitty day trying to string together before he left her house for good didn't change how she felt.

How she'd always felt.

She was attracted to Petey, maybe more than to any other man. But she'd never be with him for anything more than a few nights of hot sex.

She was too smart for anything more.

—⚬⚬⚬—

Alison met with James's parents at her office a few days after the awful incident. They all agreed that James would be better off at home for now, and Alison referred him to a therapist in the Appleton area that she'd worked with in various studies over the years.

"Please know that we don't blame you," James's mother said. "In fact, it might have been far worse if he hadn't been seeing you."

Alison shuddered to think about what she meant about the situation being worse. "Thank you for saying that."

His mother nodded. "James wanted me to tell you that he's so sorry he lied to you. He said you'd know about what."

Alison nodded. "He told me he didn't have any pills. But it's not unusual for someone in James's situation to lie to their therapist." She knew what she said was true, but it didn't lessen her deep feelings of hurt and self-doubt.

"I told him he needed to apologize to you himself, but—"

Alison cut off James's father. "That's not necessary. And something that you probably shouldn't push on him at this point. He may feel some time in the future that he'd like to come back to Tech and hopefully continue therapy. I'd like to leave all doors open. And if he's not comfortable talking to me at this point, that's fine."

212 ·§   MARA JACOBS

The mother gave the father an "I told you so" look that Alison ignored. They talked for a little while longer, then they left to pick up their son and take him back to Appleton. Alison wrote herself a note to call the psychologist she'd recommended and give him a heads-up about a possible call from James's parents.

She checked her watch and realized she was running late to meet the movers at her parents' apartment at the Ridges. Sherry and her mother were at the house seeing them off and Alison was supposed to meet them at the new place. They'd decided not to bring their mom over until the furniture was in place. They also didn't want their mother in a semi-empty house because of the possibility that she could become confused. As soon as the movers left, Sherry was going to take Nora to the hospital where they'd wait for Alison's call. Then they'd get her father, who was able to leave the hospital today, and come over to the new place together.

—⁊⁊⁊—

"Oh, look, lasagna is on the menu tonight. You both love lasagna," Sherry said to their parents as Alison was putting the last of the groceries away in their new apartment. The furniture she'd chosen fit perfectly in the small space. She'd had the movers arrange it as closely as possible to how her parents had it in their place. Familiarity was key when dealing with dementia. She'd even arranged to have painters come in and paint the walls to match what they had at home.

Alison looked up from where she had squatted to place the dish soap under the sink. Her father was nodding at Sherry, but Alison could tell he wasn't sure who her sister was.

"Lasagna does sound good," Alison said, standing up. She put the grocery bags away in the pantry. "How about if Sherry and I stay and have dinner with you tonight?" She didn't tell them about the last time she'd had lasagna—and ended up on her back on the kitchen table soon after.

Her parents looked at each other and she saw the moment her father came back to them. "That's nice of you to offer, Alison, but your mother and I would like to dine alone tonight." He took his wife's hand, raised it to his lips and kissed it. "Isn't that right, Nora, darling?"

Her mother smiled, and wove her free hand through her husband's arm. "That's right. It's been a while since just the two of us had a meal together that wasn't brought in on a hospital tray."

They smiled at each other, their intimacy obvious, and Alison felt like she had the morning Lizzie and Finn had brought Petey's truck to him. Like she was intruding on someone else's life.

Lizzie and Finn had been married only a year. Her parents, over fifty-five. And yet they shared the same sense of ease with each other, the same twinkle in their eyes when they looked at each other.

"Well, then, we'll get going and let you two have a nice romantic dinner," Sherry said, and started gathering her things.

Alison walked over to her parents and hugged her mother and then her father. "Please don't overdo. You just got out of the hospital and need to take it easy. An early dinner, then to bed with you," she said to her father.

"Yes, mother," he teased, then tweaked her nose just like he used to do when she was a child. She turned to go, but her father pulled on her hand and she looked back to him. "It's okay to be afraid, you know?"

"What?" She looked around, trying to figure out what he thought she might be afraid of.

He pulled her aside, away from her mother and Sherry. "It's okay to be afraid to love. It's natural for someone like you, Alison."

"Someone like me?" she whispered. Her body went cold. She didn't want to hear what her father was going to say because she knew he'd probably be right.

"Whatever it was? Whatever happened? It doesn't have to stop you from taking a chance on love. Only you can do that. Don't give whatever it was that kind of power."

The breath left her body, but she tried to laugh. "That sounds like something I'd say to a patient. Have you been watching reruns of Fraser again?"

He didn't chuckle at her joke, only looked at her with sadness in his eyes. "Just...just promise me you'll listen...you'll let him in."

"Daddy? Who?" But he was gone. If he'd even been there. For all she knew he could have been telling Sally to give poor Jimmy a shot.

He was looking around the room, confused, and then he saw the La-Z-Boy that he'd sat in for the past twenty years and made his way over to settle into it. He looked at the three women and smiled, a blank and benign look on his face.

"Oh, Daddy," she whispered, a lump forming in her throat.

"It's okay," her mother said. "I've got it from here. You girls go on now. You've done so much."

She grabbed her coat and she and Sherry headed for the door. As they were leaving, she turned around and saw her mother seating herself in the chair she'd sat in next to her husband for year after year, taking his hand lovingly.

Alison quietly closed the door behind her, leaving the lovebirds alone.

Twenty-Five

—∽—

There is no coming to consciousness without pain.

~ *Carl Gustav Jung*

TWO WEEKS LATER ALISON got a call from James's therapist in Appleton telling her that James wished to talk with Alison. She spoke with the therapist for a long time about the best course of action and they finally decided that she'd drive to Appleton and be present during James's session with his new therapist.

Which is where she now sat.

Cameron Rowe was a psychologist that Alison greatly admired. They'd met at a conference years ago and had conferred with each other on different cases many times. She knew James was in good hands with Cam.

"I wanted to apologize to you in person," James said to her once they were all settled in Cam's beautifully decorated room he used for sessions. It was much swankier than Alison's, but then, Cam didn't have the view that she did.

"I told your parents, and Cam, that it wasn't necessary, James, but it's good to see you."

He sighed, his hands stilled, and he looked her in the eye for the first time since he'd walked in. "It's good to see you, too."

"How are you doing?"

He shrugged. "Okay, I guess."

"Is it good to be home?"

He turned his head, like he did in her office, but there was no window here. He turned back to Alison. "Some days, yes. Some days I wish I was back in Houghton."

"Is that a goal for you, James? To return to Tech?" Alison asked. She and Cam had decided that he would stay silent as much as possible so James didn't feel they were tag-teaming him in any way.

"I guess. I've got to do *something*, right?"

"For now, you can just concentrate on yourself. I know your parents want that for you, too."

He grimaced. "I know they do. I know my mom is…"

"She loves you, James, and would like to help you. She just doesn't know how, and that's frustrating for any parent—to not be able to help their child," Alison said.

"I know. But she can't help. I'm afraid no one can."

"There is help, James. Cameron. Myself. Your parents. But mostly you. You're your own best asset James. You just need to let people help where they can."

"But you can't stop the sadness. You can't stop the pain."

"I know some days it feels like a black hole. But I also know you have good days, too. You've told me about them. We just need to concentrate on those good days. You need to stay on your meds too, James."

He looked away guiltily.

"That's imperative, James. The pain can sometimes be too big for us alone. Some pains stay with us forever, and some we can conquer and move on. The trick is to let go of the ones you can."

They talked for another hour, James contributing more than she thought he would. When he left, he said he hoped to see Alison again—back in Houghton when he felt able to return to school.

She and Cameron went to lunch and discussed the case for another two hours, then Alison started the four-hour drive home.

She'd been lucky that the roads were bare when she'd left

home early this morning. By now a heavy snow was coming down. To make it worse, it was that dense, wet snow that made the roads so treacherous.

By Iron Mountain, she was white-knuckling the steering wheel and decided to pull over for a while to see if it got any better. Still stuffed from lunch with Cam, she decided to just find a coffee shop and write down some notes from her session with James.

She saw a sign for one, but their small parking lot was filled, so she drove past it to the next parking lot, pulled in, and parked her car. Something seemed familiar and then she realized it was the same parking lot—to some insurance company—where she and Petey had been when she'd miscarried.

She quickly brushed those memories aside, grabbed her bag, and walked through the snow to the coffee shop.

Two hours later the snow had stopped, the roads were drivable, and Alison hadn't written one note in her files. Oh, she'd thought about James at first. About discussing pain. But soon the memories of the pain she'd felt all those years ago in this town—two parking lots over—dominated her thoughts as she nursed a coffee.

Her dad had been right—she had let that pain rule her choices. And what she'd said to James was right, too. That you had to learn from pain and move on from it when you could.

And then she thought about Petey. More specifically, how great Petey had been that horrible day here in Iron Mountain.

He really had been a prince to her that day. She'd been too wrapped in her own pain and fear that day to really acknowledge it. And she knew she'd been unfair to him—had known it even then.

And she'd held on to the pain, she could admit that. Not only held on to it, but morphed it into the antagonistic relationship she'd developed with Petey for the next eighteen years.

Oh, he'd given as good as he got through the years. But if she was honest with herself, he'd only been following her lead.

She'd counseled her patients about working through pain, about letting it go. And yet she never really had.

Could she? Now? After all the time that had passed?

Or was it too late for her and Petey? Had she finally pushed him away one too many times?

As soon as she saw the snow plow go by, she gathered up her things and left the coffee shop. Once in her car she took a deep breath, looked around the parking lot, and said farewell to that awful time for good.

She put her foot on the gas and headed home.

Twenty-Six

One is very crazy when in love.

~ *Sigmund Freud*

"RED WINGS SCORE!" the announcer bellowed from the television as Petey sat watching the game with his father.

It'd been over two weeks since he'd left Alison's, and there was still no word from her. So that was it. Done. Over before it'd even begun. Just like eighteen years ago.

And just like eighteen years ago, she'd ripped his heart out.

"They're going to make a run for it. I know it," Dan Ryan said to Petey.

"What?"

His father pointed to the TV. "The Wings. They're going to go all the way. You'll get your ring yet."

"Dad, I won't get a ring."

"Oh yes, you will. I looked it up. You played just enough games to qualify if they win the Cup."

"I don't want to skate by on a technicality. If they win, it will be without me, and I'm not going to show up to collect a ring." He felt so shitty about it he couldn't even enjoy the good skate pun.

His father started to say something, but looked at Petey and smartly kept his mouth shut.

It'd been a long two weeks, and he and his father had had some very tense moments. Starting tomorrow, Petey was taking a room at his friend Jules's motel for the remaining time until he could get back into his own place or until he headed to Detroit to take care of things there. He'd probably come by here for a few meals, but staying elsewhere would help ensure that he and his father didn't kill each other.

It wasn't so bad during the day when his parents were at work. And since Petey had started driving again a week ago, he'd been meeting Darío most days to discuss their new business venture.

Which he still hadn't told his parents about.

He was waiting until he could leave the house and go to his motel room for that.

"Hey, they're talking about you," his father said, pointing at the television.

"He is definitely missed, that's for sure," one announcer said to the other, presumably about him.

"The defenseman they brought up has done a good job, but Pete Ryan is a hard act to follow." Petey puffed up a little bit.

"You've got that right. I've never seen a more brave player on the ice. One who put his whole heart and body into every shift...."

The announcer went on, but Petey stopped listening. They were right—he was fearless on the ice and always had been.

So why in the hell was he so afraid of a five-foot nothing Laplander?

He got to his feet, reached for his crutches and then pushed them aside. Nope, no crutch for this job. He left the living room and went to the front foyer, where he started putting on his parka. His father followed him out. "Where are you going so late?"

"Out," he said and started to leave, then stopped. No. Do it right. He turned to face his father. "I'm going to Alison's and I'm going to beg her to give me a chance. Give *us* a chance. At a real future together."

His father looked at him with shock, then disgust. "You're just lonely, and out of circulation. You just—"

"No, Dad. It's not out of loneliness. I love Alison. I've loved her since my senior year in high school. Though there were years in there when I absolutely could not stand her—I still loved her."

"As a friend, sure. Like you love Lizzie."

"Nope. Not even close to how I feel about Lizzie."

"But...but...."

"And hopefully she's going to be in the picture for a while, so you better get used to the idea of her and me. And while you're at it, you better get used to the idea that I'm going into business with Darío. We're going to build that indoor driving range I told you about."

His father stared at him, his mouth open. Before he could spew out the words sure to come, Petey zipped up his jacket and walked out the front door. He was halfway down the stairs when he heard the door open behind him and his father shout, "Petey!"

He stopped and debated just leaving but finally turned around, ready to hear what his dad had to say.

"Be careful on those stairs," his father said to him. And then, holy shit, he just smiled, turned around and walked back inside.

—⁓—

Alison sat on her bed, Petey's note in her hand.

She read it again, for the third time in the twenty minutes since she'd found it.

Al,

First off, thanks for letting me crash here. I know it wasn't easy on you, but it sure made the last few days bearable for me.

I don't really know what happened today, but I know I blew it—again. I know the idea of us as anything more than friends with benefits scares you to death, but it shouldn't. We're so good together, Al, and in more than just sex (though that's pretty fucking great!). There's no one who challenges me more than you do. No one who I want to be at my best for.

Okay. I've been a pussy long enough. So, here it is:

I love you. I always have. I haven't always liked you...but the love was always there.

I know I wasn't the man you needed me to be at nineteen, and I've had to live with that.

All I ask is that you give me a chance to show you now the man I've become.

Please. Let's take a chance. Together.

I'll wait for you to call.

Petey

"What are you doing?" Petey said from her doorway, scaring the living crap out of her and causing her to drop the letter.

"How'd you get in here?" she asked, rising from the corner of the bed.

"You never lock the door. A habit you've got to break." He looked at the note on floor, and at her open panty drawer. "You *just* found it?"

She nodded. "I ended up staying in the guest room. I just washed the clothes I'd brought there and put them back in that dresser."

"You haven't slept in here since I left?"

She shook her head and watched as he looked at the bed, still made up the way he'd left it. He walked into the room and she noticed he wasn't wearing the brace. Or using crutches.

"How's your knee?" she asked, still stunned that he'd walked in now, like she'd conjured him up or something just by reading his letter.

"Good. I've been driving for about a week now. I'm going to take Annie skating on Saturday."

"That's nice."

He reached her and bent down, still a little stiffly, and retrieved his letter. "It's been royally messing with my head, you know, thinking you read this two weeks ago and had nothing to say."

"I'm not sure what to say *now*." She was telling him the truth.

He glanced at the open dresser drawer. "So if you're in the next room, why were you in your panty drawer tonight?"

She couldn't look at him, didn't want him to know the truth. But he put a finger under her chin and lifted her face. "Al?"

"There was one pair I couldn't find. I thought they'd be in the other room. They should have been. But they weren't, so I thought maybe they were in here."

"The black satin ones?"

"Yes. And I thought—wait. How did you know that?" Her eyes narrowed.

"Why did you need the black satin panties tonight?"

"I…I…."

"Were you going to call me tonight, Al? Even before you found the note?"

She started to deny it, to not give him the satisfaction. Then she glanced at the letter he still held. Thought about what it'd taken for him to write it. "Yes. I wanted to see you tonight. After I left my parents, I started thinking. Thinking about us. And…."

He started to grin. "Oh, all right. I was going to call you and I wanted to have those panties on if I saw you tonight."

She started to step away from him, but he reached out and held her wrist. "And do you? Have those panties on?"

She shook her head. "I saw the note and started reading it. I never really looked."

"You wouldn't have found them."

"No?"

He shook his head and set the note on the bed, then reached into his jacket pocket and pulled out her panties.

"See. There was good reason to warn you to stay out of my panty drawer, ya perv," she said, but there was humor in her voice.

And then he flashed that grin. It nearly took her breath away. He moved closer to her, still holding on to her wrist.

And then a thought hit her. "Wait. If you thought I read your note two weeks ago and didn't respond, what are you doing here? Now?"

His grin widened. He brought her wrist behind her back and then released her hand and slid his palm down to her ass, which he grabbed, pulling her close. "Because my knee is better and I'm here to make good on my promise."

She looked at him, puzzled, and then she got it. She broke from him and made for the door, but he wrapped a hand around her waist before she'd gone five feet. He picked her up off the ground and whirled her around, depositing her on the bed.

"That's right. I'm here to chase you, Al." He bent down and kissed her, long and hard. She wrapped her arms around his neck, pulling him down to her, loving the weight of his big body on top of hers. He raised his head and looked down at her.

"And this time, I'm going to catch you."

~*~

Epilogue

—⧖—

Sometimes a cigar is just a cigar.

~ *Sigmund Freud*

Six months later

ALISON READJUSTED IN THE CHAISE LOUNGE, trying to get optimal sun. She heard rustling and opened her eyes to see Katie and Lizzie next to her on the lawn doing the same thing on their loungers. She smiled at the familiarity of it all. They'd been doing this for nearly twenty-five summers. And before they'd become sun goddesses, they'd been playing games on this lawn every summer.

Some things never changed.

Sam Robbins picked that moment to start crying, which caused Peaches Luna to join in, causing their mothers to gather the babies off the blanket beside their chairs and start digging in diaper bags.

Okay, some things changed plenty.

The babies, sitting on their respective mothers' laps, reached for each other and Alison saw a possible romance in the making.

"They are so going to be high school sweethearts," Alison said, watching as Sam shared a Cheerio with Peaches.

"That won't be possible," Darío said as he left the nearby

picnic table and swooped up a cooing Peaches from her mother's arm. "You see, Peaches will not be dating until she's thirty." He took the bottle that Katie held up for him and returned to the picnic table, settled Peaches on his lap and proceeded to feed his daughter"Good luck with that," Alison said. "If she has her mother's looks she'll have to start beating them off with a stick in middle school."

Darío said something Spanish under his breath and held his daughter even tighter. Katie, apparently able to hear—and understand—her husband, laughed. "It's okay honey, it turned out okay for me. It will for Peaches, too."

The couple smiled at each other.

Finn, who was sitting at the table with Darío, came and gathered up baby Sam, bottle, the blanky that seemed glued to Sam, and joined Darío and Peaches at the table. He barely had the bottle in Sam's line of vision before the eight-month-old was tearing it away from his father and jamming it into his mouth.

"Just like his Uncle Petey—needs to get that nipple in his mouth," Petey said as he joined the group at the table. He'd been playing with Annie in the lake where she remained, swimming with strong strokes, her legs kicking wildly.

He now stood drying himself off with a towel, his amazing body glistening with water. His comment was greeted with groans from them all, thrown Cheerios and a combination head shake/eye roll from Alison.

"What?" he said, his hands up in surrender. "Just telling the truth."

Alison let out a long-suffering sigh. "Yeah, he's a total perv. But he's *my* total perv."

"And you love him," Lizzie said, almost as if she was still trying to come to terms with it, six months after they told their friends they were a couple.

"Yep. I love him," she said to her friends, though she was watching her man. He grinned that stupid, sexy grin at her and she sighed once more. This time the sigh was not of suffering, but of contentment. Then the smile grew wider, dirtier, and her sigh turned to an tiny gasp of anticipation.

Their friends had been shocked back in February when they went public with their relationship. Petey and Alison let them all believe that it had grown out of the proximity they shared during Petey's recovery. They didn't feel the need to throw in the story of their history, so they'd allowed the misconception.

Petey had moved back in with Alison and had stayed, even when his house had become vacant. They'd talked about moving there, but they both liked the coziness of her cottage, so the conversation never got much traction.

In early May, they'd made the trek to Detroit where Petey was honored at the last home Red Wings game. Lizzie had gone with them to be there for the ceremony and for meetings with her staff. They'd gotten Petey's condo cleaned out, moved what they couldn't take back with them to Lizzie's place, and met with a realtor about listing Petey's place.

Alison was thrilled to share Petey's last Red Wings moment with him, and so happy that he was able to get some closure on that chapter of his career.

And his new chapter—as a local business owner—was moving right along. He and Darío had gone into business together to build an indoor driving range. He'd even hired the engineering firm where Denise Casparich worked, and she was one of the main people on the project. Petey oversaw the project on a daily basis with Darío, Katie, and Peaches now on the road most weeks during the golf season.

Darío was having a so-so year on Tour, but didn't seem to care. Alison wondered if it might be his last—he seemed to want nothing more than to stay in the Copper Country with Katie and Peaches. At least, now that winter had passed.

Finn's horse boarding and training business had gained a few new clients, but his bread and butter was still the family strawberry farm. In fact, it was rare to even see him in the summer, he tended to be too busy with the crops.

Katie had just sold her first freelance piece to a women's magazine about becoming a first-time mother in your mid-thirties.

And Alison? Well, not much had changed in her life.

Except for Petey.

Which meant everything had changed.

"Have you told them yet?" Petey asked her as he rubbed the towel through his hair. He'd wanted to cut it when the summer began, but she'd asked him to keep it longer.

"More for me to grab on to," she'd whispered to him that night in bed.

He'd left it long.

"Told us what?" Lizzie asked as she sat up in her chair, her head turning from Petey to Alison and back again.

"Obviously not," she said pointedly to Petey. He did a "so sue me" shrug and grinned again.

Katie craned around Lizzie and looked at Alison. More specifically at Alison's left hand. Knowing what she was looking for, Alison quickly said, "We're not engaged."

"Not for lack of trying," Petey said. He threw the towel at Alison, who caught it and draped it over the back of her chair to dry.

"You've proposed?" Lizzie said to Petey and then looked at Alison with accusing eyes.

"I didn't tell you because—"

"She didn't say yes," Petey cut her off.

"You said no?" Katie said, surprise evident in her voice.

Alison put her hands up in surrender. "No. I didn't say no."

"But she didn't say yes," Petey added as he nudged her legs aside and plopped down on her chair.

She shot him a look. "This was not how this was supposed to go," she said to him in a warning voice.

"Al. Baby. When has anything with us ever gone the way it's supposed to."

She shrugged. He had her there.

"What were you going to tell us, then?" Lizzie asked.

"Well it wasn't supposed to be some big announcement or anything," Alison said, softly kneeing Petey's thigh. "I was just going to tell you guys that Petey and I...that we're going to... we're thinking about..."

"We're going to try to get knocked up," Petey finished for her.

Their friends all sat stunned for a moment, then began with congratulations and well wishes.

Alison held up a hand. "It's very early. Who knows if I'll even be able to conceive," she looked at Katie who gave her a sympathetic, and knowing, look. "And I'm certainly not telling people or anything. I just wanted you guys to know."

"Well of course we should know," Lizzie said.

After a moment Katie said, "Not that I'm one to talk, but are you guys planning on getting married, too? I mean, before you get pregnant? Or at least very pregnant?"

"See?" Petey said, addressing Alison, but motioning to Katie. "See how scarred Katie is from having a shotgun wedding? We should definitely make that trip to the altar soon, Al."

Everyone laughed, even the obviously unscarred Katie.

Alison knew that they'd be taking a trip to the altar—as Petey called it—soon. He was wearing her down with his almost daily proposals. And really, she had no doubts about marrying Petey. She loved him, knew he loved her, and they were committed to a life together.

But she did like how he begged.

"I mean, seriously, Al, we need to get cracking on this," Petey now said. "We need to have a bunch of kids."

"Ummm...a bunch?"

"Yeah. With your genetic pool, and all those concussions I've suffered, we're going to need a whole brood to take care of us in our old age."

He teased, but he knew how her parents' conditions and the risk of their heredity scared her. They'd talked about it several times, and it was probably the real reason Alison held out.

He leaned over and kissed her cheek, then whispered in her ear, "Don't worry, Al. I'll be there through it all. No matter what happens. I'll catch you if you fall."

She wrapped her arms around him and held on tight.

—〰—

Lizzie, Katie and Alison may have found their Happy Ending, but the Worth Series is not over.

Alison's client, Denise (Deni) Casparich, is featured in the next installment,

WORTH THE EFFORT
THE WORTH SERIES BOOK 4

—∞—

Try Mara Jacobs's romantic mystery series

BROKEN WINGS
BLACKBIRD & CONFESSOR, BOOK 1

—∞—

AGAINST THE ODDS
ANNA DAWSON'S VEGAS, BOOK 1

AGAINST THE SPREAD
ANNA DAWSON'S VEGAS, BOOK 2

Find out more at
www.MaraJacobs.com

Mara Jacobs is the *New York Times* and *USA Today*
bestselling author of The Worth Series

After graduating from Michigan State
University with a degree in advertising,
Mara spent several years working at daily
newspapers in Advertising sales and pro-
duction. This certainly prepared her for
the world of deadlines!

Most authors say they've been writing
forever. Not so with Mara. She always
had the stories, but they played like movies in her head. A few years ago she began
transferring the movies to pages. She writes mysteries with romance,
thrillers with romance, and romances with…well, you get it.

Forever a Yooper (someone who hails from Michigan's glorious
Upper Peninsula), Mara now resides in the East Lansing, Michigan,
area where she is better able to root on her beloved Spartans.

Mara first published in October of 2012 with 2 romantic mystery
series and the contemporary romance Worth series. You can find
out more about her books at **www.marajacobs.com**

CPSIA information can be obtained at www.ICGtesting.com
Printed in the USA
LVOW13s1525301113

363321LV00004B/90/P